A MONTH FROM MIAM[...] eBook format in 2008 and in pr[...] Publishing, Ltd. This version ha[...] original except for the back matt[...]

This edition published by Barbara Meyers,LLC 2017
Edited by Lindsey McGurk
Cover by Steven Novak, Novak Illustration
Formatted by Enterprise Book Services, LLC

ISBN-13: 978-1-951286-06-4

Meyers, Barbara
A Month From Miami
1. Contemporary romance-Fiction 2. Single dads-Fiction
3. FBI romance-Fiction 4. Jewel heist –
Fiction 5. Florida - Fiction 1. Title

Daily I thank God for the inspiration, writing and otherwise, that He gives me.

The original version of this book was dedicated to someone I thought would be a lifelong friend. I learned much of what I know about the art of persistence from her. She never gave up and she always landed on her feet.

Thank you to my husband Bill for his years of unflagging support.

Thank you to Rick for having such a heroic-sounding name.

Thank you to Christina Brashear of Samhain Publishing for furthering the philosophy, "It's all about the story."

PRAISE FOR A MONTH FROM MIAMI

"Readers will be hooked from the first scene thanks to Meyers' comedic flair, which shines in this enchanting story. The relationship between the characters seems real and warm, and there's nice chemistry."   —Romantic Times Magazine, Four Stars

"...perfect pace and fluid writing, too. A Month From Miami is fun, romantic, sincere and perfect for holiday leisure reading. I give this book thumbs up!"
—Literary Nymphs Reviews Only

"A Month From Miami is truly a treasure; an entertaining, heart-warming, engaging read."
—Fallen Angel Reviews

"The author has a real gift for bringing a real down home feel to both her characters and her story...a story that can make you laugh and put a lump in your throat at the same time..."
—Coffee Time Romance

"...a fun romance book with just a bit of mystery thrown in...Molly is cute and a well written character and I adored her. I'm looking forward to reading more books by Ms. Meyers."
—The Good, The Bad, The Unread

"If you're looking for a very light romantic beach read with a spunky main character then I'd definitely pick up A Month From Miami."
—Novelspot

A Month From Miami

Barbara Meyers

Chapter One

With no other choice, Kay Lee closed the hatch on the gas tank, retrieved her now melting drink and her sunglasses and settled herself in the seat. She popped a fresh piece of bubble gum into her mouth and turned the key in the ignition.

Nothing happened.

"No," Kay Lee pleaded with the car. "Come on, baby, come on. One more time, for Kay Lee." She pumped the gas pedal and tried the ignition again.

Nothing.

Kay Lee banged the heel of her hand on Old Blue's steering wheel. "You rotten piece of junk," she growled. She jammed the gearshift into neutral and turned the key one more time. Dead.

She got out and slammed the door shut. Lucky for her it didn't fall off. She thought about kicking the tire just to vent some frustration, but she didn't want to mess up her pedicure or dirty the mules she'd bought at the JC Penney seventy-five percent off sale. Besides, she couldn't kick Old Blue when the old girl was already down. Surely the package she'd just discovered dangling inside her gas tank wasn't causing problems already? Knowing Old Blue, something else had gone wrong.

1

For a moment she fretted over the discovery of those three glass vials filled with what had to be valuable gemstones.

Wrapped up in plastic and tied with a clear cord slipped over the base of her gas cap, they had been hidden inside the tank, yet easily retrievable.

With curiosity and no small amount of awe, she'd fished them out and unwrapped them. The question of how they'd come to be in her gas tank remained unanswered, but she'd decided they'd best remain hidden where they were. But the cord had slipped from her nervous fingers when she tried to loop it back over the base of the gas cap. She imagined the package was currently floating in her gas tank. At least she hoped it was floating.

She needed to get her car running and get to Miami ASAP.

She fought down her sense of unease and retraced her steps to the convenience-store counter where she forced her best smile at the clerk. "Hi again. Is there a garage around here? You know, with someone who can fix cars? Mine just sort of died out there."

"There's a mechanic in Perrish, just up the road there." He pointed west, away from the interstate.

"How far is that?" It didn't look like there could be a town of any size at the end of the road he indicated.

"Couple miles is all. Garage is right there on the main drag. Rick Braddock runs it. He'll fix you right up."

She purposely broadened her smile and batted her eyelashes. "Can I use your phone?"

The clerk shook his head. "Sorry, miss. Phone's been out of order all day. Word is a construction crew severed a line. Supposed to have it fixed by midnight tonight."

"Hmm." Kay Lee thought for a moment. Everything had been going so well. Until she crossed the Florida state line. "You wouldn't happen to have a cell phone I could use, would you?"

"Nope," came the clerk's helpful answer.

And here she'd thought she was the only person in the country who didn't possess a cell phone. Perhaps she and the convenience-store clerk were soul mates.

"Then how can I call this Rick whatever-his-name-is and see if he can come take a look at my car?" Kay Lee gave him her best I'm-a-helpless-southern-miss look.

"Sorry, ma'am. Can't help you there."

Ma'am. He called me "ma'am"! So much for southern charm. She sighed but she kept her smile in place. Just her luck. A broken-down car and no phone for miles. It was like being back in rural Tennessee.

Doesn't this just make my day. Kay Lee nodded and adjusted her weighty purse over her shoulder. "Thanks anyway."

Kay Lee made sure her smile remained firmly in place as she went back outside and climbed behind the wheel of her car. The humid heat closed around her like a living being. She took a breath, closed her eyes for a second, said a brief prayer, jammed the key into the ignition and turned it.

Nothing.

Apparently the answer to her prayer was no.

She got out and glanced from Old Blue to the empty stretch of road. A couple of miles. Couldn't be any farther than the walk down to Munson's Creek and back. She'd done that a million times back in Bertie Springs. Besides, the exercise would do her good.

She grabbed her drink in its wilting cardboard cup, stuffed the bubble gum in her already bulging purse and set off.

In seconds she was drenched in perspiration. Not a breeze blew. Nothing moved. It was as if everything had died on this Florida afternoon.

The heat of the sun reflected off the crumbling gray blacktop, but Kay Lee refused to stop or turn back. If she did, she'd never get to Miami. She shouldered her heavy bag and sucked on her straw, forcing herself to think cool thoughts.

Like jumping off the swing rope into the cold water at Munson's Creek every summer. Like the winter snow that clogged the curving mountain roads around Bertie Springs. Like Granny Daisy's cool, work-roughened hand pressed against her forehead to check for a fever.

Even though she'd vowed never to return to Bertie Springs or to settle for a life spent in any other little town, Kay Lee had some fond memories of home.

Pretty soon the trees on either side of the road thinned a bit and she saw a house. Then another one. A sign announced the city limits of Perrish, Florida, population twelve hundred and eight. About the same size as Bertie Springs.

She kept walking, even though her mules rubbed against her little toes and sweat trickled down her back and between her breasts. What she wouldn't give for a dip in Munson's Creek right about now.

She'd have taken the foolish shoes off except she'd spent too much of her life walking barefoot along country roads, her toes getting dusty and grimy. On the road to big-city glamour and sophistication there was no room for grubby feet. She'd impress the heck out of whoever she ran into along the way or die trying.

Pretty soon a business district came into view. A bank. A drug store. A gas station garage combo. All of which looked as deserted as the main road.

She entered the gas station which thankfully was air conditioned. An empty counter greeted her, but she loitered there anyway, taking a few minutes to cool off. A couple of vending machines hummed next to each other. Another door led to the garage. She poked her head through it. Country music wailed from an unseen radio.

"Hello?" she called. "Anybody home?"

She took a couple of tentative steps into the two-bay garage. A minivan sat elevated on a hydraulic lift in the first bay, its hood up and tires off.

She walked past it, looking for signs of life.

A pickup sat in the second bay, the front end jacked up. A pair of long legs covered in dark blue denim and work boots stuck out from under it.

A male voice sang along with the radio. Garth Brooks he wasn't, but she'd heard worse.

"Hello?" she called. "Excuse me?"

The caterwauling continued. At this rate, she'd never get to Miami. She nudged the nearest ankle with her toe. This time she was rewarded with a loud clang and an even louder curse. The rack he'd been lying on slid out from under the truck.

"What the...?" His gaze locked with hers and Kay Lee felt a tremor go through her. He was dangerous-looking, with what appeared to be a two-day growth of beard, black hair almost to his shoulders and a dark scowl. As if that wasn't bad enough, he had the kind of muscles she and other girls back home drooled over in the magazines, only his were covered by a snug, almost spotless white tee shirt.

"Sorry to disturb you, but—" Kay Lee began.

"What? Wait a minute." In one swift movement he got up and Kay Lee had to take a step back from his imposing presence, even though he turned in the opposite direction. A second later the music snapped off and he came back tapping the wrench he held against his open palm. The scowl remained.

"Can I help you?"

Words almost failed her, but her goal never did. Miami or bust, she reminded herself. "My car won't start," she told him. Nervously she blew a bubble, sucked it back into her mouth and popped what was left of it.

"Fine. Let's have a look." He shepherded her out of the garage and paused to survey the empty gas pumps and surrounding area. A few other vehicles were lined up in a row along one edge of the property. He turned back to her. "Where is it?"

"It's, uh, at the convenience store out near the interstate. I stopped to use the bathroom, and it wouldn't start." *I stopped to use the bathroom?* Too much information, Kay Lee.

"Then you'll have to wait. I've got a brake job to finish on that truck and a tire rotation on the van."

"Okay," Kay Lee agreed as if she had some choice in the matter. So Miami would have to wait another hour or two.

She'd been waiting her whole life to get out of Bertie Springs. She could wait a little while longer.

She followed him back into the garage. He repositioned himself on the rack and disappeared beneath the pickup once again. "I'm Kay Lee Walsh, by the way. You must be Rick, huh? I'm not one of those psychics like on TV or anything. The clerk at the convenience store told me your name. Rick Bradley? Is that right?"

"Braddock," came the clipped reply.

"Oh. I knew it was something like that." She leaned against the wall of the garage, although what she wanted to do was sit. Since she'd held out long enough to make an impression on Rick Braddock, she stepped out of her mules. The cool concrete felt heavenly on the soles of her feet. Her little toes were rubbed raw and ready to blister from her long walk. She blew her bangs off her forehead. The heat wasn't so bad in here. A couple of fans set on high speed swiveled back and forth stirring the humid air.

"I hope it won't take long to fix my car. I'm on my way to Miami. I've got a job at my cousin Tillie's beauty salon there. Well, she's not exactly my cousin, but we're sort of like cousins, being that our mamas were like sisters, you know what I mean?"

Kay Lee blew another bubble and popped it, the sound echoing off the concrete block walls. "At Granny Daisy's funeral, Tillie told me I could come work for her. I thought why should I stay in Bertie Springs? There's nothing for me there. Well, there was Bobby Lou Tucker. He was real sweet on me. But I just couldn't see spending the rest of my life in Bertie Springs with Bobby Lou. Eating dinner every Sunday with Bobby's family. Plus, our kids would have to have Lou as their second name. It's a Tucker tradition. Cindy Lou. Billy Lou. Donnie Lou."

Kay Lee blew a series of small bubbles, punctuating each of them with a satisfying pop. She slid down to sit, propping her elbows on her knees. This way she could see some of the white tee shirt, too. It was almost like having a conversation with a whole person.

"Lee's not any better for a middle name," she went on to her audience of one. "I'm not thrilled with the name Kay Lee. I always sort of wished my name was Kaylee, you know, all one word? It sounds more modern. When I get to Miami, I'm going to be Kaylee. In fact, I think I'll start right now. With you. You can call me Kaylee, all right?" In response, Kaylee heard a noncommittal grunt.

"You're not much of a talker, are you? Don't you have anything to say?"

Rick Braddock scooted out from under the truck and fixed her with a dark penetrating look. He caught her right in the middle of blowing a big bubble.

"Yeah. I've got something to say. Do you ever stop talking?"

Chapter Two

Kaylee was so startled by Rick's appearance and his question she forgot to suck the bubble back into her mouth before it popped. The sticky mass stubbornly attached itself to the tip of her nose. She reached up, pulled the pink blob away from her face and stuck the whole wad back in her mouth.

He was still staring at her with those dark eyes. Kaylee gulped and accidentally swallowed her gum. It got stuck halfway down her throat, and she had to swallow again. She couldn't tear her gaze away from his. All she could hear was the hum of the fans and the steady beat of her own heart.

One side of his mouth quirked up. "Guess you answered that question." He lay back down and disappeared under the truck once again.

Kaylee studied what she could see of him and kept her mouth shut. She knew she talked too much. And she chattered even more than normal when she was nervous. For some reason, Rick Braddock made her nervous. Hard to say why. She got the feeling he didn't much like her, even though he'd just met her. Well, technically he hadn't met her. She'd introduced herself. He'd grunted.

He had long legs. Lots of muscles and penetrating dark eyes. That was about all she could tell about him. At least his presence was distracting her from the find in her gas tank earlier. Almost. She went back to contemplating the possible whens, wheres, hows and whys of that mysterious package.

After five minutes or so of silence, Rick slid out from under the truck and stood. He wiped his hands on a rag, walked around and lowered the hood. "You'll have to move so I can back this out."

Kaylee scrambled up, winced as she slid her sore toes back into her shoes and tottered to the other side of the garage, her heavy bag swaying from one shoulder.

He backed the truck out and parked it at the end of the line of vehicles, then returned to the garage, picked up a tire and positioned it on the back wheel of the minivan.

"So have you lived here long?" she ventured.

"Quite a while."

An answer! That seemed like progress.

"This is a pretty small town, isn't it? Course, the town I came from back in Tennessee isn't much bigger. Tillie says there's all kinds of things to do in Miami. Stores stay open late. There's restaurants and nightclubs. I've never been in a nightclub before. Have you? I mean, I've been in Joe-Bob's Liquor Store and Lounge back home, but it's hardly what you'd call a nightclub. Folks just go there 'cause there's nowhere else to go. They have a jukebox though. Me and Bobby Lou'd dance sometimes. Not because Bobby Lou likes to dance so much; only because he knew I liked to. He figured dancing would sweeten me up for later, you know what I mean?"

Rick responded with the *rat-a-tat* of the pneumatic gun as he attached the rear tire to the wheel.

He rolled a tire to the front of the car and mounted it on the wheel. Kaylee trailed behind him.

"I don't understand why men don't like to dance. I mean, why can't they just enjoy it, instead of always looking for a reward?" Rick glanced at her.

"Do you like to dance?"

He blasted the nuts with the gun and checked to make sure they were secure. He retrieved another tire and hung it on the passenger side.

"Do you?" Kaylee pushed.

"What?"

"Like to dance?"

Again she got that quick once-over before he returned his attention to the tire.

"Depends who I'm dancing with, I guess."

She crossed her arms over her bosom. "Huh. So what are you saying? Bobby Lou didn't want to dance with me?"

Rat-a-tat. Rat-a-tat. Five times in quick succession. Kaylee tapped her toe, waiting for a response.

He rolled the final tire close to the rear passenger side and hoisted it onto the wheel.

"Well?"

This time he looked at her directly. "Bobby Lou sounds like a jerk who probably didn't know what he had until it was gone. Sounds like you're better off without him."

"That's exactly what *I've* been thinking."

When Kaylee smiled, Rick almost fell over. He yanked his gaze back to the task at hand trying to remember what it was he was doing. He put the lug nuts in place and hit them with the pneumatic gun.

He hoped there wasn't anything too terribly wrong with her car. He wanted Kaylee Walsh out of his garage, out of his town and out of his mind, the sooner the better.

He'd seen her type before. In fact, he'd married her type.

Small-town girls with big dreams and stars in their eyes. Kaylee Walsh was no different from Brenda Larsen Braddock. He'd learned from that mistake. When a woman had her sights set on city lights—and more specifically, city men—it was best not to dissuade her. Because he'd proved himself no match for the lure of Atlanta and the life Brenda had arranged for herself there.

This time it was Miami, but this woman was no different. She'd be on her way in record time if he had anything to say about it.

He lowered the hydraulic lift and backed the van out of the garage.

Signaling to Kaylee he said, "Let's go then."

She followed him to the tow truck which sat in the shade under a towering maple tree. He opened the door for her, wondering if she could even get herself into the cab in those tight pants and ridiculously high heels. She hadn't walked all the way from the interstate into town in those, had she?

Kaylee tossed her big black purse onto the high seat, grabbed the door handle with one hand, the edge of the seat with the other and set one foot on the running board.

"Need some help?" Rick asked, offering her his hand.

"No, I'm okay."

She put her other foot on the edge of the floorboard to haul herself onto the seat. Her foot slipped and she sprawled half-on, half-off the seat, dangling out the door. "Oops."

She tried to get a knee under her, but she couldn't get any purchase on the leather seat. One of her mules fell off. The other dangled precariously from the tips of her toes.

Rick groaned. At this rate they'd be here all day. Not that he wasn't enjoying the view. The jeans outlined a near-perfect derriere and emphasized the length and shape of her legs.

"Could you maybe give me a boost up?" Kaylee asked, looking over her shoulder at him.

"No problem." Rick placed his hands on her bottom. The heat of her skin through the tight denim scorched itself all the way to his brain. Old desires tugged at his memory banks, arousing the rest of him.

"Harder."

Harder? In about another ten seconds he'd be rock solid. Is that what she wanted?

Rick shook his head like a drenched puppy, recalling his circumstances and whereabouts. He gave her a shove, probably more of one than she needed. She slid up into the seat with a surprised oomph.

While she scrambled to sit up, Rick tossed her shoe in, slammed the door and stomped around to the driver's side.

Get hold of yourself, buddy. It's not like you've never had a woman before. Never had your hands on a woman's— Rick cleared his throat and his mind. Forget it. Don't even go there.

He climbed into the cab and started the engine, throwing the switch for the air conditioning on high and turning up the volume on the radio to discourage conversation. Not that it would stop Kaylee Walsh. The only thing he'd found so far that shut her up was staring right into those deep blue eyes of hers and asking her if she ever stopped talking. Only problem was, that seemed to work both ways. Because once he'd asked the question, while looking into her eyes, his mind had gone blank.

Besides, he knew where the convenience store was. What more did they have to talk about?

He pulled into the parking lot, and she pointed to her car. Kaylee's car was an American make and model that hadn't been popular when it first came out ten years ago. Sales had been so poor, and the vehicles proved so unreliable, the design had been abandoned almost immediately. Rick couldn't remember the last time he'd seen one on the road. Running.

He parked next to it and got out, leaving Kaylee to her own devices. The last thing he needed or wanted was to put his hands on her again even under the guise of helping. She opened her door and slid out without his assistance.

He held out his hand. "Keys?"

She dug through her massive purse and dropped them into his palm. He opened the door, leaned in and turned the ignition key. Nothing. Not a peep. Not a sound.

He popped the hood and looked the engine over. Except for a coating of dust and grime, nothing appeared out of place. He checked the hoses and the battery cables, unscrewed the radiator cap to check the fluid level, which looked okay. He took a look underneath the engine for leaks.

"How old's your battery?" he asked as he unwound the jumper cables from the front of his truck.

"Hmm. About six months, I think. Granny Daisy replaced it right before she took real sick."

"Been having trouble starting it?"

Kaylee nodded vigorously. "For a while now. But Old Blue never lets me down."

At Rick's look she added, "Until now, that is."

Rick connected the cables to the battery and nodded to her. "Get in and try starting it."

Kaylee complied. Nothing happened.

Damn, Rick thought to himself. That meant he'd have to tow it—*and her*—back to the station.

Chapter Three

"So what's wrong with it?" she asked the moment he put the truck in gear, with Old Blue in tow.

Rick shrugged. "I don't know for sure. Could be your alternator. Your starter. Fuel pump."

Kaylee cringed. Everything he'd named sounded expensive. She hadn't counted on car problems taking a bite out of her meager travel funds. As it was, her gas and bubble gum money would barely get her to Miami.

She'd tried to save some cash, but Granny Daisy'd been so sick. And Medicare didn't cover all the doctor bills and prescriptions she'd needed. Somebody had to take care of her, and she'd seen no alternative. All last year she'd worked Friday and Saturday nights at the Shop 'n Save in addition to her hours at the salon just to keep a roof over their heads.

There was nothing left for her back in Bertie Springs. No one there she loved or who loved her. Not anymore. She'd make a new start, a fresh start in Miami. There she'd earn some real money, enough to rent a place of her own. An apartment right on the beach. Maybe replace Old Blue one of these days. She'd save her money and open a salon of her very own. If she couldn't get to Miami, she didn't know what she'd do. She couldn't go back, and she couldn't move forward. She'd be stranded in Perrish, Florida forever.

Fuel pump. "How long will it take to figure out what's wrong?" she ventured.

Rick shrugged. "I don't know." He glanced at his watch which clung to his wrist courtesy of a worn black leather band.

Kaylee was a sucker for manly wrists. Rick's were definitely manly and capable looking, tapering down from muscular forearms lightly coated with dark hair. She yanked her gaze away.

"Do you, uh, think there could be something clogging it? Like something in the gas tank?"

Rick gave her a sideways glance. "Most people don't put anything in their gas tanks except gas, so I'd say it's highly unlikely that's the problem."

Kaylee decided maybe she should shut up. She crossed her arms over her chest and stared out the windshield.

"It's getting kind of late," he said. "I won't be able to do much with it today."

Kaylee tried not to panic at the thought of being homeless. She had nowhere to go. No money for a motel. Not that she'd seen anything even remotely resembling a motel in Perrish. She could always sleep in Old Blue, she supposed.

Rick pulled the truck back into the garage parking lot. An old red Camaro was parked near the pump. Kaylee opened her door and slid out just as Rick came around the back. A tiny, dark-haired moppet sprang from the other vehicle and ran in Rick's direction.

"Daddy! Daddy!" Rick swung the little girl up, holding her high overhead. She squealed with delight, before he lowered her. With her arms wrapped around his neck, she kissed him soundly on the cheek.

Kaylee could not have been more surprised. To say Rick Braddock did not seem the fatherly type would have been a massive understatement. He didn't look at all domestic. In fact, he looked like a cover model for one of those steamy romance novels she used to sneak peeks at in Poulsen's Drug Store and Variety back home.

Rick's daughter turned to look at Kaylee, giving her the same penetrating once-over Rick had. She had his dark eyes and straight, almost-black hair, but where Rick's brushed just over his collar, hers fell well past her shoulders.

"Who are you?" Her tone mixed curiosity with suspicion.

"Molly," Rick admonished. "That's rude. You wait to be introduced next time, okay?"

His tone was gentle, and Molly didn't seem the least perturbed by his disapproval.

Her gaze remained fixed on Kaylee.

"This is Kaylee Walsh," Rick said. "Her car broke down. Kaylee, this is Molly."

An odd sort of thrill went through her from hearing Rick address her as Kaylee instead of Kay Lee. He was the first person to do so. This was the first step on her transformation from small-town hick to sophisticated city girl.

Kaylee nodded and couldn't help but smile at the serious little girl who was so clearly a small, feminine version of her father. "Hi, Molly. It's nice to meet you."

The red Camaro drew closer and the passenger door opened. A girl who couldn't have been more than eighteen or nineteen stepped out. She nodded at Kaylee, but addressed Rick. "Hey there, Mr. Braddock."

"Hi, Tiffany. What's up?"

"You remember Joey?" Tiffany gestured to indicate the driver of the car.

Rick nodded at the kid who couldn't be much older than his passenger. Joey made a gesture that was half salute and half wave.

"Here's the thing. Joey's band got a month-long gig in Orlando starting this weekend. And well, I want to go with him. Do you think you can find someone to watch Molly until school starts? I don't want to leave you in the lurch, but this is their big break." The girl peered up at him with her big brown eyes.

Rick frowned. "Wow, Tif. That's kind of a big bomb to drop on me, don't you think?"

Tiffany's eyes welled with tears. "I know, Mr. Braddock. My mom won't let me go unless you say it's okay. She said I have to see my commitments through. But the thing is…" She glanced away, blinking rapidly, before her gaze came back to Rick's. "I've been stuck in this town my whole life. Sometimes I feel like I'll never get out. And if I don't go now, I don't know what I'll do." She sniffed. A couple of tears ran down her face. "My aunt lives in Winter Park. She said I can stay with her. Maybe I can go to school there. But if you can't find anyone else, I won't go." Tiffany held back a sob.

Rick shifted Molly to his other side. "I'm not sure I can find someone to take over on such short notice."

Tiffany nodded. Tears began to flow in earnest. "I understand. But I had to ask. It's okay, Mr. Braddock. I won't go."

A few seconds of awkward silence slipped by before Rick said, "Go."

Tiffany's head came up. "What?"

"I don't want to be the reason you're stuck here. I'll figure something out until school starts."

"Really, Mr. Braddock? You're sure?"

"I'm sure."

"Wow, Mr. Braddock. Thanks." She stood on tiptoe and pecked Rick's cheek, then Molly's.

"Bye, Molly. You be a good girl." The girl waved and drove away, leaving the three of them standing there together. Now what? Kaylee wondered.

Rick set Molly on her feet, but she clung to his hand staring up at Kaylee with undisguised curiosity. Kaylee glanced at Rick.

"I don't have—"

"There's a—"

They'd started to speak at the same time and stopped just as abruptly.

"Sorry," Kaylee said. "Go ahead."

"I was going to say there's a motel near the interstate off the next exit, about ten miles from here."

Kaylee shifted uncomfortably, her little toes protesting the movement. She involuntarily winced. She glanced at Molly. The little girl's dark eyes looked old somehow, as if they'd seen too much and she couldn't be surprised.

Nervously, Kaylee dug through her bag for her bubble gum. She offered a piece to Molly who looked at Rick. He nodded his approval before she accepted it.

Kaylee started to put the pack of gum back in her purse, but then remembered her manners and offered it to Rick.

A corner of his mouth quirked up at the gesture. "No thanks. I'm trying to quit."

Kaylee's brow puckered as she returned the gum to her purse. Could Rick Braddock, beneath his tough-guy appearance, harbor a sense of humor?

Molly busied herself with unwrapping the gum while Kaylee addressed Rick. *Honesty is the best policy.* She could hear Granny Daisy's admonition echoing in her head before she spoke.

"I can't afford a motel. I figure I've got enough cash to buy gas until I get to Miami. I wasn't counting on—" her gaze slid to Old Blue still attached to the back of Rick's tow truck,

"—car trouble."

Rick didn't appear surprised by Kaylee's revelation.

"She can stay with us, can't she, Dad?" Molly tugged on Rick's hand, speaking around her mouthful of bubble gum.

"Molly, I don't think—"

"Why not?" Molly asked. "Miss Tiffany says I need a babysitter. Why can't Kaylee babysit me?"

"Molly, I don't know—"

"You know anything about babysitting kids?" Molly demanded of Kaylee.

Kaylee grinned down at the little girl who was doing her best to get her wad of bubble gum under control by chomping on it with all her might between questions. "I sure do. Why, back home, I watched little critters like you all the time."

"You talk funny," Molly said.

"Molly." Rick's pained expression was an apology for his daughter's comment.

Kaylee could hardly be offended. "That's 'cause I'm from Tennessee. But you know what, Molly? Everyone has an accent. If I took you back home to Bertie Springs, people would say you talked funny."

"Really?" Molly's eyes widened. "I don't talk funny." Her gaze swung to Rick. "Do I, Daddy?"

"No, but you look funny."

"Daddy! I do not." Molly giggled. She clearly knew her father was joking with her.

Rick glanced at his watch again, then he looked at Kaylee. "I've got a softball game at seven. If you want to come home with us for tonight, I'll take a look at your car tomorrow."

Was Rick Braddock completely clueless? Kaylee wondered. He'd barely batted an eyelash before inviting a virtual stranger into his home. What was he thinking?

Even though she had nowhere else to go, she felt duty-bound to question his offer. "Are you sure? I mean, you hardly know me."

"You look pretty harmless to me. What are you trying to say? You're a serial killer or something?"

"No, of course not." *But I unknowingly transport valuable gemstones across state lines.*

"What's a cereal killer, Daddy?" Molly wanted to know.

Rick glanced down at her. "Somebody who uses corn flakes for target practice."

He brought his attention back to Kaylee. "You want a place to stay tonight or not?"

Kaylee chewed the inside of her lip, wishing she'd opened a piece of gum for herself when she'd given one to Molly. "Uh, what about your wife? She might have something to say about this."

Rick pinned her again with those dark eyes as if considering her question before he answered. "Ex-wife. She doesn't have much of anything to say to me these days."

"Oh. Sorry." Kaylee gave him a weak smile.

Courtesy of Rick's little girl, Kaylee wasn't homeless anymore. At least for the moment. Gratitude clogged her throat. "Thanks, then. If you're sure it's no trouble."

"I didn't say that," he pointed out.

Rick released Old Blue from the hoist and loaded most of Kaylee's luggage into the back of the truck. Kaylee sat with Molly near the front door of the station while several customers came by to retrieve their repaired vehicles. A few greeted Molly by name. All of them sent friendly but curious glances in Kaylee's direction.

Around five she heard the overhead garage doors roll down. Rick came out and locked the front door, and the three of them piled in the cab of his truck. Molly sat in the middle, chewing her gum and pointing out the local sights to Kaylee.

"That's where I go to Sunday School," she said, as they passed a small, white steepled church. Her head swiveled in Kaylee's direction. "Do you go to Sunday School?"

Kaylee nodded. "I used to. I haven't been in a while."

"How come?"

"My granny was real sick before she died. I took care of her so I sort of missed Sunday School."

Molly's little hand patted Kaylee's knee. "That's too bad." After a minute she said, "Miss Tiffany's kitty cat died. She was real sad. But I don't think she missed Sunday School."

"No, probably not."

Within minutes Rick turned into a narrow, graveled drive and parked in front of a flat-roofed house nearly obscured from view by the trees and tropical foliage surrounding it.

From inside a dog barked. Kaylee stayed behind Rick and Molly. She wasn't too keen on dogs ever since Arnie Frey's oversized mongrel got loose from his chain and came after her. Everyone knew he was the meanest dog in Bertie Springs. Kaylee had stood frozen in fear, while the dog sniffed, slathered and growled. Eventually, old Arnie hollered at the mutt and he retreated, tail between his legs, back to his chain amongst the junk littering Arnie's front yard.

She'd been ten at the time, but she recalled every detail of that encounter, from the dog's feral yellow brown eyes, to the dusty gravel road beneath her feet, to the rusted-out refrigerator on Arnie's porch. She'd detoured around Arnie's place ever since.

Rick's dog proved to be an even bigger but less vicious version of the species. Still, Kaylee froze when the dog, who Rick greeted as Brutus, sniffed her with interest. He was covered with short, reddish brown fur and had a long, whipcord tail. His ears drooped but his eyes were alert.

Rick shooed him out, and Kaylee sidled into the house breathing a sigh of relief when the door closed behind her.

Inside it was relatively cool and dim after the bright sunlight and late afternoon heat outside.

"Want to see my room?" Molly asked. Without waiting for an answer she tugged on Kaylee's hand and led her away.

Rick went in the opposite direction.

Molly's room was simply decorated with basic white furniture, cartoon curtains and a matching bedspread. A few stuffed animals sat here and there. A baby doll took a place of honor on the bed. Games and books were stacked neatly on a shelf.

"This is very nice," Kaylee said. "What's your dolly's name?"

"Josie," Molly answered proudly. "Want to hold her?"

"Sure." Kaylee sat on the edge of the bed and Molly picked up the doll as if it were a real baby. Kaylee held Josie to her shoulder and patted her back. "Oh, she's such a good baby, isn't she?"

Molly nodded. "She hardly ever cries. Except when she's sad."

"What makes her sad?" Kaylee asked.

Molly shrugged and busied herself with rearranging a few stuffed animals. "If her mommy goes away and leaves her. That makes her sad." Kaylee's brow furrowed.

Rick appeared in the doorway. "Molly, go call Brutus in and give him his food, okay? Then wash your hands for supper."

"Macaroni and cheese and hot dogs, right?"

"Right."

"Goodie," Molly said, and left to do his bidding.

Kaylee laid Josie back on Molly's pillow and rose. "Can I help?"

She followed Rick through the living room, which was furnished only with the basics: sofa and matching chair, television, coffee and end tables. She did her best to keep her gaze above Rick's belt loops, but she couldn't help but notice that in addition to his manly wrists he had a great set of masculine buns. The denim of his jeans molded nicely around them as if agreeing with Kaylee's assessment.

Bobby Lou had been sadly deficient in that department. His legs seemed to shoot right up to his belt buckle with no thought to the need for some curvature on the backside.

Kaylee sniffed. Georgia Rose Stiller was welcome to him. In fact, she hoped they'd be very happy together. Between the two of them, they'd probably turn out a couple dozen stick-legged, flat-bottomed young'uns like themselves.

Kaylee had better things to do. Like shake the dust of Bertie Springs, Tennessee off her feet and make a new life for herself in sunny Miami. One way or another Rick Braddock was going to help her get there.

In the kitchen, water was boiling and a box of macaroni stood ready on the counter. Hot dogs were heating in a skillet.

"You can set the table if you want." He handed her three plates and opened a drawer that held utensils.

She set the plates on the table. "Could I, um, freshen up first?"

"Sure. Bathroom's next to Molly's room."

"Thanks."

With the locked door ensuring her privacy, Kaylee stared at herself in the bathroom mirror. She looked a bit more worn than she had earlier at the convenience store. The hours spent driving since before dawn this morning were catching up with her. Her hair was a disaster, her face shiny from perspiration. Her halter top and jeans still felt a bit damp after her trek into town earlier. Her shoulders and the tip of her nose were sunburned.

She washed up as best she could, touched up her makeup and clipped her hair up off her neck. She glanced behind the shower curtain to see fairly clean facilities. If Rick were a single father, as he appeared to be, at least he was not a slovenly one.

Kaylee slid out of her shoes and left them near her purse in Molly's room. Her little toes were rubbed raw. The cool terrazzo felt wonderful beneath her bare feet.

In the kitchen, Rick was slicing tomatoes. Kaylee finished setting the table.

"Ketchup, mustard and relish are in the door of the refrigerator. Oh, and ranch dressing. Molly likes that with her vegetables." He added broccoli flowerets and celery sticks to the plate of tomato slices.

Kaylee gathered the condiments and set them on the table. She held on to the bottle of salad dressing a little longer. "Ranch dressing! I love this stuff. Granny Daisy never would buy it. Too expensive, she said. I guess she was right. We had other more important things to spend our money on."

She turned to find Rick regarding her quizzically. She'd spoken the truth and further words escaped her for a few seconds. "Should I get Molly? Are those hot dogs about ready?"

Rick directed his gaze back to the stove. "Yeah. Make sure she's washed her hands, would you?"

Kaylee nodded, and Rick berated himself as he scooped the macaroni into a serving bowl and plopped the franks into buns. It wasn't like he'd never had a woman in his house before. But Kaylee Walsh had pushed all kinds of sensitive buttons ever since she'd walked into the garage and nudged him.

In some ways she reminded him of his ex-wife, Brenda, which in itself was a little scary. Except Kaylee was genuine in a way Brenda had never been. Or at least she appeared to be.

Shoot, he felt like he knew half of Kaylee's life story after only a few hours of acquaintance. Orphaned, probably, raised by a grandmother who had fallen ill. Kaylee'd done what a devoted granddaughter would do. Taken care of her sick grandma. Rick tried to imagine Brenda nursing an ailing grandparent and couldn't.

Kaylee'd had some sort of unsatisfying relationship with one of the hometown boys that had probably started in high school. Her cousin in Miami offered her escape from what she perceived to be a dreary future in Bertie Springs, Tennessee, and Kaylee had grabbed it.

That's what Brenda had done, too, except Rick had gone along for the ride. For a while. Once they had saved enough money to move to Atlanta, they both worked and Rick trained to become a certified mechanic. From the beginning they'd planned to return to Perrish where Rick would take over the garage from his uncle.

Except it didn't work out that way. Brenda had a secretarial job she liked. She loved Atlanta. She didn't want to leave. Then she became pregnant with Molly. Neither of them had planned on that.

Rick gave in to Brenda's pleas to remain in Atlanta. He was sure after the baby came, she'd want to return to Perrish and settle down like they'd talked about. Until then he got a job at Atlanta's biggest import-car dealership. The money was decent. Molly was born. Brenda got a promotion. Discussion of returning to Perrish temporarily ceased.

Then Brenda met Jim Madigan, the owner of the dealership, at the annual Christmas party. The signs had all been there, and sometimes Rick still kicked himself for not recognizing them earlier.

He poured a glass of milk for Molly, trying to ignore the sounds of water running and Kaylee and Molly chattering to each other in the bathroom.

Within six months of meeting Jim, Brenda divorced him and gave him custody of Molly without blinking an eye. She was traveling a lot for the company she worked for by then.

He and Molly hardly ever saw her anyway. A year later she married Rick's former boss.

After pestering him about taking over the garage, his uncle Steve was only too happy to retire when Rick returned to Perrish permanently with four-year-old Molly in tow.

In the two years since, Rick had all he could do to manage the garage and take care of Molly. The last thing he wanted or needed was another woman in his life to trample on his heart and dump him for a glamorous career and a city guy with more money.

Molly and Kaylee arrived at the table and took their seats. Molly's hands were washed, her face scrubbed clean; her normally tangled hair had been brushed. Kaylee smiled at him as he sat across the table from her.

Yes, he warned himself, the last thing he needed in his life was Kaylee Walsh.

Chapter Four

After grace, a recitation by Molly which included thanks for everything from macaroni and hot dogs to Kaylee's presence at the dinner table, they began to eat.

Kaylee was starving. She helped herself to a hot dog, macaroni and vegetables. She did her best to ignore Brutus who, having wolfed down his own dinner in a matter of minutes, was sprawled close to Molly's chair, his eyes alert and watchful. No doubt the dog had figured out that of the three of them, Molly was the most likely to drop crumbs his way.

Molly selected several celery sticks and broccoli flowerets and arranged them on her plate. Rick squeezed a dollop of ranch dressing out next to them, then offered the bottle to Kaylee.

"Thanks." She followed suit, squeezing some onto her plate to use as vegetable dip, then dribbled another portion over her hot dog.

Molly's eyes grew round. "You put ranch dressing on your hot dog!"

Kaylee set the bottle back on the table. "It's yummy." She picked up her hot dog, took a bite, closed her eyes for a second and chewed. "Oh, that is so good." She opened her eyes to find both Rick and Molly regarding her with equal expressions of mystified horror.

She grinned. "Don't knock it 'til you've tried it." She took another bite.

Rick ignored her remark and pointedly ladled mustard and relish onto his hotdog. Molly picked hers up and tentatively dipped it into the pool of dressing on her plate. She watched Kaylee take another bite of hers then stared at her own hot dog regretfully before taking a bite.

She chewed as if considering the impact on her taste buds, then she swallowed and shook her head. "I don't like it. Ranch dressing is for vegetables only."

Kaylee winked at her. "At least you tried it, Molly. Granny Daisy would say that means you have an adventurous soul."

Molly took a bite of dip-covered celery. "What's adventurous?" Molly asked.

"Don't talk with your mouth full," Rick reminded her.

"Adventurous means you're not afraid to try new things," Kaylee answered. "Go new places. Explore possibilities. You're the adventurous type. Like your dad, I'll bet."

Rick shook his head. "Not me. Not any more."

Kaylee gazed at him wide-eyed. "You mean you invite virtual strangers into your home on a regular basis?"

"Un-unh," Molly answered for him right after she took a bite of macaroni. "We hardly ever have company. 'Cept for Grandma and Grandpa. And Daddy doesn't have a girlfriend, either."

"Molly," Rick warned. "Don't talk with your mouth full."

Molly made a big show of swallowing. "Are you going to stay here and babysit me?"

Kaylee glanced at Rick. "I don't know, Molly. I think your daddy and I need to talk about that."

"But you already said you knew how to take care of craters like me."

"Critters," Kaylee corrected. "But it's not up to me, Molly. Your dad has to decide if he wants me to babysit you."

"I'll need references," Rick put in. He concentrated on putting condiments on his second hotdog.

"Folks in Bertie Springs will vouch for me."

"We can talk about this later." He shifted his gaze in Molly's direction and Kaylee nodded.

"Bertie Springs. That's a funny name for a town."

"It was named after Albert Hoffermeyer a way long time ago. He discovered the springs bubbling out of the mountains and he decided to settle there in Tennessee. Pretty soon other folks came to live there, and they turned it into a town. Albert's nickname was Bertie and since he discovered the springs first, they named the town Bertie Springs."

Rick pushed his chair back and picked up his plate. "Molly, you need to stop talking and eat, okay?" He stood. "I gotta get ready for the game. You're welcome to come if you want," he said to Kaylee.

"Thanks. I'd like that."

"We can get popcorn," Molly informed Kaylee. "And if I'm real good, Daddy lets me have a candy bar. 'Cept he only lets me eat half and I have to save the other half until tomorrow, because he says too much sugar isn't good for me."

Rick put his plate and utensils in the sink. "Molly, don't talk with your mouth full. And if you're not done with your dinner in—" he glanced at his watch, "—ten minutes, no candy bar at all."

As soon as Rick left the kitchen, Molly began scooping macaroni into her mouth.

While Rick changed and Molly ate, Kaylee cleared the table and tidied the kitchen. The kitchen window overlooked a screened porch and a sizable back yard complete with a swing set and a small playhouse.

The spreading branches of two live oaks shaded the yard. Giant shadows marched across the sparse grass as the sun drifted lower in the sky.

Kaylee wished she had time to take a shower, but it would have to wait. She'd change into shorts and a tank top, and more comfortable shoes.

Molly brought her almost-empty plate to the counter as Rick reappeared. He wore a striped baseball uniform. The bill of his cap had been molded into an upside down U-shape.

"Thanks for cleaning up," he said.

Kaylee gave the counter a final swipe while Brutus sniffed the table edges, the chairs and the surrounding floor. "It's the least I could do."

Rick glanced at his watch. "We need to get going. The game's in Jannings Point."

Kaylee had no idea where Jannings Point was, but Rick made it clear she didn't have much time.

"I'll be ready in a couple of minutes."

She scooted into Molly's room and rummaged through her big suitcase. She hadn't packed very well. Her things were haphazard and wrinkled. She grabbed a yellow tank top and an old pair of denim shorts and flip-flops.

Perrish, or Jannings Point for that matter, was a far cry from Miami. She didn't have to dress to impress.

She reappeared in record time. Rick's eyes widened at the sight of her. Uh-oh. Something was wrong. What was it? She smoothed the tank top with her hand. "Is this okay? Everything in my suitcase is wrinkled, but—"

"It's fine." He tossed his keys in the air and caught them. "Ready?"

Kaylee hoisted her purse. "I'm ready."

"Me too!" Molly chimed in. She slipped her hand into Kaylee's on the way to the truck.

Rick did his best to ignore the way Molly seemed to have taken to Kaylee Walsh on such short notice. He also did his best to ignore the way Kaylee filled out the snug yellow tank top and the shape of her long legs. Even the dime-store flip-flops couldn't detract from her appeal.

She'd piled her mass of dark waves on top of her head earlier, but tendrils escaped and curled around her temples and nape in the humid air.

Her blue eyes sparkled and her southern drawl washed over him as she and Molly chatted. By the time they'd reached the park in Jannings Point, Molly had told Kaylee almost every detail that comprised her life in Perrish. Kaylee'd asked leading questions about Molly's best friend Hannah, her days at Miss Tiffany's house during the summer and her kindergarten experience last year.

Rick thought himself to be a pretty good judge of character. Kaylee seemed genuinely interested in Molly. And Molly was practically glowing as a result of Kaylee's feminine attention.

Kaylee offered Molly more bubble gum when she unwrapped a piece for herself.

"Better ask your dad if it's okay first," Kaylee whispered to Molly.

Rick glanced at the two of them. "It's okay. But don't swallow it," he warned Molly.

"Why? What happens if I swallow it?"

That was a good question. Rick remembered being admonished in his childhood not to swallow gum. He vaguely recalled a warning that he'd sink if he went swimming because of the gum in his stomach. As an adult, he doubted that could possibly be true.

"I don't know," he told Molly.

Kaylee chuckled. "Nothing happens. Trust me, I've swallowed lots of gum in my time. It's harmless."

Molly patted Rick's arm. "Don't worry, Daddy. I won't swallow it."

Sometimes Rick wondered who was the parent and who was the child. Molly had grown up fast, too fast, he thought. She seemed to have as much a need to protect him as he felt to protect her.

Rick parked the truck. He pointed to the bleachers. "You guys can sit over there. Molly knows the ropes," he assured Kaylee.

"Here." He opened his wallet and handed Kaylee a five dollar bill. "Molly gets popcorn and a small soda. No caffeine," he warned, giving his daughter a stern look.

"And if she behaves herself, she gets a candy bar."

"But she only gets half of it, right?" Kaylee asked.

"You can have the other half," Molly told Kaylee.

"Why thank you darlin'," Kaylee said as they turned and started toward the bleachers. "But maybe we better wait and see if I behave *myself*."

Molly giggled delightedly. Rick watched until they disappeared around the corner of the bleachers, trying once again not to recall how Kaylee Walsh's firm buttocks had felt beneath his hands.

Kaylee's eyes nearly glazed over from boredom and her butt began to go numb from sitting on the hard metal bleachers. Molly amused herself by playing with some of the other children close by. Kaylee made certain she was within view at all times.

The only saving grace to a men's softball game, Kaylee decided, was the sight of Rick Braddock in the striped baseball pants. Each time he took a turn at the plate, Kaylee sat up and took notice of the way the pants clung to his physique, outlining his form, tickling her imagination.

When the coach called time, Rick took the opportunity to glance her way. His gaze skirted the immediate area until he spotted Molly running around with other little ones. Then his gaze connected with Kaylee's. He gave her that penetrating, assessing look once more. Kaylee swallowed her gum. A slight nod was his only indication that he'd zeroed in on her specifically.

Flustered, Kaylee glanced around to see if anyone else had noticed. The sprinkle of spectators was oblivious as was Molly, who was playing tag with her cohorts.

Great, Kaylee thought. At the rate she was swallowing gum, she would probably sink to the bottom of the Atlantic off the coast of Miami her first time out.

Rick's team won, thanks in part to his two singles. On the way home, Molly leaned against Rick and closed her eyes. Kaylee wished she could do the same. Her eyes were gritty from exhaustion. All she wanted was a quick shower and a pillow beneath her head. It was only nine o'clock.

Kaylee gasped suddenly.

Rick yanked his foot off the accelerator. "What?"

"I have to call Tillie and tell her what happened. I forgot all about it."

Rick put his foot back on the accelerator. "Geez, you scared the hell out of me."

"Sorry. I just remembered. I don't want her to be worried."

"You can call her when we get home." Home, Kaylee thought. Hmm.

"So what do you think about staying until your car's fixed? Babysitting Molly?"

"What do *you* think?"

Rick glanced her way. "I think I better take a closer look at your car tomorrow. But I still need a babysitter. Do you have references?"

Kaylee grinned and leaned her head back against the seat. "I should have brought the Bertie Springs telephone directory with me. You want references, practically anyone in town can give you one."

"Three will probably be enough. Molly likes you."

Kaylee glanced down at Molly. Her mouth was open, but her eyes were closed. "I like her, too."

"She doesn't usually warm up to new people so quickly."

She probably learned that from her father, Kaylee thought. She recalled Rick's initial assessing stare that afternoon at the garage. Making a new friend had not been on his list of priorities.

"If you can give me some names, I'll call them tomorrow," Rick continued. "And if you can stay until school starts, and assuming there's nothing major wrong with your car, I won't charge you for the repairs and we'll call it even."

Kaylee glanced Rick's way. "I sure hope it's nothing major. And when does school start? A month from now?"

"I'd have to check on the exact date. In two or three weeks I think. Something like that."

"So I could be stuck here for almost an entire month?"

"Unless you get a better offer." Rick's tone indicated he didn't think that was likely to happen.

Kaylee crossed her arms over her chest. "Maybe Tillie can come and get me."

"Maybe she can," Rick agreed.

"But then what will you do about Molly?"

"I'll work something out."

Kaylee didn't much like her options. She already felt obligated to Rick for giving her a place to stay. He clearly needed a temporary babysitter for his daughter. If she stayed, Old Blue would be up and running again, and it wouldn't cost her a dime. Only a month. A month from Miami.

Chapter Five

While Rick tucked a sleepy Molly into bed, Kaylee made up the couch with sheets and a pillow. Brutus, who lay with his head on his paws, tracked her every move.

Rick reappeared as Kaylee tucked the last fold under the cushions.

"I'm going to grab a shower and then the bathroom's all yours," he informed her.

Kaylee nodded, suddenly aware that for the first time they were alone with each other. The glow from the single lamp cast shadows around the room. Night settled in around them. An odd sort of anticipation bubbled in her tummy.

She wondered if Rick felt it too. He gestured toward the sofa. "Think you'll be okay out here?"

Her glance slid to where Brutus lay observing them. "Fine."

Rick chuckled, clearly unimpressed with her efforts to hide her discomfort with the dog. "Don't worry. He sleeps with me." Rick patted his thigh. "Brutus. Come on, boy." The big dog dragged himself up and trailed over to Rick.

"Night," Rick said.

"Good night."

The shower came on a few minutes later. Kaylee dug through her purse and located her address book. From the phone in the kitchen she dialed Tillie's number.

After the fourth ring Tillie picked up. "Hi Tillie, it's me."

"Girl, where are you? I thought you'd be here by now. You get lost or something?"

"No. My car broke down and I'm stuck in a little town near the Florida state line. I'm about out of money, too. Can you come and get me?"

"Dang, girl. You know how far that is, the Florida State line? That's a good day's drive from Miami. And the same coming back. Plus, what are you going to do about your car if I come get you?"

Kaylee hadn't thought of that. She'd somehow have to make a return trip to get Old Blue once it was fixed if Tillie came and got her now. She sighed. "I guess it doesn't make any sense, does it?"

"That depends," Tillie replied in a reasonable tone. "What's wrong with your car and how long will it take to get it fixed?"

"That's the problem. I don't know what's wrong with it. Or how long it will take to fix it or how much it will cost."

"Oh, baby, what are you going to do in the meantime? I can send you some money. Where are you staying?"

"No, look, it's okay. The guy that owns the garage said he'd fix my car for free if I babysit his little girl for a couple of weeks."

"Hmm. Sounds suspicious to me," Tillie said. "Has he had a good look at you? I bet he wants more than a babysitter."

Kaylee laughed. "I doubt it. He seems like a nice guy and his daughter is absolutely darling. It'll be fine, but it'll be a couple of weeks before I get there. Will I still have a job?"

"It's slow as molasses here in the summertime, baby. Most of my regular clients head up north to stay cool. Don't worry about it."

Kaylee sighed in relief. Tillie always came through for her. "So how's everything else going?" She twisted the phone cord around her finger. "How are things with that guy? Marcus, was it?"

"Marco. Marco DiPaulo. It didn't work out."

Tillie's tone was flat and unemotional, which didn't surprise Kaylee. None of her *relationships* ever seemed to work out. "Well, cheer up. Maybe the guy from the bar will appear and sweep you off your feet."

"Maybe, hon. You never know," Tillie agreed, her voice lighthearted. She was probably smiling at the thought.

It was an old joke between them. The guy in the bar was someone Tillie had met in Knoxville years ago while she was still in beauty school. They'd hit it off immediately.

The attraction, according to Tillie was mutual. They'd danced and talked over the too loud music the entire night and when they'd parted, Mac, for that was the guy's name, had Tillie's phone number securely tucked in his pocket.

He'd never called, but Tillie had never forgotten him. He was her ideal in looks and personality. She'd convinced herself of it. She was equally convinced someday they'd meet again and he'd have a perfectly believable excuse for not calling. He'd still be single, of course, as would she. They'd never look back at the time they'd lost, but forge ahead into the future together and live happily ever after.

Kaylee believed Tillie purposely sabotaged her relationships with other men, holding them to the standard of Mac, a man surely after all this time she could barely remember. But Tillie was her best friend, closer than a sister, so she willingly humored her fantasy. In a way she admired her. Tillie had found what she wanted and was willing to hold out for it against all odds. She refused to settle for anything less.

"Okay, so I'm going to be here for the next couple of weeks, then."

"You stay in touch, okay? If you need anything, you call me. Let me know if that guy tries anything with you. I'll find a way to come get you if I have to."

"Okay, Tillie, but I'm pretty sure it won't come to that." Kaylee hung up with a sigh of relief. She'd still have a job with Tillie as soon as she could get to Miami. Tillie would help her figure out what to do about the package in the gas tank. And in the meantime, there was no reason why the arrangement with Rick shouldn't work out for all concerned.

While Rick occupied the bathroom, Kaylee quietly dug through her suitcase in Molly's room. By the glow of a nightlight, she located her nightclothes and robe. She yawned. She couldn't wait to wash the dust and perspiration off her skin, scrub her makeup off, brush her teeth and crash on Rick's couch.

The bathroom door opened and she heard Rick padding along the short hallway to his room. She waited half a minute, then scooted into the bathroom.

Two clean bath towels, obviously meant for her use, occupied one corner of the counter. The bathroom smelled freshly soapy and damp. Homey. Somehow Kaylee felt comforted by the sloppy familiarity of it. Toothbrushes, Rick's and Molly's were side by side in a holder. Two tubes of toothpaste, one with cartoon characters and one to fight plaque and whiten, stuck their white-capped heads up from behind the brushes.

A razor and a can of shaving cream sat near the sink. From the looks of Rick, however, Kaylee was pretty sure he didn't shave every day.

She turned on the shower, and stepped under the spray. On the narrow ledge at the back of the tub were several bottles of bubble bath lined up like small femininely dressed soldiers. Surely they belonged to Molly, but a wave of longing swept over Kaylee. She picked up the bottle nearest her and sniffed. Unbidden tears came to her eyes as the scent of vanilla wafted from the open container. Granny Daisy's one weakness had been bubble baths. If she found a brand on sale, she would squeeze the pennies from her pocketbook to pay for it. Granny Daisy'd had so few luxuries in a life of hard work. For every birthday and Christmas, Kaylee somehow managed to save her own pennies to buy bubble bath for Granny.

She recapped the bottle and set it back in its place, shaking off memories of her past. She must concentrate on her future. Her future in Miami.

At the edge of her thoughts was the unpleasant business of the gems in Old Blue's gas tank. Like Scarlett O'Hara, she pushed them away.

Kaylee dreamt she was outside, beneath the trees, on a summer day. A warm rain sprinkled down on her face, the droplets running over her lips and onto her tongue. She turned in a circle, arms spread wide, embracing the moment. The rain on her face became more insistent, falling with more force, more pressure. It was no longer rain. It was slimy, like saliva.

Kaylee's eyes fluttered open to the feeling of decidedly wet slobber being applied to her face. A tremendous weight pressed on her chest.

Kaylee screamed and sat up, throwing the weight off. She shrieked as she rushed to untangle the sheets from her legs and swipe at the wetness on her face at the same time. She hobbled up, stumbled over a warm, hairy body, and reached for the lamp on the end table.

The switch escaped her grasping fingers as she tripped and cried out again. The lamp tumbled to the terrazzo floor and Kaylee followed.

Overhead light flooded the room and Kaylee blinked, her heart racing.

"What's going on? What happened?" Rick, in a pair of not-quite-zipped jeans, clutched a baseball bat and stared at her questioningly.

Near the couch, Brutus stood between her and Rick, his tail wagging like a flag in a dying breeze.

The dog. That darn dog, Kaylee thought. With his sloppy pink tongue and his oversized paw on her chest. That's what woke her up.

From her undignified position on the floor amidst broken pieces of ceramic from the lamp, Kaylee attempted to rise gracefully. She almost made it too, except her foot came down on a broken shard and she yelped.

"Aw, geez. Watch it, would you?" Rick dropped the bat across a chair and carefully made his way to where Kaylee was balancing on one foot.

Drops of blood dribbled onto the floor.

He took her arm to steady her, making Kaylee all too aware of their half-dressed states. Even the pain in her foot couldn't drown out the sensation of his fingers when they wrapped around her bare upper arm, the tips slightly brushing the side of her breast.

For a second he didn't move, and she couldn't help but look up into his dark, impassive gaze. Anticipation crawled along her spine at his nearness. She drank in the sight of his bare chest, covered with swirls of dark hair, his broad shoulders, the unshaven whiskers.

It seemed an eternity. Kaylee thought she'd stopped breathing, but apparently she hadn't. Brutus yawned and stretched, then ambled away, his nails clicking along the terrazzo before he disappeared down the hallway.

"What have you got to say for yourself?" Rick asked in a husky whisper.

"Ow?" As if a spell had been broken, the pain from the cut in her foot quite suddenly reasserted itself.

"We better have a look at that."

With Rick's aid, Kaylee limped to the bathroom. He lowered the lid on the toilet. "Have a seat."

Kaylee sank down gratefully, her limbs not quite steady, but whether that was from the shock of her rude awakening or Rick's touch, she wasn't sure.

Rick wet a washcloth and hunkered down in front of Kaylee.

She rested her injured foot on top of her knee for inspection. Rick wiped at the dribble of blood. The cut was long, slashing below her instep, but it wasn't very deep. "Doesn't look too bad. I think you'll live."

"Can't say the same for your lamp." Her gaze flickered to his and held. Again Kaylee had that feeling like she couldn't breathe.

"Yeah, well."

Rick stood and rinsed out the washcloth, and handed it to her. "Why don't you hold that on there for a minute."

Kaylee complied, barely looking at her cut. She couldn't tear her gaze off Rick. And it wasn't just his bare chest, the well-developed biceps or the corded muscle in his arms. It was the area directly below the waistband of his jeans. The fly to be exact. The not-quite-zipped fly from which a glimpse of white briefs teased her imagination.

What would it be like, she wondered, to slide that zipper down ever so slowly. To ease that denim down over those briefs. To explore at her leisure what lay beneath.

Heat swept over her. Unable to fight the feeling of lightheadedness, she swayed slightly on the stool. "Oh!" She gripped the counter with her free hand to steady herself.

"You okay?" Rick bent closer, peering at her. His fingers touched her ankle as if that would keep her upright.

"I'm—I'm okay," Kaylee breathed. Okay, if she didn't count the hot spot that had developed on her ankle.

"Let me see." He covered the hand that held the washcloth and lifted it. The cut had stopped bleeding. Kaylee relinquished the washcloth without a fight.

"How about some of this antibiotic ointment on there?" Rick held up a tube. "And we'll wrap it in gauze for tonight. Tomorrow you can put bandages on it."

"Sure. Okay." If he'd said, how about coming to bed with me and letting me kiss it and make it better, Kaylee knew she'd have agreed just as easily.

With his forefinger, Rick spread a thin line of ointment along the narrow gash. Kaylee felt it as if his finger was touching not her foot, but somewhere much more sensitive.

She held onto the counter as her eyes rolled back in her head.

Her thoughts ran wild.

Such tenderness. Such attention to detail, Kaylee thought. Is that how Rick would be as a lover?

Stop it, she warned herself. It's not like you'll ever find out. She was here because of Old Blue. Which Rick would fix while she babysat Molly. For a month. No longer. Because she had bigger, more important places to be than Perrish, Florida. And no man, not Bobby Lou Tucker, and certainly not Rick Braddock, was going to hold her back from her dreams.

Rick wrapped a strip of gauze around her foot and secured it. "I think you'll be okay now." He tapped her ankle and stood.

Kaylee did too, and that put them eye to eye and almost chest to chest in the tiny bathroom. She'd never been so aware of herself, of her own body, as she was standing in close proximity to Rick Braddock. She could feel every breath she took, felt her breasts swell and her nipples tighten beneath the thin fabric of her pajama top.

The ribbed cotton taunted her with its light pressure. She needed more. Much more. Like Rick's hands cupping her breasts, his thumbs rubbing her aching nipples, his tongue flattening against them.

"You okay?" he asked in that husky nighttime voice of his.

Moisture pooled between her thighs.

"No. Yes."

Rick gave her an odd look. "Come on. Let's get you back to bed."

"Yes." *Your bed. With you in it.*

Rick helped her to a chair then went for a broom and dustpan. Kaylee watched while he swept up the mess she'd made.

"I'm sorry about your lamp. I'll—I'll replace it." Even as she said it, she wondered how.

Rick's mouth quirked up in his now-familiar half smile.

"Don't worry about it. I'll put it on your tab."

He dumped the broken pieces into the kitchen garbage can and returned. "Sorry about Brutus. He's not usually so affectionate with—"

"Strangers?"

"Yeah." Rick seemed confused by his dog's uncharacteristic behavior. "He's usually out like a light on the floor by my bed, and he never moves."

"What can I say? Kids and dogs. They love me." With men, however, it was an entirely different story. "I can't believe all the ruckus didn't wake up Molly."

"She'd sleep through a Category Eight hurricane. A broken lamp is nothing."

Kaylee nodded, glad she hadn't disturbed anyone else. She crawled back to her makeshift bed and rearranged the sheet over her.

Rick gazed at her for a moment, then took a couple of steps closer. "Will you be okay?"

"Fine." She forced a smile. "Good night."

He nodded, though he didn't look terribly convinced. He moved away and turned off the overhead light. "Night." He disappeared into the darkness.

Rick stepped over Brutus and crawled back into bed, punching his pillow in frustration. Great, Braddock, just great. The first woman who's turned you on in two years just happens to be Kaylee Walsh. Kaylee, who didn't want to be stuck in a small town with a small-town guy any more than Brenda had.

She'd hightail it to Miami as fast as that old car of hers could get her there once he had it up and running. Like Brenda, she wouldn't look back at what she'd left behind.

Rick flopped over onto his back and stared at the ceiling.

He'd known the moment he'd set eyes on her that Kaylee Walsh was nothing but trouble for him. He'd had an instantaneous gut reaction when he'd slid out from under Frank Selby's pickup and spotted her standing over him.

Tonight's fiasco had done nothing but confirm his initial reaction. For as long as he lived he'd never forget the sight of a scantily dressed Kaylee sprawled on the floor amidst the shattered lamp. Her brunette hair cascaded around her shoulders; her blue eyes were dazed and confused.

The moment he'd touched her to help her into the bathroom, he'd reacted all the way to the tips of his toes. His fingertips had accidentally brushed the side of her breast and instantly longed to do more.

The entire time they'd been in the bathroom, he'd had all he could do to act unaffected and stick to the business of dressing her wound.

Rick rolled to his side, bunching the pillow until it was hard as a rock. If the rest of his body wasn't getting any relief, why should his head?

Kaylee's nightclothes consisted of a ribbed cotton undershirt that hugged the curves of her generous breasts and vividly outlined her nipples, and a pair of equally well-fitting boxers that did fabulous things for her hips and exposed her legs in all their glory.

Rick groaned and rolled to his stomach again. No. Bad idea. Too much pressure from the mattress. He flipped to his back and stared at the ceiling some more.

What would it be like to have Kaylee's curves pressed up against him? To feel the heat of her skin beneath his? To lift that skimpy shirt away from her breasts and slide a hand below the waistband of her boxers?

He knew how it would be. In his heart he knew how it would be with Kaylee. Hot and glorious and passionate.

Steamy, great sex. She'd give and she'd take in equal measures. And when she left, she'd take a piece of him he'd never get back.

He couldn't let that happen.

Chapter Six

Never willingly an early riser, Kaylee came awake even more slowly than usual.

She could hear the low murmurs of Rick and Molly from the kitchen, hushed morning tones, the hum of a country music radio station in the background, the rustle of newspaper, the clink of a spoon against a bowl.

She turned her head and opened her eyes. A sliver of the kitchen came into view like a slice of life.

Rick and Molly sat side by side at the table as they'd done last night. The newspaper was open between them. Rick was reading the comics to Molly, his dark head bent close to hers. *Peanuts. Garfield. Dennis the Menace.*

A lump formed in Kaylee's throat as she watched the two of them together. While Molly might lack a mother's presence in her day-to-day life, she'd won the jackpot when it came to her father. Rick clearly was doing his best to parent his daughter.

She sat up and reached for the robe she'd laid at the end of the sofa. Another new purchase, a cheap polyester imitation of silk in a blinding shade of fuchsia, she wrapped it around herself and wandered into the kitchen.

"Hi, Kaylee," Molly greeted around a mouthful of cereal.

"Hi, Molly." Kaylee smothered a yawn and fought the urge to rub her eyes with her fists. She shoved a handful of hair away from her face.

Rick's penetrating gaze made her wonder if he possessed X-ray vision, if he could see right through the thin material of her robe, through her pajamas to the skin underneath. She flushed, a full body wave of heat she couldn't control.

"There's coffee there if you want some." Rick tilted his head in the direction of the counter.

"Thanks."

Kaylee moved past him. She could swear the temperature of the room shot up as she did so.

"Mugs are in the cabinet there on the left."

Kaylee found a mug with the name of a local bank on it and poured coffee. She doused it with milk from the refrigerator and sugar from the bowl on the counter before returning to the table.

She sat across from Rick as she had last night and took a tentative sip.

"Want something to eat?" he asked.

"I'm not...hungry." Liar, her subconscious argued back, while her gaze ate Rick up.

Rick cleared his throat then glanced at his watch. Kaylee's gaze shot in the same direction. Yep, same turn-on reaction as yesterday. No doubt about it. She was a sucker for manly wrists. She needed professional help.

"Do you have those references? It's almost eight; that means it's seven there. Do you think it's too early to call?"

Kaylee shook her head. "No. Country folk are early risers."

Rick assessed her disheveled state in silent disagreement. His mouth quirked up slightly at the corners.

Kaylee grinned. "Except for me, that is. The only reason I ever got up early was to throw rocks at Granny Daisy's old rooster to get it to shut up."

Rick chuckled. "Did it work?"

Kaylee shook her head. "No. Like a lot of my plans it backfired. Since I was up so early, Granny Daisy found chores for me to do."

"You shouldn't throw rocks at birds," Molly informed her.

"You're right. It was a mean thing to do."

"What was the rooster's name?" Molly wanted to know.

"He didn't have a name. He wasn't a pet."

"Then why did you have him?"

Kaylee's gaze clashed with Rick's. She bit her lip. "Umm, he was good company for the other chickens."

"Did you throw rocks at them, too?"

"No. Just the rooster."

"Where are they now?"

Again, Kaylee's gaze crossed Rick's. She didn't want to get into a discussion of where the chickens had finally ended up any more than she wanted to explain the facts of life. She didn't want to lie to Molly either. "They're um, they're in chicken heaven," she blurted on a burst of divine inspiration.

Molly nodded solemnly. "That's where Mr. Whiskers went. Only he's in kitty heaven."

Molly slid off her chair and took her cereal bowl to the counter near the sink.

Rick lifted a brow as she passed the table. "Molly? What do you say?"

"'Scuse me."

She marched into the living room, plopped herself in a chair with the television remote and found a channel with cartoons.

"Uh, about those references," Rick said as he stood. He put a pad of paper and a pen in front of Kaylee. "If you can give me two or three, I'll call before I leave."

"Sure." Kaylee picked up the pen, stuck the end in her mouth while she thought. "Call Maxine Palmer first. She's the secretary at the elementary school. Mr. Palmer up and died real sudden and left her with five little ones."

Kaylee wrote down the name and phone number. "She won't be leaving for school for another half hour or so. Then you can call Anna May Jarvis. Anna May's House of Beauty. She's Bobby Lou's second cousin on his mama's side. I worked in her shop all last year."

After adding the second number, she thought for a moment while tapping the pen on the pad. "Let's see, then. Oh, I know. Call Martha Stewart. Not the Martha Stewart that's on TV with the sheets and towels. Martha Stewart that runs the Shop 'n Save back home. She'll vouch for me." Kaylee scribbled down the name and store number. "Her and Ed get into the store pretty early most days."

She handed the list to Rick. She took a sip of coffee while he looked it over. "Okay, then." He shifted from one foot to the other and looked over her head at the wall phone behind her. He glanced at his watch again.

Finally, Kaylee got what he wasn't saying. He wanted some privacy while he phoned her references. She shot out of her chair, almost spilling her coffee in the process. "I'll go get dressed, then."

He moved to let her by, but she moved in the same direction. Then they both moved again, so he still blocked her path.

"Want to dance?" Rick asked.

He was so close Kaylee caught his scent. He'd shaved earlier, the heavy growth of whiskers removed now, the clean fragrance of shaving cream and soap blended with virile male. She laughed nervously. Hell yes, she wanted to dance with him. And a whole lot more. But she wouldn't. Not today. Not any day.

He stepped back and bowed with an exaggerated flourish and a sweep of his hand, leaving room for her to pass by. Kaylee hightailed it to Molly's bedroom.

"Kay Lee Walsh? Well, I'll swan. She's down there in Florida, you say?" Maxine Palmer's Tennessee accent poured into Rick's ear in a slow gentle wave. "Broke my heart to see that girl up and leave. 'Course after Daisy passed on, and that no-good Bobby Lou Tucker broke her heart, I guess there weren't no reason for her to stay 'round Bertie Springs."

"Yes, ma'am," Rick interrupted politely. He glanced at his watch again. He'd be late opening the station. He had a feeling if he didn't get Maxine Palmer to the point he'd be on the phone with her the better part of the morning listening to a detailed history of Bertie Springs' residents.

"I'd like to hire her to take care of my daughter, Molly. Do you think she's qualified?"

"Oh my lands, yes. Folks 'round here been having Kay Lee Walsh look after their little ones almost before she stopped bein' a little one herself. I don't know what I'd have done without her after Mr. Palmer died. The twins, Garth and Dwight, well they was barely out of diapers. That Kay Lee, why she came over every afternoon after school. She wouldn't take no money from me neither, even though I know good and well between her and her granny, they didn't have two nickels to rub together. My girls, Loretta, Patsy and Tammy, why they adored Kay Lee."

"So you feel Ms. Walsh is qualified to babysit my daughter?"

"Yes, sir! Didn't I say so? You better snap her up while you can, mister. Kay Lee Walsh is a rare gem. Your daughter'll be lucky to have her."

"Well, thank you, Mrs. Palmer. You have a good day. Good-bye now."

Rick dialed the next number on the list. Clearly, Maxine Palmer led the Bertie Springs chapter of the Kay Lee Walsh Admiration Society.

Anna May Jarvis and Martha Stewart gushed in similar style. Kay Lee Walsh was reliable, responsible and possessed a heart of gold. She was sorely missed by the residents of her hometown, although a similar note of understanding of why she left threaded through the responses to Rick's questions.

By the time he hung up after the third call, he noticed the TV was off and Molly was not in the living room. He pushed open the door of her bedroom. Kaylee, in a pair of cut-off denim shorts, was bent across Molly's bed, smoothing the wrinkles out of the bedspread. The well-worn shorts hugged her bottom, bringing back to Rick the recent and clear memory of helping her into the truck yesterday afternoon. The palms of his hands itched to offer similar assistance once more.

"Kaylee says I should make my bed and brush my teeth before I watch TV," Molly informed Rick. She smoothed the bedspread on the other side and scooted past him to the bathroom.

Kaylee finished with the bed and straightened. Above the shorts she wore a faded pink tee shirt. She'd restrained her hair in a ponytail and she was barefoot. Rick licked his lips. Kaylee gave him a tentative smile.

"Looks like you're hired," he informed her.

She smoothed her hands down over her shorts. "O-Okay."

They stood staring at each other for what seemed a long time. Molly reappeared. "What are you guys doing?" She tilted her head back, her gaze sweeping from Rick to Kaylee and back.

"Hiring you a new babysitter, squirt." Rick hunkered down next to Molly. "You be good and do what Kaylee tells you, okay?"

"'kay," Molly agreed.

He glanced up at Kaylee. "If you have any problems, call me at the station. The number's by the phone."

"'kay." She grinned, purposely mimicking Molly's response.

He ruffled Molly's hair and hugged her and kissed her good-bye. "See you later, alligator."

"In a while, crocodile," she responded from long habit.

She held up her hand for Rick to high five.

"Be good." He gave Kaylee one last glance and left. The door closed behind him.

Outside, the truck engine rumbled. Kaylee sighed in relief.

While Molly busied herself with a puzzle, Kaylee sat with the newspaper in one hand and the remote control in the other. She found a cable news channel on the television and turned up the volume slightly. Although a jewel heist might not make the national news, it might make the ticker-tape news that ran across the bottom of the screen. Those gems in Old Blue's gas tank had to be stolen. By someone. From somewhere. And hidden in Old Blue for a reason. If she figured out the who and the where, maybe that would lead her to the why.

Kaylee kept one eye on the TV and with the other she scanned the headlines of each page of the *Jacksonville Times.*

She found the section where there was a list of each state's most noteworthy news. At almost the same moment the item from Tennessee caught her eye, the television newscaster snagged her attention. "Disguised as a security guard, a jewel thief in Knoxville, Tennessee apparently made off with precious gems estimated at over five million dollars. The FBI and local authorities are investigating."

Kaylee heard a loud roaring in her ears. She stared at the TV while the anchor went on to read other headlines. Her gaze refocused on the newspaper item which repeated virtually the same information. A jewel heist. Knoxville, Tennessee. The day before yesterday.

Kaylee's heart sunk to the pit of her stomach as reality set in. The day before yesterday. Her last day in Bertie Springs. Bobby Lou had asked to borrow her car because his pickup had a flat tire. He needed to drive into Knoxville to pick up a new one. Kaylee had told him no. She was packing to leave. She needed to load her things in the car so she could set out early in the morning.

Bobby Lou being Bobby Lou had sweet-talked her with his slow, honeyed drawl. Then he'd bribed her by promising to wash Old Blue, check the oil and the tires and bring it back with a full gas tank.

Kaylee knew the tank was almost as empty as her cash reserves. The promise of a free tank of gas had clinched her decision. Who was she to look a gift horse in the mouth?

Besides, Bobby Lou owed her something, didn't he? After he broke her heart by taking up with that stick figure, Georgia Rose. He'd even offered to help her load her things in the car so she'd be ready to go.

Kaylee agreed and off Bobby Lou had gone to Knoxville, returning as promised with a full tank of gas. He'd fetched and carried her boxes and bags, helping her arrange them in the trunk and the backseat. Then he'd wished her luck in Miami, dropped a kiss on the top of her head and joined his cousin Dwayne who'd come to pick him up.

Kaylee had known Dwayne Holcomb her whole life and she'd never liked him. He'd teased her unmercifully during her childhood and made lewd comments about her developing body during her teen years. He'd been in and out of trouble since his adolescence, leaving his poor parents at their wits' end before he was finally sent up to the state prison a couple of years ago for armed robbery.

Even as she'd said good-bye to Bobby Lou, she could feel Dwayne's gaze on her, ogling her, giving her that creepy feeling she always got around him. He continued to stare hard at her as he backed the truck out of the yard. Kaylee, refusing to give him the satisfaction of knowing he made her uncomfortable, stared back until the truck turned onto the road and disappeared.

Dwayne was a creep and a criminal, but Bobby Lou wasn't. At least he never had been before. But Bobby Lou had always hero-worshipped his older cousin. Dwayne was the bad boy Bobby Lou was too decent to be. Dwayne crossed the line. Bobby Lou only ever came close to toeing it. Until now.

Kaylee turned off the TV and got up from the couch. She went into the kitchen, found a sponge and some spray cleaner. Cabinets, refrigerator, sink. Cleaning helped her think, calmed her agitation.

What if Bobby Lou went to Knoxville and Dwayne was with him? Had the whole scheme been Dwayne's idea? Hard as she tried, Kaylee couldn't picture Bobby Lou robbing anyone. She'd loved him since childhood, dated him all through high school and beyond. He wasn't the brightest begonia in the flowerbed, but he had an inner sweetness, an innocence that didn't jive with her picture of a criminal element. Dwayne even teased Bobby Lou about his easygoing nature. Dwayne was a small fish in an even smaller pond. Not too many people put up with him these days. Bobby Lou was the one remaining member of the Dwayne Holcomb fan club.

Kaylee didn't know what to do. Should she call the FBI?

Sic them on Dwayne? And by doing so, send them after Bobby Lou as well? What if Bobby Lou was innocent? What if the jewel theft was all Dwayne's doing? But the gems were in her car. And Bobby Lou had borrowed Old Blue. Still, she couldn't send the authorities after Bobby Lou. Even after he'd dumped her and taken up with Georgia Rose, she couldn't generate that kind of vindictiveness toward him. She still felt a certain sense of loyalty to him, maybe only because of their past history.

Maybe Bobby Lou had found out what Dwayne had done? Maybe he stole the jewels away from Dwayne and planned to turn them in anonymously. But then why hide them in the gas tank when he knew she was leaving for Miami the next day?

She scrubbed the sink, moving the sponge round and round, mimicking the way her thoughts kept circling in her head. Maybe for right now she would do nothing, as she'd thought yesterday when she'd first found all those sparkling stones. She'd wait until she got to Miami. She trusted Tillie. Tillie would know what to do.

Chapter Seven

Kaylee peered over Molly's shoulder. "That looks good, Molly." Molly continued to happily stir the mixture of brown sugar, flour, cinnamon and oatmeal.

"And then we sprinkle this on the apples, right?"

"Yes. But first we have to add some butter."

Kaylee opened the refrigerator and removed a stick of margarine. Measuring the correct amount, she placed it on a cutting board and handed Molly a butter knife. "Now cut this up into little pieces and put them in the bowl there."

"'Kay." Molly went to work.

The phone rang. Kaylee wiped her hands on a towel and answered it. "Hello? Braddock residence."

"Braddock residence?" came the surprised female voice at the other end of the line. "Who is this?"

"Who's this?" Kaylee demanded. One could never be too careful these days. She knew better than to give out any information over the phone to a stranger.

"Who *is* this?"

Kaylee frowned. "Who is *this*?"

Molly glanced up. Kaylee covered the mouthpiece with her hand. "You're doin' good, sugar." Molly grinned at the compliment.

Kaylee blew an extra large bubble and returned her attention to the telephone.

"I don't know who you are, but I don't have time for these games. I called to leave a message for Rick."

Kaylee picked up a pen and the pad of paper she'd written her references on earlier. "Okay. Shoot."

"Who are you?"

"Who are you?" Kaylee grinned. She was beginning to enjoy this little game. She could almost hear the woman silently fuming.

Kaylee thought she heard the caller mutter something that sounded like "ridiculous", but she couldn't be sure. She blew another bubble and popped it loudly.

"Listen you, you tell Rick I want Molly this weekend. Jim and I want to take her to Disney World. I'll be there Friday around seven to pick her up. If he's got a problem with it he can call me." The phone slammed so hard in Kaylee's ear she jumped.

She hung it up and came back to the counter where Molly had succeeded in mixing the tiny lumps of margarine into the dry ingredients. "Who was that?"

"I'm not sure, hon. They didn't exactly say." Kaylee blew a big contemplative bubble and sucked it back into her mouth. "Now you can sprinkle this over the apples." She demonstrated for Molly then backed off to let her do it herself.

The caller had to be Molly's mother. Rick's ex-wife. She looked down at Molly's dark head bent in concentration over her task and tried to reconcile the voice on the phone as being related to such a pleasant little girl.

Oh, well. She snapped out of her thoughts. It wasn't any of her business. If all went as planned, Rick would fix her car. She'd spend no more than a month in Perrish, Florida. School would start. She'd bid Rick and Molly good-bye. Then she'd be on her way to Miami. Tillie would help her figure out what to do about the jewel-heist mystery.

Only a month to Miami, she repeated to herself. Only a month to Miami.

Rick walked in the door shortly after six. Kaylee ignored the flutter of excitement that rippled through her. Molly had no such compunction, however, and neither did Brutus.

The dog, who'd been fairly complacent all day, gave a couple of deep woofs in greeting while Molly squealed her delight as Rick swung her up into his arms and held her overhead for a moment.

Kaylee gave the skillet of potatoes and ground beef a quick stir and turned around as the three of them entered the kitchen. She sucked in a quick startled breath as Rick's dark gaze held hers. He stood there with Molly in his arms and Brutus happily wagging his tail. They looked like a ready-made family. The thought was in Kaylee's head before she could stop it. A family waiting for some lucky woman to come along and complete it.

Not me, she reminded herself. No way. No how. Her future was in Miami. Beaches, cruises, fashionable hair salons, eligible bachelors. She was so close she could almost taste it.

Rick's an eligible bachelor, her subconscious told her. Not exactly, Kaylee argued silently. He hardly comes unencumbered.

Molly wiggled out of Rick's arms and came over to Kaylee.

"Can we eat now?"

"We sure can, darlin', if your Daddy's ready."

"You made dinner."

"It's this ground beef and potato dish I make, nothing special. Brown the ground beef, cut up some potatoes, a can of cream of mushroom soup, salt, pepper, parsley flakes. It's real simple. I thought you'd be hungry. Molly helped—"
Kaylee cut off the flow of words this time all by herself. No doubt about it. Rick Braddock made her nervous. Especially

when he pinned her with his gaze the way he was now, as if he didn't know quite what to expect from her next.

"And we made apple crisp for dessert too, Daddy. Kaylee let me help."

Rick gazed around the kitchen as if he'd landed on some foreign planet. The table was set with placemats, the blue checkered ones his mother had bought on sale along with a few hand towels and dishcloths when she'd seen the sorry state of his kitchen linens on her visit last year.

A bunch of wildflowers, their tiny white and yellow heads poking up valiantly from the thin stems, held place of honor in a tall, narrow vase in the center of the table. Rick was quite sure he'd never seen the vase before.

"I made green beans too," Kaylee informed him. "Molly says you like green beans." Rick shook his head as if he'd been doused with cold water.

"Yeah, but she doesn't microwave them like you do, Dad," Molly said. "She put onions and butter in first and she cooked it all together with the beans."

Kaylee winced as though Molly had blurted all of her culinary secrets.

Rick transferred his attention to Molly, needing the distraction of his daughter to tear his gaze away from the woman in his kitchen. "I'll go wash up then, squirt, how about it?"

"Kaylee made lemonade, too," Molly called after him.

"From the lemons off our tree. And I helped!"

Rick closed the bathroom door on Molly's peal of laughter and the clink of glassware.

He gazed around the room as if he'd never seen it before. Something was different, but he couldn't put his finger on what. The same towels hung on the racks, the shower curtain still hung from the overhead rod. He picked up the same bar of soap he'd used this morning and washed his hands, trying to figure out what had changed.

"Nothing," he told his mirrored reflection. "Nothing has changed." *Except Kaylee's here now,* his subconscious reminded him. *Not for long,* he insisted in return. *Not for long.*

Rick's gaze clashed with Kaylee's once again as they held hands across the table during Molly's pre-dinner blessing. His hand, where it held hers, felt unnaturally warmed, like an electrical charge was transmitting itself from her fingertips to his.

The scent of hot food rose up from the meat and potato dish and the bowl of onions and green beans to tickle his nostrils. By the time Molly finished thanking God for apples, lemons, green beans and potatoes, Rick's mouth was watering. His stomach growled, his lunchtime sandwich a distant memory.

Kaylee had also emptied a can of peaches into a bowl and sprinkled them with cinnamon. Apparently Molly had informed her that she did not share her father's love of green beans.

He took generous helpings from every bowl on the table, including two slices of bread which he topped with margarine. He concentrated on his meal, vaguely wondering why he was so hungry and why everything tasted so good. Probably because he didn't have to cook it himself. He had the same feeling when his parents arrived for their semiannual visits and his mother took over the cooking for a week.

He spooned up the last bite of meat and potatoes from his plate and reached for the bowl. "This is good," he told Kaylee, sliding a glance in her direction.

"Daddy, you're not supposed to talk with your mouth full." Molly crossed her arms and frowned at him, her delicate brows furrowing in disapproval.

61

"Well, excuuuuse me," Rick drawled in a semi-imitation of the comedian, Steve Martin. He poked her in the ribs. "You must be a bad influence on me."

Molly giggled and uncrossed her arms. "What's a bad influence?" She speared a peach slice and popped it in her mouth.

Rick's gaze flickered in Kaylee's direction. "Somebody who makes you do things you know you shouldn't do," he answered. *Or someone who makes you feel things you'd rather not feel?* his subconscious asked.

Rick cleared his throat and gazed down at the enormous second helping he'd piled on his plate without realizing it. Somehow the small mountain of food echoed his sentiments about Kaylee. As if he'd taken on more than he could handle.

Absently, he picked up his fork and dug in. He'd met her yesterday, he scolded himself. How was it she'd gotten under his skin in less than twenty-four hours? Could it have something to do with seeing her sprawled on the floor in her pajamas last night? Or being squeezed into such close proximity with her in the bathroom? Holding her injured foot in his hand? Or maybe it was the way she'd wandered into the kitchen this morning in her brilliant fuchsia robe with sleepy eyes and rumpled hair.

Rick jabbed at the chunks of ground beef and potato, shoving them into his mouth and chewing, his agitation threatening to get the better of him.

"Daddy?" Molly patted his arm insistently. "Daddy!"

Rick jerked himself out of his wandering thoughts and looked at his daughter. "What?"

"I said can I be 'scused?"

Rick's glance automatically went to Molly's plate, which for once, was clean.

"Yes. And it's 'can I be *ex*cused'."

"Well, excuuuuse me," Molly said with a giggle, darting out of reach when Rick tried to playfully swat her behind as she passed by with her empty plate.

His grin faded as he caught Kaylee watching him from across the table, her chin propped in her hand, her empty plate pushed to one side.

Molly skipped into the living room and turned on the television. Vaguely Rick wondered what children had done for after-dinner entertainment before the Cartoon Network and Nickelodeon came along.

He sat back from the table. "What?" he demanded of Kaylee.

He seemed to have startled her out of her own thoughts. "Hmm?" Kaylee shook her head which sent the tendrils of curling hair around her ears and temples flying. "Nothing. Sorry."

She stood and began clearing the table.

Rick stood as well. He put his hand on her arm, then dropped it quickly as that same surge of warmth leaped from her skin to his. "I didn't expect you to cook and clean house, too. I'm sorry if I didn't make that clear."

Kaylee straightened. She was so close. Rick could count the few freckles sprinkled across her nose and the tops of her cheeks. He noticed two of her bottom teeth overlapped slightly. She had small, delicately shaped ears that hugged her head and sported a tiny blue earring in each lobe.

"It's okay. I don't mind. Molly likes to help. All I did was clean the kitchen. Oh, and the bathroom. Not that the bathroom wasn't clean before. Or the kitchen, either. I didn't mean that. You had a package of ground beef in the freezer. Molly showed me where the potatoes and onions were. And she told me you like green beans…"

Rick's gaze seemed to be transfixed on Kaylee's mouth as she spoke. The full, soft-looking lips, slightly smudged with the remnants of mocha lipstick. He hadn't processed a word she'd said. Something about clean bathrooms and green beans. He leaned in closer, a part of him wondering what in the hell he was doing. Another part not caring at all.

Beep! Beep! Beep!

Was it some kind of internal alarm system, Rick wondered.

Warning him away from Kaylee Walsh?

Beep! Beep! Beep!

Kaylee took a deep breath and stepped back as Molly raced by and slid to a stop in front of the oven.

Beep! Beep! Beep! went the oven timer insistently.

Kaylee crossed to the stove and turned it off.

"It's done! It's done!" Molly jumped up and down in excitement.

"Stand back," Kaylee warned. "The oven's hot. You don't want to get burned."

Kaylee opened the oven door releasing the strong aroma of apples and cinnamon which had hung only faintly in the air before.

Using a pair of pot holders, she lifted the baking pan out of the oven and closed the door.

"Mmm." Molly sidled up close to her. "It smells good."

"We'll let it cool for a little bit and then—"

"And then we put vanilla ice cream on it. And it's all melty and warm. Just like you said, right?"

Kaylee touched the tip of Molly's nose with her forefinger.

"Right."

Molly giggled and scooted back to the living room and the television.

Rick shooed a snuffling Brutus into the other room and started to clear the table, Kaylee's warning to Molly reverberating through his head. *Stand back. You don't want to get burned.*

Had he, he wondered, been saved by the bell?

Chapter Eight

Rick helped Kaylee clean the kitchen, maintaining as wide a berth as possible considering the limited space. The entire time he was aware of the apple-cinnamon aroma mixed enticingly with the scent of strawberry bubble gum that clung to Kaylee.

She still wore the tee shirt and cut-offs from this morning. Her feet were still bare. Most of her hair was clipped on top of her head, but a few loose strands curled enticingly around her nape and temples. She was entirely too appealing, Rick decided. And entirely too sexy for her own good. Or his.

As soon as possible he escaped to the living room and joined Molly on the couch. He pretended to read the paper and keep an eye on the cartoon as Molly chuckled from time to time, but in truth he could focus on neither. Awareness of Kaylee Walsh hummed through his system. He could hear her still puttering in the kitchen. What could she be doing? Cleaning out his cabinets? Cleaning the refrigerator more likely. Rick wasn't much of a housekeeper, and he'd be the first to admit it.

The cartoon ended and yet another commercial break started. He set the paper aside. "I'm going to walk Brutus.

Then it'll be about time for your bath, right, squirt?" he asked as Kaylee came into the room.

Molly's eyes lit up. "Can Kaylee give me a bath?"

Rick shook his head. "She's your babysitter when I'm not here. Just like Miss Tiffany. Plus she cleaned the bathroom, made dinner *and* dessert already today. We don't want to wear her out."

"I don't mind," Kaylee mouthed to Rick over Molly's head. "But it's up to you," she added.

"See, Dad, she doesn't mind," Molly chirped, having picked up on what was intended to be Kaylee's silent communication. Kaylee rolled her eyes. So much for diplomacy.

She grinned at Rick and shrugged in apology.

"Okay, I guess. If Kaylee doesn't mind."

"She said she didn't, Dad," Molly pointed out as she slid off the couch. She grabbed Kaylee's hand and tossed her head. "Men!" She sniffed. "Come on, Kaylee. Grandma gave me bubble bath for my birthday. It smells like strawberries."

Kaylee allowed herself to be led to the bathroom. She ran warm water into the tub and added the bubble bath while Molly undressed. Molly dumped a plastic container of bath toys into the tub before she joined them, holding onto Kaylee's arm. She held up a bedraggled Barbie doll who looked like she'd had one too many bubble baths.

"This is Olympic Gold Medal Barbie," Molly informed her. She stood the doll on the side of the tub and posed her as if she were a high diver.

"Whoo!" She squealed as Barbie made her dive. Molly pretended the doll swam under water to the edge of the tub where she resurfaced. "Six-eight. Six-two. Six-two. Six-five. And look, a six-nine from the Swedish judge. You did all right, Barbie." Molly high-fived the doll's tiny hand.

Kaylee knelt at the side of the tub, thoroughly amused by Molly's game. While Molly splashed and played and chattered, Kaylee ran a soapy washcloth over her. A lump formed and tightened in her throat. A memory from her own childhood surfaced. Her mother bathing her like this. Oh, she hadn't had anything as fancy as an Olympic Gold Medal Barbie to play with in the tub. Mostly she had cast-off plastic containers and a couple of floating toys.

But she could remember the scent of the soap, her mother's gentle hand on her skin. As a child, she'd probably chattered like Molly, making up her own games, playing with her few toys. And like Molly, she'd had to do without a mother, although she'd been twice Molly's age when Lenore had hightailed it out of Bertie Springs with that traveling chickenfeed salesman, Russ Gantry.

It was okay, though, Kaylee reminded herself. Granny Daisy had stepped in and finished the job Lenore had started. And Molly? Well, Molly had Rick as a father. If Molly herself were any indication, he was doing an admirable job of raising his daughter without the help of a wife.

As the last of the bubbles disappeared, Kaylee managed to coax Molly out of the tub with the promise of apple crisp and ice cream. Once dry, Molly wiggled into her nightgown.

Rick returned with Brutus as they were dishing up dessert. He joined them at the table, trying not to ogle Kaylee's chest where she'd been splashed during Molly's bath. The damp tee shirt clung enticingly to the curves of her breasts. Vaguely Rick wondered if Kaylee'd ever entered a wet-tee-shirt contest. She'd win hands down, he thought.

Oh, good. A new fantasy for his repertoire. Kaylee in a soaked tee shirt parading in front of a bunch of men in some sports bar. No, he told himself. Kaylee wasn't that type of woman. And if she were with him, he wouldn't allow ogling of any sort by another man.

Brows knit in confusion, he spooned up ice cream and apple crisp, wondering where this possessive feeling regarding Kaylee Walsh had come from. He squelched it, refused to think about it. Shoved it way down deep where he kept all the other feelings he preferred not to think about. Like what it felt like when Brenda announced she wanted a divorce. Or how lonely he was sometimes at the end of the day, when

Molly went to bed and he had only Brutus for company. As much as he loved the dog, conversation was not one of the animal's strong suits.

He ate the dessert, noticing on some level the chewy sweetness of the topping mixed with melting ice cream, the tartness of the warm apples. But mostly what he noticed was the way Kaylee smiled at Molly in between bites of her own dessert. He also noticed the way the tip of her tongue darted out of her mouth a time or two to lick her lips.

Damn! He didn't want to be noticing her lips any more than he wanted to notice her damp tee shirt.

He scraped the last drops of ice cream and apple from his bowl and pushed his chair back.

"All done, squirt?" he asked Molly.

She'd eaten all of the ice cream and the topping. Most of the apples remained in the bottom of her bowl.

"Did you like it, Daddy? You know what's in it?" Molly slid off her chair and followed him to the sink. He set his bowl down and spooned up what was left in hers. "Oatmeal and sugar and brown sugar and cinnamon and butter," Molly told him. "I made that part."

"It was dee-licious," Rick told her, polishing off the last bite. He bowed low at the waist. "My compliments to the chefs." He caught Kaylee's eye, including her in the praise.

Molly giggled and grabbed his hand, tugging him out of the kitchen. "Story time.

Story time."

"Brush teeth time. Brush teeth time," Rick answered back.

"Story first."

"Teeth first."

"Oh, Dad," Molly groaned.

Kaylee carried her own bowl to the counter, smiling at their banter. Brutus followed her, head raised, inquisitive nose sniffing the air. After spending an entire day with him, she knew the dog was harmless. But he seemed to have a neverending curiosity about what was on the kitchen table, and a hypersensitive alert system to the tiniest crumb that fell to the floor. She glanced down at his woeful, hopeful brown eyes as he looked from her to the dish she held. "Okay, one little taste." She swiped her finger around the bottom of the bowl and offered it to him. His warm pink tongue licked the goo off that finger and continued on to the rest of her hand before she pulled back. "All gone," she informed him, though the look he gave her was one of pure disbelief. Kaylee chuckled. Like everything else in Rick's house, she seemed to have adjusted almost immediately to his dog, her earlier discomfort around the animal forgotten.

She rinsed the bowls and put them in the dishwasher and covered the remainder of the apple crisp for the refrigerator.

She went to the bathroom to straighten up and retrieve Molly's discarded clothes. In doing so she saw another slice of Rick and Molly's life together. Rick, looking entirely too big and masculine for Molly's twin bed, was stretched out on it nonetheless, pillows bunched up behind his head. Molly was tucked in the curve of his arm, her dark head and pink nightgown in vivid contrast to his white tee shirt and jeans. From a book of fairy tales, he was reading Rumpelstiltskin. He was even doing the voices of the characters. A high-pitched, comical falsetto for the miller's daughter, a deeper throaty voice for Rumpelstiltskin. Kaylee felt that lump in her throat again.

She stepped out to the garage to add Molly's clothes to the pile in the laundry basket next to the washer. Was that what she was trying to do? Spin straw into gold? Turn herself into something she wasn't? She was a small-town girl from the hills of Tennessee with the accent to prove it. Her plan was to become slick and sophisticated once she arrived in Miami. But sometimes she wasn't so sure it was what she wanted.

All she knew for certain was that nothing remained for her in Bertie Springs, Tennessee. But what would she find in Miami? Would it be any better? Or just different?

She leaned against the washer, arms crossed.

No. She wasn't going to start doubting herself now. She'd made a decision. She'd stick to her goal. Miami or bust.

Her thoughts scattered when Rick appeared in the doorway. His dark gaze trapped her, and she couldn't look away. It seemed they stood there, staring at each other for a very long time, but probably it was only a few seconds.

"Molly wants to tell you good night."

Kaylee snapped out of the slightly hypnotic trance Rick's gaze imposed on her.

"Okay."

She slid past him, all too aware of the heat from his body as she did so.

Molly's bedroom light was still on. Molly herself had been tucked under the covers.

"Good night, Molly," Kaylee said as she approached.

Molly tracked her as she came close to the bed. She lifted her arms up and Kaylee bent to hug her. Molly squeezed her neck tightly, and that mysterious lump appeared once again in Kaylee's throat. It occurred to her that it had been a while since anyone had hugged her. Not since Granny Daisy's funeral, in fact. And those had been hugs of sympathy, which felt entirely different from Molly's hug of affection.

She kissed Molly's forehead and turned out the lamp, leaving only the glow of a small nightlight. "Sweet dreams."

Chapter Nine

Rick took up most of the couch, although he didn't seem very interested in the baseball game playing on the television screen.

Kaylee perched on the edge of a chair and pretended to be fascinated by the Florida Marlins lineup. After about fifteen minutes, she asked, "Is it okay if I take a shower? Or would you like the bathroom first?"

"You go ahead."

Kaylee retraced her steps to Molly's room, hoping by now she'd be asleep. She was and Kaylee found her pajamas and robe easily.

She stood under the shower, letting the warm water wash over her. She needed to ask Rick if he'd had a chance to look at her car. And she needed to tell him some woman, presumably Molly's mother, had called.

She returned to the living room to find Rick idly flipping channels with the remote control. She sat once again in the chair and pretended to be interested in the parade of commercials. She crossed her legs. She had no idea what Rick's normal evening routine was. She wasn't especially tired, but Rick was occupying her bed anyway. She could hardly kick him off his own couch in any case.

After a few minutes, he sat up. "I think I'll take Brutus for a walk."

"Didn't you just take him?"

"Huh? Oh, yeah, right. I need to go outside for a while."

Rick escaped out the front door and stood for a moment breathing in the steamy night air. No rain today, which meant the humidity hadn't broken even temporarily. It was probably twenty degrees cooler inside, but even the air conditioning couldn't override the heat he felt whenever he and Kaylee were in the same room.

The scent of her clean skin had wafted through the air to tickle his senses. Out of the corner of his eye, he'd watched her relax back into her chair and cross her legs. She had stunning legs. The hem of her short robe had ridden up to mid-thigh, which churned up even more memories of what lay beneath that robe. The thin cotton undershirt and boxers.

Rick took a deep breath, feeling as if he were underwater. The warm air did nothing to cool his skin or his thoughts. What was he doing out here anyway? That was his house in there. His couch. His television. Why had he suddenly felt such a need to escape?

Not from the house itself, certainly. But from Kaylee. Before his fantasies took hold and he did something stupid like try to turn them into reality.

Where was he supposed to go now? He had no inclination to take a walk. But he couldn't go back inside yet, either. Not until he got himself under control.

His keys were still in his pocket. He went to the truck and climbed in. He lowered the windows and turned on the radio. Leaning his head back against the seat he stared at the ceiling. Night had fallen. There were no streetlights. Only the glow of light through the windows of the neighboring houses pierced the dark.

He forced himself to think about nothing, letting the lyrics of the country singers whine through his head. Why was it, he wondered, country singers seemed to have only two subjects?

Getting dumped or getting a new truck.

He had no idea how long he sat like that. Long enough to attract a mosquito or two, before the door to his house opened and Kaylee stood for a moment, looking out before she spied him. She closed the door and crossed the yard in bare feet. The passenger door opened and she climbed up next to him, closing the door behind her. But not before he got another nice glimpse of legs and cleavage when the interior light came on.

"Hi," she said.

"Hi."

"What are you doing?"

"Nothing. Just sitting here."

"Do you come out here and sit by yourself a lot in the evenings?" Kaylee asked.

"No."

"Is it a special occasion?"

Rick turned his head sideways and looked at her without answering. He couldn't tell her he'd come out here to get away from her, could he?

Kaylee didn't seem to mind that he ignored her question. "Did you get a chance to look at my car today?"

"Yeah," Rick said. "It looks like your starter's bad. I'll have to locate a replacement."

"Will that take long?"

"Probably not. But they don't make them anymore. Most likely I can get one from a salvage dealer."

"Are you sure that's what's wrong with it?"

"I'm sure. But if you want to get a second opinion, be my guest. Wouldn't be the first time a woman had doubts about me."

"Oh. No, I didn't mean... Never mind. I trust you." Kaylee was quiet for a minute.

Then, "I wanted to tell you a woman called today. She wouldn't give me her name."

Rick looked at her again. "Oh?"

"Yes. She said to tell you she wanted to take Molly to Disney World this weekend with somebody named Jim, and she'd pick her up on Friday." Kaylee hesitated. "She sounded kind of annoyed."

Rick snorted. "That was Brenda. I don't know why she wouldn't give you her name, though."

"That might sort of be my fault, actually."

Intrigued, Rick asked, "How so?"

"When I answered the phone she said, 'Who's this?' and I said, 'Who's this?' We went back and forth with that for a while and I think it ticked her off."

Rick laughed. Kaylee felt encouraged. "So then she left the message about picking up Molly and hung up."

Rick chuckled. "That sounds like Brenda all right."

"Your ex-wife, I guess? Molly's mother."

"Yep."

"How long have you been divorced?" Kaylee asked.

"Almost four years." Rick tapped his fingers on the steering wheel, but he didn't seem annoyed by the question.

"Was it hard for you? Being divorced, I mean?"

Rick shrugged. "At first. But the truth is, Brenda and I wanted different things. We always did, but it took us a few years of marriage before we realized it. Splitting up was for the best. We'd only have made each other more miserable if we'd stuck it out."

"Wow, that's a really mature thing to say."

Rick grinned, a slash of white teeth in the dark which was broken only by the glow of the radio dial. "Thanks. I've been practicing."

Kaylee smiled. "Molly's a wonderful little girl."

"Yeah. She's a good kid."

"You're a good dad."

Rick shrugged. "Sometimes I wonder about that."

"Are you kidding? You're teaching her manners. She goes to Sunday school. She eats right. You read to her. What more could a kid want from a dad?"

Rick lifted his shoulders again. "I don't know. Maybe a dad who's capable of finding her a new mother?"

"Hey, I grew up with only one parent around, and I turned out okay. I think."

"I'd say you turned out great."

Kaylee leaned toward Rick and grinned, her hand on his forearm in a gesture of genuine appreciation. "Thanks."

His expression, virtually unreadable in the dim light, held her suspended in fascination. He leaned closer and so, somehow, did she. Their lips touched in mutual curiosity which lasted only a second. Heat exploded and the gap between them closed as Rick hauled her closer. Their mouths melded, their tongues touched. Kaylee moaned deep in her throat as Rick's arms wrapped around her. How she'd longed to be held again. She was in his lap, straddling him, their kisses long, slow, deep and hot. Kaylee clasped her arms around Rick's neck, every sense on full alert. She could feel the soft denim of his jeans against her bare legs. Her breasts were smashed against the width of his chest. He tasted vaguely of apples and cinnamon and smelled of before-dinner soap and man. The silk of his dark hair slid over her fingers. She ached to get closer to him.

She wiggled around, her lips never leaving his, yanking his tee shirt up and out of the way, splaying her palms against the heat of his skin. Her foot hit something. The turn signal lever, maybe, but who cared? Maybe it was a sign. Her relationship with Rick Braddock was about to take a turn for the better.

Kaylee and Rick were rasping for air, concentrating only on each other. Rick firmly planted her in his lap, holding her tight against his arousal. She heard his groan of frustration and smiled even as they kissed. His hands slid up to cup her breasts through the thin material of her robe and pajama top. She moaned in anticipation as his thumbs grazed her nipples.

She could hardly breathe. The temperature inside the cab must be over a hundred. Her brain had overheated along with her body. Between the two of them, they'd started a fire in

Rick's truck. Kaylee hoped they didn't have to call out the volunteer firefighters.

She smiled again.

"What?" Rick whispered against her mouth, feeling her lips curve beneath his.

"Fire. Hot," Kaylee whispered back, not caring if he understood her explanation or not.

He murmured his agreement from deep in his chest.

He untied her robe and pushed it back, the palms of his hands skimming up the tops of her thighs before he reached behind her and held her tightly as they ground against each other.

Kaylee could feel Rick's arousal and she knew at that moment she wanted to go to bed with him. She wanted everything he had to offer and then some. She didn't care if he thought her cheap or easy. She wanted this man. Right here.

Right now. For all time.

She tore her mouth away from his. "Rick, I—"

The driver's side door popped open. The interior lights came on. Kaylee blinked in confusion as Rick held her slightly away from him. She stared down into the brilliance of a flashlight trained directly on her before looking away, holding up a hand to shield her eyes.

"What the—" This came from Rick.

"Rick? That you in there?"

"Hell, yes, Kevin. Get the light out of my eyes, would you?"

The light lowered and Kaylee blinked owlishly, still afraid to look at the intruder. Rick eased her off his lap and back onto the seat next to him. For the first time she became aware of a flashing yellow light overhead. Rick reached over to the lever near the steering column and turned it off.

"Sorry, Rick. Irv and me, we saw the light flashing.

Thought it was some kids messing with your truck."

"Didn't expect you'd be out here, sitting in the dark, running your wrecker lights." This came from another individual. Kaylee could make out two grizzled heads beyond the open door.

"It's me, and uh, a friend," Rick assured the two. He snapped the door shut. "Thanks for looking out for me."

"No problem, Rick. It's our week for the neighborhood watch, anyway. We don't want no trouble. Kids, you know."

"Yeah. Right, Irv. Kevin." He gave a half salute of dismissal. Kaylee squinted into the darkness as the two elderly men shuffled away, back to their house, apparently next door to Rick's. Belatedly, she realized her state of dishevelment. She straightened her pajamas as best she could and retied the sash on her robe.

Her cheeks burned. What had she been thinking? Coming out here in her nightclothes? Making out with a man she'd known for barely twenty-four hours? Granny Daisy was probably spinning in her grave thinking she hadn't raised her granddaughter any better than a common floozy.

"Oh." Kaylee didn't mean to release her expression of distress, but it escaped somehow, clearly audible over Toby Keith on the radio asking, "How do you like me now?"

Rick exhaled on a heartfelt sigh. "Yeah. 'Oh'."

Kaylee chanced a look his way, but he was staring straight ahead. She didn't know what to say. She couldn't seem to think clearly. It was like her normal common sense had somehow been short-circuited. Rick Braddock had that effect on her. All of a sudden her brain stopped functioning. Happened pretty much every time he looked at her or got too close to her. It wasn't good not to be thinking when a man like Rick was around.

Without another word, Kaylee opened her door and slid to the ground. The gravel drive prickled her feet. In comparison, the grass felt dewy and cool. Kaylee ignored it all. She went back inside and resolutely made up her bed on the couch. She turned off the TV, and got under the covers before removing her robe.

She pretended to be asleep when she heard Rick open the door. She thought he hesitated, but maybe it was her imagination. Her lips still tingled from kissing him.

"Brutus," he whispered. She heard the dog's nails click across the terrazzo.

She held her breath until she heard Rick's bedroom door close. Then she opened her eyes and stared at the ceiling.

Chapter Ten

The following evening Kaylee exited the bathroom after her shower and couldn't help but notice Rick was on the phone in the kitchen. He'd insisted on cleaning up after dinner. That was done, but Rick looked none too happy.

He listened, the receiver wedged between his shoulder and his ear while he flipped through a stack of mail on the counter. Kaylee didn't know if his frown was due to the mail or the conversation. She wished she could give him more privacy, but there was virtually no place for her to go.

The television buzzed on low volume. Kaylee busied herself making up the couch for the night.

"You don't know anything about her, Brenda, so why don't you knock it off," Rick said.

He listened for a minute or more. "I told you. She's a friend. She's taking care of Molly until school starts."

Kaylee could only imagine what Rick's ex-wife was saying. She was glad she'd told him about their phone conversation already.

Rick snorted, that half-laugh, half-disgusted sound he made every now and then as if he didn't want to be amused but couldn't help himself.

"Brenda, my love life is none of your business. We're divorced, remember? I'll have Molly ready Friday at seven."

He hung up as Kaylee straightened after tucking the edge of the sheet under the cushions. They looked at each other. Kaylee didn't want Rick to think she'd purposely eavesdropped. She'd done her best not to. In fact, she'd done her best to avoid him all day. This morning she'd pretended to wake up only after Molly turned on the cartoons.

Then she'd stayed on the couch under the covers until Rick left.

She'd prepared dinner once again, but when Rick offered to clean up afterward, she didn't stick around to help. Instead she took Brutus for a walk around the neighborhood. It amazed even her how quickly she'd become accustomed to the big dog, who was mild mannered in spite of his size.

"I guess Molly's going to Disney World," she said.

Rick came toward her. "Not necessarily. Brenda has a habit of promising things she doesn't deliver on. I've learned never to tell Molly what Brenda has planned. Instead, I pack for every possible eventuality and hope for the best. That way Molly isn't disappointed."

"Oh." Kaylee didn't know what to say. Surely Molly wasn't the only person disappointed by Brenda.

"She can't wait to meet you," Rick said.

"Me! Why on earth would she want to meet me?"

Rick took a seat in one of the chairs, stretching his legs out in front of him, arms crossed behind his head. A corner of his mouth quirked up in a half smile. "She thinks there's something going on between us."

Kaylee plopped onto the neatly made-up couch. "But you told her—I heard you tell her—we're just friends."

"Yeah. That's what I said."

Kaylee bit her lip. "Sorry, I didn't mean to eavesdrop."

Rick gave a slight shrug of indifference. "Hey, if I'd wanted privacy I'd have used the phone in my room. I didn't say anything you shouldn't have heard."

Kaylee chewed her lip some more, wishing she had a piece of bubble gum to chomp on instead. What was Rick trying to tell her? That they were friends and that was it? Maybe he was ready to forget that incredible interlude in his truck the other night. Yeah, right! Rick Braddock had been ready to jump her bones then, and she bet if she gave him the slightest bit of encouragement he would now. Who was he trying to convince?

Her?

Himself? Or his ex-wife?

Kaylee fought the apprehension she felt all day Friday. She wanted to make a good impression on Rick's ex-wife. No, that wasn't exactly it. She wanted Rick's ex-wife to be jealous of her. She wanted Brenda to think there was more to her relationship with Rick than mere friendship.

But she wasn't sure why. She'd be gone as soon as Rick fixed her car. As soon as school started, she would be on her way to Miami, and she planned to never look back at what she left behind. Not her life in Bertie Springs, Tennessee, or this temporary stop on the way to her dreams.

Why did she give a hoot what the former Mrs. Rick Braddock thought of her?

Darned if I know, she told herself irritably. As if to prove her point she blew a big bubble and popped it loudly as she cleared up the remnants of pizza and soda glasses from the table. Frozen pizza from the supermarket, to be sure, because there wasn't a take-out place in Perrish. But Friday was apparently the night where the rules were relaxed a bit. Molly got soda with her pizza, wasn't expected to eat any vegetables and she chose a cherry Popsicle for dessert. A glance at the kitchen clock told Kaylee Molly's mother would arrive any minute.

Rick was in Molly's bedroom with her, probably giving her last-minute instructions on how to behave and packing her Power Puff Girls duffel bag.

Kaylee firmly clamped down on the butterflies racing around in her stomach. Maybe the reason she was so nervous was that once Molly left, she and Rick would be alone.

Maybe that's what you're afraid of, her subconscious niggled at her.

"Maybe it is," she muttered back as she gave the counter a final swipe.

The doorbell rang. Kaylee swallowed her gum in a nervous gulp.

"Kaylee, can you get that? We're not quite ready in here," Rick called from the bedroom.

Kaylee smoothed down her denim skirt and checked her red gingham blouse for dribbles or splashes as she fluffed her hair on the way to the door. She'd worn her uncomfortable high-heeled mules, because she knew they made her legs look great beneath the short skirt.

She opened the door to a woman who could have stepped out of a photo shoot for the cover of *Vogue*. Rick's ex-wife was a fashion plate to say the least. Her almost-black hair was cut fashionably short in a chic style that clung to her head.

She wore white hip-hugger slacks cinched with a silver belt and a multicolored clingy top. Her make-up was flawless, her jewelry elegant. In her spike-heel sandals she was almost the same height as Kaylee.

Kaylee pasted a smile on her lips and forced herself to speak. "Hello. You must be Molly's mother. Won't you come in?"

Won't you come in? Even to Kaylee the words sounded out of place. Stop it, she warned herself. Stop trying to be someone you're not.

Oh, but she wanted to be someone else at that moment.

She wanted to be someone cool, slick and sophisticated. Like Rick's ex-wife. She wanted expensive clothes and a trendy haircut and—she glanced beyond Brenda—a bright red Jaguar parked on the street with a man behind the wheel. She wanted that, too. A nice car and a man that came with it.

Somehow she managed to keep her wits about her and move out of Brenda's way and close the door. "I'm Kaylee." Not knowing what else to do, she offered her hand.

Brenda took it in her own slender, perfectly manicured one. "Brenda Madigan." Kaylee wasn't immune to the not-so-subtle once-over Brenda gave her.

Thank goodness for movement in the hallway. Molly stepped forward. "Hi, Mommy." Kaylee noticed the lack of enthusiasm in Molly's voice.

Brenda turned and stooped to embrace Molly. "Hi, sweetheart. All ready to go?" Her note of false cheeriness hung in the air.

"I guess." Molly patted Brenda's shoulder the same way she'd patted Rick's arm the other night, as if she had to take care of her parents and not the other way around.

"Hi, Brenda." Rick's tone matched Molly's. Clearly, no one was happy to see Brenda.

Brenda straightened. She nodded in his direction. "Rick."

Brutus chose that moment to pad past Rick and Molly. He stuck his nose near the zipper of Brenda's slacks, leaving a string of drool across the previously spotless fabric.

"Oh! Get away from me, you!" Brenda stepped back, pushing the dog away at the same time. Her heel came down on Kaylee's instep. Kaylee, who hadn't been expecting Brenda to back into her, automatically tried to give her room, but somehow the heel of Brenda's sandal caught on the strap of Kaylee's mule. Hopelessly intertwined, Kaylee reeled back, reaching for something, anything to prevent a fall. Her arm found the lamp on the end table near the couch and sent it crashing to the floor. She joined it with Brenda in a sprawl on top of her.

Kaylee's head hit the unforgiving terrazzo and she saw stars before everything went black.

Her eyes fluttered open to see Rick frowning, genuine concern in his expression and Molly's little hand patting her cheek.

"Are you okay?" Rick asked gruffly.

She started to nod, but groaned instead at the pressure of the floor against the back of her head.

"Come here." Before she realized his intention, Rick slid one arm under her shoulders and the other beneath her knees and stood, placing her gently on the couch.

"Sorry about your lamp," she whispered as he laid her down.

He gave her that half smile. "I'll put it on your tab."

"Well, thank you for your concern. I'm fine." This came from Brenda, who had regained her footing and appeared unharmed.

Rick stood, hands on hips. "Let's be realistic, Brenda. You're hardly the injured party here."

Brenda sniffed and brushed imaginary soot off her slacks and top. "Perhaps not. But this outfit is ruined. Not that you'd care about that, even though it cost more than you make in a week."

A muscle ticked in Rick's set jaw and his eyes darkened even more if that were possible. He switched his attention from his ex-wife to his daughter. "What do you say, squirt, about time for you and Mommy to go, don't you think?"

Molly looked anxiously at Kaylee. "Are you going to be okay? You're not going to die, are you?"

"I'll be fine. My head's way harder than this floor. In fact, I might fall down a couple more times while you're gone to teach it a lesson."

Molly giggled in relief and threw her arms around Kaylee's neck squeezing tightly.

Kaylee hugged her back and whispered something in her ear.

"I love you too," Molly said in a not-so-soft whisper.

Kaylee blushed. She saw Brenda's look of competitiveness and Rick's of astonishment before Molly released her.

"Let's go, Mol." Rick picked her up and carried her out the door, stopping for her duffel bag on the way. Molly waved to Kaylee over Rick's shoulder and Kaylee waved back.

Only Brenda remained. She gave Kaylee a pitying look. "I guess when a man can't hang on to a woman like me, he has to settle for whatever cheap imitation that comes along."

She turned on her heel and disappeared through the door. Tears welled up in Kaylee's eyes even while she told herself she shouldn't be hurt by Brenda's words. *A cheap imitation.* The description whirled through her throbbing head. Is that all she was? All she was destined to be? Surely she was good enough in her own right. She couldn't spend her life chasing after something better, trying to be something other than what she was.

Chapter Eleven

A few minutes later Rick reappeared. He looked down at Kaylee. "Are you all right?"

"I'm fine."

She blinked back the shimmer of tears that she didn't want to let fall.

He sat on the coffee table. "You're hurt, aren't you? We'll go to the hospital. They'll do a CAT scan, probably. Maybe you've got a concussion."

He was ready to scoop her off the couch and into his arms, but she blocked the move with a hand on his chest. "Rick, stop it. I don't have a concussion."

He peered at her unconvinced. "Are you sure? How can you be sure?"

"It's a bump on the head, is all."

"Fine. Let me see."

Kaylee half sat up and bent her head. Rick's fingers were gentle as he parted her hair. "That's a helluva lump."

Kaylee nodded and sank back on the cushion, careful not to lie on the injured area. "Want some ice for it? How about some aspirin? Or I've got Tylenol."

Kaylee nodded. "That'd be great."

Rick went to the kitchen and Kaylee was left alone with her thoughts once again.

What was she doing? She was going to Miami, she reminded herself. Yes, but what did she expect to find in Miami? Something she hadn't found anywhere else? Certainly not in Bertie Springs. Maybe what she was looking for didn't exist.

But what was she looking for? The respite provided by her broken-down car and the past few days spent mostly with a six-year-old had given her way too much time to think. She was second-guessing herself, something she swore she wouldn't do once she made the decision to head for Miami.

She couldn't shake the feeling that she was running away, even though she tried to convince herself she was running to something. But what?

Surely the key to happiness did not lie in a place or a thing.

Why had she thought things would be different once she left Tennessee? She thought *she'd* be different, suddenly transformed somehow, once she got to Miami. She was more than halfway there and nothing had changed. *She* hadn't changed. One visit from Brenda Madigan had brought that point home to her.

Rick returned with ice and aspirin and a glass of water. She swallowed the tablets and he sat, rearranging the cushions so she could lie down and he could hold the ice pack on her head. "Better?" he asked after a few minutes.

Kaylee nodded, trying to will away the tears that filled her eyes. Her usual spunk had evaporated, whether from the blow to her head or the blow to her ego, she couldn't have said.

All she knew was that Molly's hug and now Rick's kindness were taking some kind of toll on her, breaking down her defenses.

"Mind if I watch TV?" Rick asked.

Kaylee shook her head.

He clicked the set on and moved through several channels until he found a movie to his liking. She could feel him settle down next to her, still holding the ice in place.

Kaylee must have dozed off for the next thing she knew she woke up feeling groggy and disoriented. From the TV came a low buzz of sound and flickering light. Rick was standing over her with a blanket which he laid on top of her.

"What time is it?" she whispered.

"After eleven," he whispered back, although there was absolutely no reason for such hushed tones. "How's your head?"

"It hurts."

"Want some more aspirin?"

"Yes."

Rick shook out two tablets from the bottle on the table and handed her the water. Kaylee swallowed them and lay back down. She had no plans to get up and get ready for bed. Rick left and returned shortly with her bed pillows and waited until Kaylee was settled.

"Think you'll be okay?" He laid a hand on her head, his thumb feathering down to stroke the skin near her eyebrow. Even in the dim light Kaylee could see the genuine concern in his expression. She felt the heat from his hand flood through her. A lump of longing settled in her throat.

"I'm fine," she managed once again.

He gave her that half smile that had become so familiar to her. "Okay. See you in the morning."

He removed his hand and Kaylee watched him retreat to his bedroom with Brutus trailing behind him.

After going to sleep so early, Kaylee was the first one up the next morning. She took a shower, dressed and made coffee before Rick made an appearance.

He shuffled into the kitchen looking a little bleary-eyed, his hair still rumpled, whiskers darkening his jaw. He had on a ribbed undershirt and baggy shorts. Kaylee thought he looked divine.

"You're up early," he grumbled as he helped himself to coffee.

Kaylee looked up guiltily from the newspaper she'd been reading. Every day she scoured the newspaper as well as the cable news networks for more information on the Knoxville jewel heist. So far, she'd found nothing other than the original mention of it.

Rick took a seat at the table across from her and scrubbed his hands across his face before taking a sip from his mug.

"I went to sleep early, remember?" She smiled. She felt a hundred percent better than she had last night.

"How's your head?"

"Better, thanks. Want some breakfast?"

Rick shook his head. "Not at the moment."

He yawned and stretched his arms overhead, the muscles of his arms and shoulders exuding sleepy strength.

Kaylee grinned. "So this is what you're like when Molly's not around."

"This is what I'm like on Saturday mornings whether she's here or not," he corrected. He picked up his mug.

"Does her mother have her every weekend?" None of your business, Kaylee, she told herself, but darn it all, she was intensely curious about Rick's relationship with his ex-wife.

"Technically, she gets Molly every other weekend, two weeks in the summer and alternate school holidays."

"Technically?" Kaylee echoed.

Rick shrugged. "Brenda knows she can see Molly whenever she wants, no matter what the custody agreement says. Let's just say Brenda's not always available and leave it at that."

"Okay." Kaylee couldn't understand why Brenda would give up custody of her little girl. If Molly were hers, Kaylee knew she'd want to spend as much time as possible with her. Her confusion must have communicated itself to Rick.

He swallowed more coffee and set his mug down.

"Brenda and Jim travel quite a bit. Cruises, shopping trips to New York, vacations to Europe and Hawaii. Having Molly around would cramp their style."

Kaylee's jaw dropped. *That's* why you have custody? So Brenda can travel with her new husband?"

Rick lifted one shoulder and let it drop. "That's part of the reason."

"And the other part?" Kaylee had a hard time hiding her outrage.

Rick squirmed in his chair then got up to pour himself more coffee, clearly uncomfortable with the subject.

Kaylee backed off. "I'm sorry. It's none of my business."

"The other part is I did a lousy job of choosing a mother for my child."

He sat back down and challenged her with a look to argue the point. Kaylee took the bait. "Last I heard, it takes two to tango. I don't know how you can blame yourself because your ex-wife isn't a great mother."

"The signs were there. I just refused to look at them."

"So now you're beating yourself up because of it?"

"Nah. I quit doing that a couple of years ago. Mostly I feel guilty as hell that Molly doesn't have a mother around to take care of her."

"So what are you doing about it?" Kaylee asked. She took a sip of her lukewarm coffee and regarded him over the rim of her cup.

"Doing about what?"

"Finding Molly a full-time mother? If you feel so guilty about it, why aren't you out looking for one? Molly says you hardly ever date. What good is guilt if it isn't motivating you to take some action?"

"This may have slipped your notice, but in order to find Molly a new mother, I'd have to get married again."

"Oh. So that's it. You don't want to get married again."

"You got that right. Scares the hell out of me," Rick admitted.

Kaylee propped her chin in her hand. "Why?"

Rick evaded her gaze. He stared down into his coffee. "I don't know. What if I screw it up again?"

"Who says you screwed it up the first time? It takes two to—"

"Tango. Yeah, I got that part." He met her gaze. "I don't think I can handle another divorce. I sure don't want to put Molly through one."

Kaylee'd inadvertently touched on some sensitive ground. She now knew way more about Rick Braddock than she'd expected to learn. She backpedaled as quickly as she could. "Well, then, all you have to do is make a woman fall head over heels in love with you and Molly. How hard can that be?"

Rick raised his mug in a mock salute. "Should be a piece of cake."

Kaylee giggled, glad she'd managed to lighten the mood. "You don't have to work today?" She rose and set her mug in the sink.

"Nope. I've got a kid that comes in on Saturdays and I close the place up on Sundays." He regarded her for a moment. "Would you like to go to the beach, maybe? If you feel up to it?"

"The beach? I didn't think we were that close to the beach."

"It'll probably take us about an hour to get there, but it's not a bad drive."

Kaylee couldn't contain her excitement. She bounced up and down on the balls of her feet. "I'd love to go."

Rick rewarded her with what was, for him, almost a complete smile. "Let's pack a cooler, then. You've got a swimsuit?" Kaylee's head bobbed in answer.

"Bring a change of clothes too. There's an outlet mall on the way. We can stop and shop for new lamps."

"Goodie! Goodie! Goodie!" Kaylee clapped her hands. "I can't believe I get to go to the beach." She raced past Rick. "I'll be ready in five minutes."

Rick chuckled. "Well, I won't be, so take your time."

Chapter Twelve

Kaylee stared at herself in the restroom mirror. She was having definite reservations about her swimsuit purchase. Sure it was a designer label. She loved the color. Best of all it had been drastically reduced in price when she'd bought it in anticipation of her dramatic debut on the Miami beaches.

The only problem was, it was almost an entire size too small. The cherry red one-piece clung tightly to her waist and hips. It didn't quite cover every square inch of her buttocks, either. And the Lycra didn't expand far enough to accommodate all of her bustline. Instead, it smushed her breasts together, and pushed them up creating lots of cleavage and the expectation that they both might topple overboard at any moment.

In the store, she'd promised herself she could lose a couple of pounds before she had to wear the slightly too-small swimsuit and convinced herself it wasn't too tight. It was a designer suit at a fabulous price. So much for bargain basement shopping, she thought as she stared into the mirror over the sink in the public restroom at the beach knowing Rick was waiting for her.

The restroom was sparsely populated at the moment. She bent over from the waist and wiggled around a bit, then straightened. Her breasts surged higher but didn't spill out of the suit. The leg openings rode up even more, threatening a complete and very uncomfortable wedgie if she wasn't careful.

"So I'll have to be careful," she reminded herself, yanking the leg openings down as far as they'd go.

She shoved her sunglasses into place and wrapped the beach towel Rick had given her around her waist.

Still not entirely secure in her appearance, she stepped out of the restroom and peeked around the corner.

Rick was leaning against the railing, arms crossed over his chest waiting for her. He wore a baggy pair of swimming trunks that rode low on his waist and reached almost to his knees. He had on a pair of mirrored sunglasses and appeared oblivious to the admiring glances he was getting from the various females who crossed his path.

He spied Kaylee and straightened away from the railing.

"Ready?"

She didn't budge an inch. "I'm, uh, not too sure about this suit."

"Why? What's wrong with it?"

"It's, uh…" How did a woman explain the discomfort of an ill-fitting swimsuit to a man she hardly knew? "It's new." As an explanation, that told him nothing.

"I'm sure it's fine." He gestured for her to come closer.

I'm sure it's *not*, Kaylee thought, but she hadn't come all this way to hide in the restroom, either.

She stepped forward.

Rick said an immediate prayer of thanks that he was wearing mirrored sunglasses. He had to consciously clench his jaw to keep it from dropping when he saw Kaylee.

The red swimsuit did wonders for her already impressive bustline, and Rick couldn't have kept his gaze off her chest if he'd tried. His mouth was dry by the time he got his gaze under control. "Looks fine to me," he said. He quickly turned and started down the ramp toward the sand.

Whoa. Kaylee Walsh had the hottest body he'd ever seen. And somehow, her insecurity about her own appeal made her even more appealing. He needed to be underwater, cold water, and lots of it. Soon. Otherwise, he'd be burning up from looking at her in that swimsuit.

He paused next to the cooler to toe off his sandals and remove his sunglasses. "You've got sunscreen on, right?" he asked Kaylee. "This sun can be brutal, especially when you're not used to it."

"I put sunscreen on," Kaylee assured him.

She slid out of her flip-flops, still clutching the towel around her waist.

"We're going in the water, right?"

"Sure," she agreed brightly.

"You might want to lose the towel, then."

"Okay. Yeah, I guess."

He knew he didn't imagine her reluctance as she unwound the terry-cloth covering and dropped it on top of the cooler. He also knew he was staring at her. Like in the movies, his eyes had turned into circling spirals. He couldn't look away. Not from Kaylee's impossibly tiny waist or the flare of her slender hips and long, shapely legs.

He tried to cover the strangled sound he made by pretending to clear his throat.

"Let's go then."

He fell into step behind Kaylee. Another mistake. The snug suit gave him an impressive view of her backside which was almost as distracting as the view from the front. His palms itched.

They reached the shore not a moment too soon. Rick ran a few feet ahead of Kaylee and made a shallow dive. Her suit might be making her uncomfortable, but it was nothing compared to what it was doing to him.

He surfaced after a few feet and turned to look back, shoving the water out of his hair and off his face.

Kaylee was taking her time getting wet. Probably afraid her suit would shrink.

Which wouldn't be a bad thing as far as Rick was concerned.

"Come on. Jump in. You can swim, can't you?"

Kaylee splashed water in his direction, though the droplets fell several feet short. "Yes, I can swim. Do I have to rush into it? Can't I savor the experience?"

It occurred to Rick the longer she took to submerge herself, the longer he'd have to look at her. "Sure. Take your time."

"It's colder than I thought it would be."

Her proudly erect nipples were outlined beneath the suit as if to punctuate that statement.

"Yeah. Cold," Rick agreed. The water seemed to be having a similar effect on him. Correction. Kaylee Walsh in the water was causing parts of his body to stand at attention as well.

She came closer, the water lapping above her waist. A wave rolled in and slapped them both, splashing water in Kaylee's face, wetting her suit entirely. She giggled and licked her lips. "Salty."

"We can jump the waves," Rick told her.

"Jump the waves?"

"Yeah. A wave comes in, and you jump into it and sort of go along for the ride."

He turned to look at the relatively calm sea behind him. "Not too much action today. Sometimes you have to wait awhile."

Kaylee turned to look back at the shore. A couple walked by hand in hand. "Maybe we could go for a walk on the beach."

"Sure. We can walk if you want to."

They sloshed their way back to shore. Rick did his best to keep his attention averted from the water sluicing off Kaylee's skin. Her suit clung to her, leaving very little to the imagination. But his imagination was already working overtime as it was.

He retrieved their sunglasses, glad to be able to hide his eyes and hoping the mirrored lenses hid his thoughts as well. He had to cool it where Kaylee was concerned. The last thing he needed was an entanglement with a woman who'd be out of his life in a couple of weeks.

If he was going to get involved with someone, it was going to be someone who wouldn't be looking to relocate a couple of hundred miles away. He needed to find a woman who wouldn't mind living in Perrish, who was okay with a guy who owned a gas station and repaired cars for a living. Someone who didn't mind that a six-year-old came with the rest of the package.

He'd be the first to admit, he didn't have a lot to offer a woman. He couldn't spring for fancy vacations or major shopping sprees. No luxury sedans, and designer clothes were out of the question. Yeah, Rick, he reminded himself. You're a real catch. Any woman would be lucky to be with you.

Lost in his thoughts, he fell into step beside Kaylee. After seeing her in that swimsuit he knew without a doubt she'd be swarmed by men the moment she set foot on any of the beaches in Miami. Rich, available, unencumbered men who didn't have one strike against them in the marriage department.

If that's what Kaylee wanted, and why shouldn't she? Wasn't that what all women wanted? Money? Nice cars? Lots of expensive clothes?

Where was he going to find a woman who'd settle for less? Loyalty and faithfulness, those were old-fashioned traits. Where would he find a woman who'd prefer to watch him play softball than attend the opera or the ballet on the arm of some rich guy in a tuxedo? What woman would prefer his flat-roofed little house to a three-story mansion or his tow truck to a stylish foreign import?

He'd made a bad call with Brenda, and he hadn't trusted his judgment since. Truth be told, he was afraid to take that kind of chance with his heart again. Especially when he now had Molly's well-being to consider, too.

But Molly needed a mother. And he needed a wife. His reaction to Kaylee Walsh from the moment he'd met her made that fact glaringly obvious.

He'd just have to make some kind of an effort. Start looking. Start dating again.

Hope for the best.

"Rick! For heaven's sake. Could you slow down?"

Kaylee's hand on his arm startled him. He'd been marching along at his own pace, oblivious to her efforts to keep up. She was panting, her chest heaving, expanding and contracting the seams of her swimsuit.

He wanted to kiss her. Wanted to take her in his arms, right there in the wet sand, hold her close, taste the salt on her lips, the sweetness of her mouth. He stared at her from behind the lenses of his sunglasses, lost in the vivid fantasy, the memory of what it felt like to have all those curves pressed up against him.

"What's the matter?" she asked.

Rick's tongue had glued itself to the roof of his mouth. He stared at Kaylee trying to recall what it was she'd asked him.

"Are you embarrassed to be seen with me?"

"No!"

"I wouldn't blame you if you were—people are staring at me."

Two buff young men strolled by, ogling Kaylee. One let out a low whistle. Rick glared at them.

"I look ridiculous in this swimming suit."

"You do not."

"It's too small."

"That might be why you look so good in it." Rick smiled, a genuine smile, displaying all of his teeth. Kaylee sucked in a breath that sent her breasts surging farther upward.

"Then why were you walking about three feet ahead of me?"

"Sorry." He couldn't confess that he'd been lost in thought or tell her what he'd been thinking about. He reached for her hand. "I'll walk slower."

She fell into step beside him and Rick felt an absurd sense of pride as other beachgoers nodded or smiled, obviously assuming they were a couple.

Another guy stared at Kaylee as they walked by. Rick tightened his grip on Kaylee's hand. *Not today, buddy,* he thought. *She's with me.*

Chapter Thirteen

Kaylee decided to pretend her swimsuit fit and that more than half of her rear end was not exposed for all the world to see. Assured that her breasts weren't going to pop free of their restraints at any moment, Kaylee relaxed. Rick holding her hand as they walked the beach bolstered her confidence.

"There's a concession stand down there," Rick nodded in the direction they were headed. "They have pretty good frozen lemonade."

"That would be wonderful. I can't believe how hot it is."

Kaylee thought she might melt into a puddle of overheated skin and sweat. Even strolling along in the shallow water near the shore wasn't enough to keep her cool.

"It's not so bad in the winter," Rick told her. "Of course, then the beaches are packed with tourists, so the natives stay away."

"The humidity is what I can't seem to get used to," Kaylee admitted. The relatively cool hills of Tennessee were starting to look pretty good right about now.

"You'll have to get used to it, if you stay in Miami. Don't forget it's farther south, and probably a few degrees hotter than north Florida."

"Have you ever been there? Miami, I mean?"

"Nope."

"How come?"

"Never had a reason to go, I guess. What's Miami got that's so special, anyway?"

"I don't know," Kaylee admitted. "Tillie's been there for five years. She's always going on about the shopping and the restaurants. Nightclubs. Parties. Beaches. Boating. She makes it all sound so exciting."

"Maybe it is at first. I thought Atlanta was pretty exciting when Brenda and I first arrived. But a big city is like anything else. You get used to it. The novelty wears off.

"When you work for a living, you're usually too busy to take advantage of nightclubs or theatres."

"But there's more to do. More to see," Kaylee argued. "When you're stuck in a small town, you've done everything there is to do before you're out of diapers."

Rick chuckled. "Yeah, but all that stuff, nightclubs and shopping, boating, shows, it all costs money, too."

"Maybe in a bigger city you can make more money. Then you have more money to spend."

"You'd think so, wouldn't you? The thing is, the cost of living is higher in a city. Even though you make more money, you end up spending it on rent or transportation, stuff like that. Maybe in a small town you live close to where you work. Maybe even within walking distance. But in a city, you have to drive twenty or thirty miles, so you have to have a car. Or maybe you take the bus. So you're no further ahead."

"You have a thing against living in a big city, don't you?" Kaylee ventured.

Rick shrugged and tugged on her hand as he trudged through the sand toward the concession stand. "No. I'm saying it's all relative. Sometimes people think relocating is the answer to everything. What they don't realize is their problems follow them wherever they go. At some point you have to face the real issue and deal with it. Running away isn't the answer."

Kaylee waited until Rick handed her a frozen lemonade. She took a grateful sip through the straw and felt the icy coldness melt all the way down her throat. They fell into step for the return trip along the shore.

"So is that what you think I'm doing? Running away from my problems?"

Rick shook his head. "I didn't say that. I was sort of thinking about what happened with Brenda and me. Things weren't that great between us before we moved to Atlanta. She pushed for the move, and I thought if I went along with it, it would make her happy. Obviously, it didn't."

"But some good came out of it, right?"

"Oh, sure. I finished school, got my certification, got a lot of mechanical experience I wouldn't have otherwise had."

Kaylee smiled. "I was thinking more along the lines of Molly's arrival."

"Yeah. I gained a daughter and lost a wife."

"Do you miss her?"

"Who? Molly? Sure. But it's nice to have a break every once in a while."

"I meant Brenda."

"Brenda?" Rick slanted a gaze down at Kaylee. "Hell, no."

"I thought men liked glamorous women like her."

"Glamour isn't everything, Kaylee. Brenda sure doesn't wake up in the morning looking the way she did the other night. And maybe you noticed her reaction when someone comes along and messes it up. I'm glad this time it was Brutus and not me. Truth is, every time I see Brenda I get a whopping reminder of how I don't want to make the same mistake I made with her."

"Do you think you'll ever get married again?"

"I don't know. I try not to think about it." Rick knew that was both the truth and a lie. He hadn't been thinking marriage. Had avoided thinking about it. Until Kaylee Walsh came along and reminded him of all the reasons why a man, especially a single father, ought to consider getting married again.

"You're starting to burn," Rick pointed out when they returned to the place where they'd left the cooler and towels. Kaylee looked at her shoulders. "Am I?"

"Yeah. You better put more sunscreen on."

She rummaged in her bag for the tube and opened it.

"Here, let me." Rick took the sunscreen from her. "Turn around."

Kaylee did as he instructed, shivering in the heat when his lotion-covered fingers touched her shoulder. Every nerve ending she possessed screamed in reaction to his touch. The sunscreen slithered over her skin beneath his strong caress, and Kaylee had that sensation that she was melting all over again.

She'd known Rick Braddock for less than a week.

Amazing that he could affect her this way. She'd known Bobby Lou Tucker her whole life and he'd never inspired this tingling kind of excitement and heat in her. Mostly what Bobby Lou inspired was annoyance and frustration.

Rick recapped the tube of sunscreen and handed it back to her. "We better not stay too much longer or you'll be burnt to a crisp."

Kaylee busied herself stowing the lotion back in her bag. For once her chattering tongue was still. She hoped the sunburn would hide her blush.

Rick stood nearby. Kaylee had the sense that he was watching her every move. "Want to eat?"

She straightened. "No. I'm not very hungry." She was glad she was wearing her sunglasses, because she was lying. Again. Hungry? Oh, yes. But not for food. From behind the dark lenses, she could look all she wanted, keeping her thoughts hidden from Rick.

He picked up the yellow Frisbee he'd brought along and twirled it between his fingers. "How about a game?"

"I'm terrible at Frisbee. I never learned how to throw it to get it where I want it to go, and I never seem to be able to catch it, either."

"Perfect. Come on. I'll teach you."

Kaylee followed him back into the water, her focus on his backside, her mouth watering in spite of the heat. The swim trunks weren't quite as sexy as his baseball uniform, but in her opinion, Rick Braddock had nothing to be ashamed of. He was gorgeous. His former wife was an idiot. No matter what her new husband looked like or how much money he had. Kaylee knew without a doubt that had she been lucky enough to be married to a guy like Rick, she'd never leave him. No matter what. Not for money or city lights or a more exciting life.

Rick Braddock had made his decisions and appeared completely content with his life. He was a great dad. He owned his own business and a home and made a decent living. He took pleasure in the simple things. And what's wrong with that? Kaylee asked herself. Nothing, came the answer as Rick paused waist-deep in the water, and she almost ran into him. She couldn't seem to direct her attention to his words. Water had splashed and beaded and rolled down the dark skin and through the swirls of black hair on his chest. She realized she was staring.

"I'm sorry, what?" She got her chin up and focused her gaze on his face.

"I said you throw from the side, see, like this." He demonstrated, crossing his right arm in front of his body, holding the Frisbee. "And then you sort of flick it. Like this." He let go. The Frisbee sailed about twenty feet then came to rest in the water. He swam over to retrieve it and tossed it to her. Of course she didn't catch it.

It landed with a plop about two feet away.

"You're trying too hard," Rick called to her. "Let it float to you and grab onto the edge."

"I told you I wasn't good at this," Kaylee reminded him.

She flung the wet Frisbee back in his direction. It sailed far to his left. Once again he swam to retrieve it and came back to Kaylee.

"Okay. Lesson number two. Keep your arm and wrist level. Don't throw it. Fling it. Here, I'll show you."

He led her into shallower water and stood behind her. He put the Frisbee in her right hand and folded his right arm around her. "Relax," he said.

Relax? Oh, sure. Relax. With the heat of his damp body pressed up behind her? With her skimpy swimsuit and his trunks the only thing separating them? With his chest and her bare back touching? Not to mention his arm wrapped around her and his lips so close to her ear? Relax. Sure. No problem.

Kaylee took a deep breath. Her breast brushed Rick's arm. She couldn't tell if he was having any reaction at all to their current position. All she knew was what it was doing to her.

She tried to concentrate. She did. She fixed her gaze on a point on the water. There. She'd make the Frisbee land right there. If she ever let go of it. She felt suspended in time. Rick's left hand at her waist steadied her as the waves rolled around them.

She licked her suddenly dry lips and turned her head a little bit. Rick was so close. So close. She could kiss him. If she moved a little bit closer, turned her head a little bit more.

"I don't think I want to play Frisbee any more," she said.

"Me either." He was going to kiss her. Kaylee was sure of it. They'd both left their sunglasses on, so she couldn't see his eyes. She wasn't the only one turned on, though.

She felt evidence of that as he pressed against her.

His head moved closer. His lips were almost touching hers.

Whomp! A wave slapped her hard, knocking her backward into Rick. They toppled over together.

Rick let go of her. She lost her footing and went under only to come up sputtering and coughing with Rick supporting her.

Another wave came up and washed over them. Kaylee felt disoriented, as if she'd awakened from a lovely dream that had turned into a twisted nightmare.

Rick's grip on her elbow helped keep her upright as he led her back to shore. "You okay?" Rick asked as he spread out a towel on the sand. "Here. Sit."

"Here." He opened a cold soda and handed it to her. She took a grateful sip.

Rick joined her on the towel, holding a cold soda against his lip but not drinking.

Kaylee drained half her soda before she noticed.

"Aren't you going to drink that? What are you doing?"

Rick lowered the soda. His top lip was swollen on one side. "Oh, no. Did I do that?"

He shook his head and finally took a drink from the can. "It wasn't your fault. That's what I get for having my lips where they probably shouldn't have been."

"Where's that?" Kaylee asked, barely getting the words out. She stared at Rick's mouth. Even with the swelling, he had a darn sexy mouth.

"I think they were about right here." He leaned forward until he was only an inch or two away.

"Maybe I should kiss that and make it all better," Kaylee whispered.

"Maybe you should," Rick agreed.

Chapter Fourteen

Her lips, as sweet and hot as he'd remembered from that night in the truck, touched his, exciting and soothing at the same time.

Teasing him, he thought, she backed off much too soon. Or maybe she was as startled by her behavior as he was by his. Rain clouds were beginning to move in anyway. They packed up their things, showered and changed at the facilities there at the beach, and headed home.

But first they had to find some new lamps. Usually the outlet mall had good deals on everything, but so far they hadn't found what they were looking for. Rick didn't mind. Normally he hated to shop, but today he was perfectly happy following Kaylee's lead as she exclaimed over bargains and chattered on about the selection of goods. The memory of that kiss was uppermost in Rick's mind as they wandered through the shopping center.

She didn't buy anything, although she gazed longingly at clothes and shoes and costume jewelry. He ought to be paying her to watch Molly, he thought guiltily. Even though the parts and labor for a new starter would about equal what he paid Tiffany for three weeks of babysitting.

"If you see something you like, let me get it for you," he said. "As a thank-you gift from me and Molly. How about those earrings?" He indicated the delicate pair of silver ones she was holding in front of her ears, checking her reflection in the counter's small mirror. Surrounded by her dark hair, they dangled enticingly, catching the light and subtly sparkling.

Kaylee considered for a moment but then shook her head and put the earrings back in the display. "You don't owe me anything. You did me a favor, remember? I'd be out on the street if not for you."

"Kaylee—"

"We're even," she told him firmly. She took his arm and steered him into a home furnishings store. "Come on. I'll bet they have lamps in here."

They did. Kaylee discovered two ginger jar lamps decorated with Oriental designs and pronounced them perfect. Rick agreed.

"You know," she said, as they exited the store, Rick carrying the lamp bases and Kaylee the shades, "if you want to buy me something, I have an idea."

Uh-oh, Rick thought. Here it comes. Shades of Brenda loomed all around him. He'd be regretting his offer as soon as Kaylee told him which overpriced outfit she wanted, or which pair of expensive Italian shoes she had to have.

"I'm listening," he said, inwardly gritting his teeth, preparing for some outlandish demand which far exceeded his budget.

"We passed a fabric store before. Could we look and see if they have remnants? I was thinking I could make some curtains for Molly's playhouse. And maybe some doll clothes."

Rick nearly dropped the lamp bases. He stopped in his tracks and turned to stare at her. "You want what?"

"Remnants. You know, the scraps of material that are left over from the bolts. Fabric stores usually roll it up and sell it cheap. It won't cost very much." Rick continued to stare at her.

"Forget it. I guess it's a bad idea." She continued toward the mall exit.

"You sew?"

She stopped and turned back. "Of course, I sew. Doesn't everyone?"

"You want to make curtains and doll clothes?"

"What'd you do, get water in your ears? Forget it. Let's go."

She turned away. Rick followed her all the way to the truck. Kaylee didn't want anything for herself. She wanted material. So she could make curtains and doll clothes. For his daughter.

Carefully they stowed the lamps and shades. Kaylee started to climb into her seat, but he stopped her.

"Kaylee, wait. If you want to look for fabric, that's fine with me. Get whatever you want. I'll pay for it."

She rewarded him with one of her beatific smiles. She hardly waited for him to close the truck door and lock it. "I think Molly would like something cute and girlish for the playhouse. Maybe flowers? Or cartoon characters? She likes those Power Puff Girls, but that's not what I had in mind. Maybe something with animals."

Rick hustled to keep pace as Kaylee darted back into the mall and swerved unerringly in the direction of the fabric store. Rick had to grab her hand to slow her progress. He had an idea. "You go look for what you want." From his back pocket he removed his wallet and handed Kaylee several bills. "I'll meet up with you here when you're done, okay?"

"Yeah, sure. Okay."

He watched her walk away, her mind on her mission. He turned in the opposite direction. He had a mission too.

Rick couldn't help smiling inside and out. It took very little to make Kaylee happy. But for some reason when Kaylee was happy, he was happy. At the moment, she was ecstatic.

On the drive home, she exclaimed over her bag full of goodies from the fabric store, bits and scraps which had cost Rick next to nothing.

"And this! Look at this!" She held up a narrow strip of shiny gold material. "A Barbie doll gown. This, I'm thinking, is good for a baby doll. Maybe a pinafore."

Rick did his best to make admiring noises while keeping his eyes on the road.

"This is perfect for curtains. Kittens and puppies on a yellow background. And look, teddy bears here, in the same colors. A little tablecloth maybe."

"Are you hungry?" Rick interrupted.

Kaylee stopped scrounging through her purchases and looked at him. "You know you seem to ask me that a lot." Her voice was huskier than usual, but Rick couldn't tell if it was intentional or not.

He nodded at a billboard. "We're two exits from our turnoff and there's a good restaurant up here. Live band on Saturday night, too. And in case you forgot, we haven't eaten all day."

"Yeah," she agreed in that same husky tone. "I'm hungry. Starving, in fact."

Was that a—what do you call it? Rick tried to remember the term. Double something. A French word. When you said something but it was full of meaning on an entirely different level. A sexual level. Like when Kaylee said she was hungry. Did that mean she was hungry for a hamburger and fries? Or did it mean she was starving for some male attention?

Rick cleared his throat as he took the exit ramp. He flipped the switch on the a/c up a notch. Maybe he needed to add some Freon to the truck's air conditioner. He'd noticed the past couple of days it didn't seem to be cooling as efficiently as it should.

Damn, you look good, girl, Kaylee told herself in the bathroom mirror. Not that she was wearing anything special. Shorts and a tee shirt and a pair of cheap sandals. She had most of her hair swept up in a clip leaving tiny tendrils curling nicely around her temples, nape and ears. The humidity in Florida did wonders for her curls. Her cheeks were sunkissed, the tip of her nose the tiniest bit burnt. Her eyes sparkled.

"I'm starving," she whispered to her reflection. A woman washing her hands at the next sink eyed her suspiciously. Kaylee grinned at her as she applied lip gloss.

That tingling sense of excitement was back. Not that it ever completely went away. Not when Rick was anywhere around. She kept thinking about that first day she'd met him, when he'd hardly said two words to her and given her that once-over with those penetrating eyes of his.

She could admit he'd intimidated her a little. But Rick Braddock was nothing like the persona he'd exuded that day. She thought she'd have to push and prod him to say two words to her. But the more time they spent together, the more he opened up. If he wasn't careful he'd be chattering away, telling her all his secrets, giving away too much information. He'd be just like her.

Her stomach growled. She was starving.

"Do you want to dance?" Rick asked.

The music from the country-western band was loud enough to discourage most dinner-table conversation, which hadn't mattered earlier. She and Rick were too busy devouring their cheeseburgers and fries to talk. But now they were finished. The place was in full swing. A dense crowd obscured the bar. The dance floor was filling up.

"I—uh—I got the impression you didn't like to dance."

Rick waggled a finger at her. "I never said that. What I said was, it depends on who I'm dancing with."

"Well, in that case…"

He stood and she offered him her hand.

By the time they'd worked their way to the edge of the dance floor the tune had ended.

The female lead singer announced, "We're going to slow things down for a bit with a real pretty tune ya'll are familiar with made famous by Miss Patsy Cline called 'I Fall To Pieces'."

Okay. So Rick Braddock could slow dance without stepping on her toes. She'd give him points for that. She wondered if he knew the two-step or the tush push. Probably not. He was probably a one-trick pony.

Not that Kaylee was complaining. Oh, no. Slow dancing with Rick beat slow dancing with Bobby Lou Tucker any day of the week. For one thing, there was more to Rick. Bobby Lou was one of those thin, wiry guys—strong, but sort of all bones.

Rick, on the other hand, had a lot of muscle and sinew wrapped around his sturdy physique. Lots more meat on them bones. Kaylee blushed at the thought, glad for the dim lighting on the dance floor.

She snuggled closer and Rick accommodated, pressing his arm tighter against her back. He smelled like sun and heat and male. She couldn't get enough of his scent. Geez, it was hot in here. She couldn't ever remember being so hot.

The slow song ended and her question was answered. Rick knew how to dance. He might have been a bit rusty and not terribly light on his feet. But he knew the steps. Kaylee lost count of the dances. She was hot and thirsty, but she was having the time of her life.

Rick smiled. A lot. She liked it when he smiled. The band ended the set with another slow tune. Rick's tee shirt was as damp as her own, but Kaylee didn't mind. He held her close again and she couldn't think. Couldn't think of anything except how good it felt to be held close by a man. How good it felt to have that man be Rick.

"I'm about ready to get out of here. How about you?" he asked as the song neared the end.

Kaylee nodded. If she didn't get cooled off soon she might burst into flame.

He led her outside, but it was only slightly cooler than the dance floor. She leaned against the truck while he dug his keys out and unlocked the door. She pulled the collar of her tee shirt away from her neck. "Whew. I am so hot."

Entendre. That was it, Rick thought. Double entendre. He still couldn't decide if that's what Kaylee was aiming for with that comment about being hot, but he was damn well ready to find out.

"Yeah. You are hot." He kissed her. Not a gentle kiss like the one she'd given him on the beach. Unh-uh. This was a fullout, let's-see-how-hot-you-are kind of kiss involving tongues and teeth and mouths. Rick got his answer. Kaylee was as hot, if not hotter than he was. They traded fire, almost as if they were in competition with each other to see who had more heat.

In the end it didn't matter. Kaylee had one leg curled around his calf, her arms twined around his neck, her back against the truck and him pressed against her front.

"Get a room," came the disgusted comment from a female passerby. The giggles of her drunken companions faded away before the words penetrated Rick's brain.

He slowly extricated himself from Kaylee's arms, taking note of her moan of disappointment. He curved a hand around her jaw. Her eyes glittered up at him, a passionate blue fire. "We should go, huh?" He almost didn't trust himself to keep his voice steady. Kissing Kaylee like that shook him up.

He opened her door and helped her climb in. Then he opened the cooler and withdrew two still-cold bottles of water. He handed one to Kaylee and downed half of his own before he put the truck in gear. The water did nothing to put out the fire. He drove home feeling like he was sitting next to a ticking time bomb. Kaylee didn't say a word, but surely she was as ready to explode as he was.

They managed to get all the way inside the house where an excited Brutus greeted them. Rick opened the door for the dog so he could go out and do his business. When he turned back, Kaylee was there. Right there. In his arms, her mouth on his.

Rick forgot about the dog. Forgot about everything except her kiss, her body pressed up against him. He buried his fingers in her hair, tugging on it until it loosened. The clip fell with a clatter to the floor.

She wrapped her legs around his waist and he carried her to his bedroom. He lowered her to the bed, which he never bothered to make. He was operating on autopilot, his brain focused on one thing and one thing only. Kaylee. In his bed. Kaylee in his bed. He'd marvel over that fact later, but for right now...

Kaylee's hands found their way beneath his shirt. She pushed it up and wanted it off. Rick obliged, tossing it aside. Then she started on his shorts, fumbling with the waistband.

"Off," she moaned. "Hurry."

Well, okay. He kicked off his Docksiders while he was at it. Kaylee'd already managed to get rid of her sandals. When had she done that?

He was still wearing his briefs, but she didn't object. Her fingers delved into his buttocks as his tongue delved into the heat of her mouth. She was still fully dressed, but her legs were wrapped around him, holding his arousal firmly against her.

They were both slick with perspiration. She was holding onto him so tight, he could hardly peel her tee shirt away from her skin. It seemed all she wanted to do for the moment was hold him close and kiss him. Long, slow, deep kisses that stoked the fire they were building between them.

"Kaylee," he choked out. He managed to get hold of her tee shirt and yank it up and over her head. He buried his face between the fullness of her breasts, but she whimpered and nudged his mouth back to hers. He held a breast in each hand, running his thumbs back and forth against her straining nipples, feeling her reaction all the way to his toes.

Her vocal responses left no doubt that he wasn't supposed to stop. He unsnapped her bra and tossed it away. Filling his hands with the full softness of her breasts made it his turn to groan. He had to taste as well as touch. First one, then the other, while Kaylee arched and writhed beneath him. "Rick! Rick!" she cried.

"The hell with this." He got her shorts off along with her panties. His briefs were next. He joined her once more, sealed together, skin to skin, front to front.

"Now this is more like it." He grinned in the dark. Only a slash of moonlight through the curtained window helped him see her answering smile.

"Mmmm. Yeah."

He kissed her, more gently than he had before, but without losing any of the fire. He felt her relax in welcome beneath him, felt the intimate touch of the heat and moisture between her legs. "Kaylee."

Woof. Woof.

"You drive me crazy."

Woof. Woof.

"Damn dog."

"What's that? Where are you going?" Kaylee's desperate tone did wonders for his ego.

"Brutus. I left him outside. He'll bark all night if I don't let him in." He dropped a quick kiss on her lips. "Be right back."

"Great timing, you lousy mutt," Rick scolded the dog. Brutus trotted past him and headed down the hall toward the bedroom. Rick locked the front door and caught the dog's collar. "Oh, no, you don't." He closed the bedroom door in the dog's face.

Rick was fully erect and Kaylee was waiting for him in his bed. He turned the closet light on and opened the door a few inches.

"What are you doing?" Kaylee whispered.

119

"I want to see you."

Kaylee had pulled the sheet over her, at least over the important parts. Rick tugged it off.

"You're staring," Kaylee pointed out after a few seconds.

"You're beautiful," he answered.

She held out her hand and he came back to her.

"Remember where we left off?" he asked.

"I remember. I remember everything."

Chapter Fifteen

Kaylee resisted waking up. No, she thought, it can't be morning already. It was. Late morning. Probably close to noon. She could tell by the strength of the light pressing against her closed eyelids.

No, no, don't let the night be over. Not yet.

Rick's arm lay across her waist. She could feel the heat from his body close behind her, the even rhythm of his breathing. She ached pleasantly in odd places. Her head throbbed slightly. And why shouldn't it? Terrazzo floor plus too much sun. She had a few tender areas elsewhere. The sunscreen she'd applied so liberally had been no match for the Florida sun. Her shoulders and back tingled with a rosy pink sunburn.

She felt Rick shift positions. He lifted a lock of her hair and let it sift through his fingers before moving on to another one.

She smiled without opening her eyes or moving a muscle.

"I can't believe you're awake already."

"I can't believe you're here. I thought maybe I was dreaming." He trailed a finger along her shoulder and down her arm to her elbow.

It tickled. Her lips twitched. "No dreams. I'm the real deal."

He kissed her shoulder. "What about the shower? Did I dream that?"

Kaylee blushed from the bottom of her toes to the roots of her hair at the erotic memory. "No," she choked out. Reality was being driven home full force with Rick's questions.

"And the kitchen table? Did we—?"

"Yes," Kaylee hissed, wondering if all of her skin was now the same shade as her sunburn.

"How did we—?"

"Water," Kaylee reminded him. "We were thirsty." "Oh, right." Rick rearranged her hair to nuzzle her neck. He flicked his tongue against her earlobe. "That was the third or the fourth—"

Kaylee rolled to her back and opened her eyes. "Does it matter?"

She stared into the dark glitter of his eyes, her earlier embarrassment forgotten. She was completely mesmerized.

Under his spell.

"No."

He kissed her and Kaylee forgot all her odd little aches and pains, her headache, her sunburn. Rick's kisses obliterated her thought process. She knew what he was thinking. Molly was due home around four this afternoon. They had until then to squeeze in all the lovemaking they could.

Already she could feel him hard and ready pressing against her thigh. She was ready as well. It didn't take much, as they'd learned last night.

Everywhere he touched she burned. He was like an arsonist setting off little fires with his fingers and his lips and every touch of his skin against hers. She'd melt if he didn't save her.

"Hurry. Now. I want you now," she cried, wondering who this wanton woman was demanding that Rick Braddock make love to her immediately. It wasn't her, was it? It wasn't Kaylee Walsh. It couldn't be.

Rick had a condom out, the package opened.

"Hurry, hurry, hurry," Kaylee whispered.

He had it on. He was ready. She was ready. He kissed her once again as his body covered hers. He hovered at the edge for a split second.

Ding dong.

Rick froze.

Kaylee clenched her fingers against his buttocks. "Rick!" *Ding dong.*

Knock. Knock. Knock.

A high-pitched female voice sounded outside, the words indecipherable.

Ding dong. Ding dong.

Someone was leaning on the doorbell.

"Dammit!" Rick swore. He rolled off the bed, tossing clothes and bed covers every which way until he located the shorts he'd worn last night.

He dragged them on and disappeared. Brutus was barking now, Kaylee realized. Panic replaced passion. She hoped against hope it wasn't too late. Maybe like last night, Rick would return and they could pick up where they'd left off.

She listened intently. Rick had opened the front door. A woman's urgent, anxiety-ridden voice responded to Rick's greeting.

Then came the unmistakable sound of a distressed child's wail. "Daddy."

The female voice could be heard above the child and Rick's low rumbles of response.

Molly! Kaylee threw off the sheet and scrambled off the bed. She heard Molly say "Kaylee" in the same moan of distress she'd used to say "Daddy" and stepped up her efforts to find her clothes.

Where were they? Rick's bedroom was a disaster of tossed linens, damp towels and hastily discarded garments.

She found her shorts and yanked them on. Where was her tee shirt? The edge of something white peeked out from beneath a corner of the bed. She yanked it over her head. It didn't fit exactly right and the tag was in front, but she didn't care. Molly's cries had escalated toward hysteria.

She ran down the short hallway and came to an abrupt stop next to Rick who had Molly in his arms. Molly spied Kaylee and reached for her, crying her name brokenly through her tears.

Rick and Brenda turned startled glances in her direction as if both were surprised to find her there, but Kaylee hardly noticed.

Molly scrambled over Rick's shoulder and Kaylee took her, holding her close. Molly squeezed her arms tight around Kaylee's neck and sobbed on her sunburned shoulder.

Automatically, Kaylee soothed her.

"Shhh. Shhh, sweetheart. It's all right. You're home now. It's all right."

Her gaze met Rick's then clashed with Brenda's. Brenda's mouth was set in a thin line of irritation and disapproval. Rick's brows were knit with worry. Kaylee turned around with Molly and took her to her bedroom.

Molly's tears had almost stopped and she hiccupped in relief as Kaylee sat on the edge of the bed and held her. Kaylee smoothed the damp hair back from Molly's forehead. Molly felt warm to the touch.

"Sweetheart, I think you have a fever."

"I-I threw—threw up—up in Jim's car. Mommy's mad at me." The tears started up again.

"Shhh. Shhh." Kaylee rocked her. "I'm sure your mommy's not mad at you. She was probably worried about you. Mommies get upset when they're worried."

"They do?" Molly hiccupped and stopped crying.

"Sure they do. Sometimes it sort of sounds the same is all. Your mommy loves you. She's not mad at you. She wants you to feel better."

Molly leaned her head wearily against Kaylee's shoulder and sighed.

"How about a nice cool bath?" Kaylee suggested. "And some nice clean pajamas?"

"Okay."

"Here, you lay down here for a minute and I'll go run some water in the tub and we'll get you out of these clothes, okay?"

Molly nodded and Kaylee's heart went out to the little girl with the dark eyes and the tear-streaked face. She turned to find both Brenda and Rick in the doorway.

"Excuse me." She edged her way between them and went into the bathroom.

She turned on the water and stayed there. Brenda probably needed to tell Molly good-bye. She hoped the woman had sense enough to reassure her daughter that she hadn't done anything wrong.

She wondered if Rick had any ginger ale on hand. She could heat it up to get rid of the effervescence. Molly might want some later.

She left the water trickling out of the faucet into the tub and headed toward the kitchen. She could hear the murmur of voices from Molly's room.

"Excuse me."

A man stood uncertainly near the front door holding Molly's Power Puff Girls duffel bag.

He looked to be in his late thirties, was dressed expensively, had a slender build and thinning blond hair. "Where should I put this?" He indicated the duffel bag.

"Oh, here. I'll take it." Kaylee took it from him then wondered why. What was *she* going to do with it? She set it down outside the hallway. "You must be Jim. I'm Kaylee. Kaylee Walsh." She held out her hand.

She thought she saw appreciation in his gaze as he shook her hand. "Jim Madigan."

"I was going to get some ginger ale for Molly. Would you like something?" He followed her into the kitchen. She found a two-liter bottle of ginger ale in the pantry.

"No, I'm fine. Is Molly okay?"

"I think so. I'm running a bath for her."

"Poor kid. She's a real trooper. We should have pulled over when she first said she didn't feel well, but Brenda—" He cut himself off.

"Too bad about your car."

He waved a hand in a gesture of dismissal. "It's upholstery and carpeting. It can be replaced."

Hmmm, Kaylee thought. Jim Madigan was not exactly the kind of guy she had pictured. Not at all. She set a pan of ginger ale on low heat and excused herself.

She met Brenda in the hallway. She still looked upset. Her mascara was slightly smeared. Kaylee braced herself. "That was a very nice thing you did, telling Molly I wasn't angry with her."

"I told her the truth."

Brenda seemed to consider this even as she looked Kaylee over again, taking in her rumpled hair and what Kaylee now realized was the too big tee shirt of Rick's that she'd hastily donned.

"Thank you," Brenda said. "I'll call when we get home to see how Molly's doing."

"Okay."

Jim appeared and escorted his wife to the door. He looked over his shoulder and winked at Kaylee.

Rick was helping Molly undress. Water still trickled into the tub.

"Do you have a thermometer?" Kaylee asked. She laid her palm on Molly's forehead. "She feels warm to me."

"Yeah." Rick rose and as if they were dancing, he and Kaylee changed places. Kaylee helped Molly into the tub while Rick rummaged in the medicine chest for a thermometer.

"How's your tummy feel?" Kaylee asked Molly as she wet a washcloth and sloshed water over the little girl's shoulders and chest.

"It hurts."

"Bad? Do you feel like you have to throw up again?"

Molly shook her head. "No. I threw up twice in the car. I think I'm done."

Kaylee glanced over her shoulder and caught Rick's gaze. A flash of mutual understanding and amusement passed between them. Jim and Brenda were going to be leaving the windows down on the trip back to Atlanta.

Rick shook the thermometer and held it in front of Molly.

"Under the tongue, squirt."

Molly obediently opened her mouth and clamped the glass tube tightly beneath her tongue.

Gently, Kaylee bathed her face.

"I left some ginger ale on the stove. I need to turn it off."

"I'll do it," Rick said.

Molly started to speak, but Kaylee smiled and tapped her on her nose to stop her. "Thermometer first. Then you can talk."

When Rick returned she removed the thermometer from Molly's mouth and handed it to him. He held it up to the light and rolled it around so he could read it.

"Over a hundred. Congratulations, kid. You're sick."

"I feel better now," Molly informed him. "Why are you cooking ginger ale?" she asked Kaylee.

"To get the bubbles out. I thought you might want some later. It might make your tummy feel better."

"Want to get out and get dried off now?"

Molly nodded. Rick stood ready with a towel. He wrapped her in it and picked her up and carried her to her room. Kaylee opened a drawer and found a Little Mermaid nightgown and underwear.

"I'll have some ginger ale with no bubbles now," Molly told Kaylee once she was dressed.

"Please," Rick prompted her. "And you'll be getting into your bed and taking a nap."

"But I'm not tired," she insisted. She turned to Kaylee. "Please?"

Kaylee knelt down next to her. "How about if I go get you some ginger ale and you get into bed. And maybe I can read you a story if you don't feel sleepy. How would that be?"

"Goodie." Molly climbed into bed and pulled the sheet up to her chin. "I'm ready."

"Maybe you and Daddy can pick out a book."

Kaylee went to the kitchen marveling at the ability of children to bounce back so quickly when they'd been sick. Marveling too at how she and Rick were behaving like a well-oiled parental machine. She ran the bath, he took the temperature. He dried Molly off, she got out the pajamas. He put Molly to bed, she went for ginger ale.

"I haven't even been here for a week," she whispered to herself in amazement as she poured the ginger ale into a cup. Yet she could hardly remember a life that didn't include Molly and Rick. She felt like she somehow fit into *their* lives, like a perfectly sewn seam.

But you don't belong here, she reminded herself as she passed through the living room. Tonight she'd be back on the couch where she belonged, as befit a guest passing through.

Nothing had changed. She had to remember that. Rick would fix her car. Molly would start school. Kaylee would be on her way to Miami.

Chapter Sixteen

Rick and Molly had decided on *Cinderella* by the time Kaylee returned to the bedroom.

Rick stood and Kaylee took his place on the bed, handing the drink to Molly. She sipped the flat soda, which Kaylee had cooled with several ice cubes, then licked her lips.

"I need to go to the grocery store. I was going to do it before Molly got back, but..." He frowned.

"You can go. We'll be fine. Won't we Mols?"

"Mols." Molly giggled. "That's my new name. Mols." She grinned up at them.

"I think she's feeling better," Kaylee informed Rick.

"Yeah. Hey, squirt. Okay if I make a run to Publix without you this time?"

"I guess. But will you still buy me a treat? Cherry Lifesavers, okay?"

He ruffled her hair. "Okay." He looked at Kaylee.

"Anything in particular I should get?"

She shrugged. What fun it would have been going grocery shopping with Rick, finding out his likes and dislikes, his buying habits. Apparently this was a chore he and Molly did together and knowing Rick, Molly surely got a reward for being on her best behavior.

"I could make pot roast. Or roast chicken. If you get chicken, get some rice. And if you get a roast get carrots, potatoes and onions. And you're almost out of apples, I think."

"Hang on. I'll make a list."

Rick returned from his shopping expedition to find the house as quiet as a tomb. Even Brutus did not make his usual appearance. Rick made several trips to haul all the grocery bags to the kitchen. He stowed the perishables and frozen foods, put the staples in the pantry and folded up the paper bags. He could hear the tick of the kitchen clock and the distant hum of the air conditioner outside.

He tiptoed down the hall and edged the door to Molly's room open. Molly was sound asleep, her glass of ginger ale empty on the nightstand. Brutus was snoring on the floor next to the bed. And Kaylee was asleep too, her arm keeping Molly cuddled close to her.

My family. The thought was in Rick's head before he could stop it. A lump settled in his throat and wouldn't go away.

If only, he told himself. If only he had a complete family. A wife. One who would stay with him for always. One who would be a mother to Molly when Brenda wasn't around. Which was most of the time. Kaylee Walsh could be that woman if only he would let her. If only she weren't on her way to Miami.

"I'm hungry."

Kaylee unglued her eyelids and peered up at Molly. For a moment she wasn't sure where she was, but then she knew she was in Molly's bed. Molly had been sick, returned early, she'd read her a story and they'd both fallen asleep. She wondered how long ago that had been. Judging from the slant of the light coming in through the half-closed blinds, it was now early evening.

Kaylee sat up. Her head weighed a ton and her eyes were gritty. Her mouth was dry.

She wanted a shower, a toothbrush and a good night's sleep in a real bed.

Molly giggled. "Your hair looks funny."

Kaylee mussed the hair on Molly's head. "So does yours." Molly's silky straight hair fell back into place.

"Can I have peanut butter and jelly?"

Kaylee yawned. "Oh, Molly, I don't know. Maybe you should start out with something simple. Like saltine crackers."

"But I want peanut butter." Molly stuck her bottom lip out and looked up at Kaylee from beneath her lashes. Kaylee recognized the face for what it was. An attempt at a pretend pout.

"How about if you eat a couple of crackers and have some more ginger ale. And if your tummy says it's okay after about ten minutes, I'll make you peanut butter and jelly."

"Okay."

Hand in hand they padded down the hall. Brutus trailed behind them. Rick was sacked out on the couch sound asleep. The television volume was on low. Kaylee put a finger against her lips.

As quietly as she could Kaylee prepared a snack for Molly. She poured a glass of ginger ale and ice for herself and sat at the table while Molly munched on her crackers.

"Your tee shirt's on the wrong way," Molly observed.

"The tags go in the back on the inside. Even I know that."

"I know that too. But I heard you crying, and I was in a hurry when I got up."

"Were you sleeping?"

"Sort of."

"On the couch?"

131

"How's your tummy feeling? Still want peanut butter and jelly?"

Molly nodded and Kaylee got up to make the sandwich, hoping her tactic would derail Molly's interrogation. What was she supposed to say? *No, I was in bed with your daddy?*

"How come you weren't on the couch when Daddy opened the door?"

"I don't know, Molly." Kaylee didn't want to lie to Molly. Nor did she want to tell her the truth. Evasion seemed the best option at the moment. The more she thought about it, she didn't know how she'd ended up in bed with Rick last night. Ever since she'd arrived in Perrish, everything seemed to happen so fast. Last night was still so new and it had ended so abruptly, Kaylee hadn't had much time to mull it over. If she couldn't give herself an answer, how could she give one to Molly?

Rick appeared at that moment looking as groggy and rumpled as she felt. Their gazes met and Kaylee wondered if he was thinking the same thing she was. How great it would be if they could curl up together in his bed and get some real sleep. Kaylee knew she wasn't functioning on all cylinders. Molly, on the other hand, was sharp as a tack after her nap. The child saw entirely too much as it was.

"Hi, Daddy. I'm all better now."

"Good news, squirt." Rick ruffled her hair. "What's for dinner?"

"Peanut butter!" Molly informed him happily. She held up her cup. "More ginger ale, please."

"You remembered to say please. Extra points for that."

Rick took her cup and joined Kaylee in the kitchen. He brushed against her as he reached for the ginger ale and Kaylee felt the sensation of tingling heat race through her body. How, she wondered, was she going to be able to pretend nothing had happened with Molly watching her and Rick's every move?

"So how was Disney World, kiddo?" Rick asked. He set Molly's drink down and returned to stand next to Kaylee at the counter. He took a knife from the drawer and bread from the loaf, then opened the jar of peanut butter Kaylee had closed.

Kaylee tried to concentrate on spreading jelly on bread, while listening to Molly's answer, but Rick's nearness drove every ounce of concentration from her brain. It wasn't her imagination. The air around them seemed to be charged with sexual awareness and something else. Mutual longing?

She passed the jelly in his direction, but he'd already finished his plain peanut butter sandwich. She made a mental note.

She sliced Molly's sandwich into quarters and set it on the table. Rick poured himself a glass of milk.

"I think I'll go take a-a shower."

He glanced up and she knew, as clearly as if he'd spoken out loud, what he was thinking. That if he could he'd join her there in a minute and there'd be a replay of one of last night's encounters.

Kaylee backed away from the desire in his eyes and fled.

In the bathroom she turned on the spray full force and stepped under it, hoping the blast of water would pump some sense back into her malfunctioning brain.

What must Rick think of her? That she was easy? That she'd known him less than a week and been only too willing to go to bed with him? That she was a small-town floozy? Any port in a storm?

She knew better. Granny Daisy had taught her better, but all of Granny Daisy's warnings and dire predictions hadn't prepared Kaylee for an encounter with a man like Rick Braddock. It had seemed like the most natural thing in the world to give in to the lightning hot attraction that had developed between them. She hadn't felt one iota of hesitation, not one qualm about making love with him. She could have backed out easily when he'd left to let the dog in last night. She could have yanked her clothes back on and told him she'd changed her mind. But she hadn't. Oh, no. She'd wanted him. She still wanted him. She was afraid she'd done something very stupid. She was afraid she'd fallen in love with Molly's dad.

After Rick and Molly finished their sandwiches, Molly found a rerun of *Mr. Ed* on TV. Rick had the kitchen straightened up before he heard the water in the bathroom turn off.

Kaylee took the longest shower on record. He wondered if she was in there thinking about last night and how awkward things were between them now. Maybe she was thinking about leaving. With or without her car.

No, he chided himself. She wouldn't do that. They had a deal. Kaylee would stay until school started. She wouldn't abandon him and Molly. At least he hoped she wouldn't.

But how do you know? he asked himself. You hardly know her. You only met her, sheesh, not even a week ago. And you're already imagining this future with her. Thinking she'll want to stay. Believing she'll forget all about Miami.

Not too likely, he scolded that hopeful part of his heart. Nice move, Rick. Get involved with her, go to bed with her so you won't be able to forget her. That way when she leaves, you can be extra miserable.

Rick scrubbed every inch of counter space, every groove and grain in the table. He wiped down the chairs and the front of the refrigerator, wishing he could wipe his thoughts away as easily as the crumbs and fingerprints.

Kaylee was convinced she had a future in Miami. Rick couldn't ask her to stay in a small town like Perrish. Correction. He *wouldn't* ask her to stay. He wouldn't give her the same opportunity he'd given Brenda, to trample on his heart and walk away. No way. No how. If Kaylee wanted to stay, the choice was hers to make.

When Kaylee appeared, she was dressed in one of her own tee shirts—right-side-out, tags in back—and a pair of faded jeans that fit her like a second skin.

Rick abruptly announced his plans to take Brutus for a walk and made his escape. With Molly as a constant guardian, the ease of the weekend had evaporated. He wished with all his heart they could get it back.

Chapter Seventeen

Kaylee spent an uncomfortable night, not in a bed, but back on the couch. For once she did not fall asleep easily. Her thoughts tumbled over themselves as if seeking escape from the confines of her mind. But there was nowhere for them to go, just as there was nowhere for her to go.

She wouldn't, couldn't, sleep with Rick again. Not with his daughter in the room across the hall. *Not ever*, Kaylee told herself. She shouldn't sleep with Rick again under any circumstances. She shouldn't, *but oh, how she wanted to.*

Jumbled in with the memories of making love with Rick was the warm sense of security she felt waking up next to him in the morning. She'd felt loved, darn it all, something she hadn't felt in a very long time. Not that Rick had said he loved her. It was too soon. She had to keep reminding herself that they barely knew each other. Yet in her heart she felt like she'd known Rick forever, even while she was still discovering him.

Dummy, she told herself. It doesn't matter anyway. A couple more weeks and you'll be on your way to Miami. Life in Perrish, Florida will go on without you.

The thought saddened her. She'd be a mere blip on the radar screen in Molly and Rick's life. Gone and forgotten.

Kaylee bit her lip. She wondered how long it would take her to forget them.

Kaylee made sure she was up and dressed before Rick made an appearance the next morning. She made coffee. While Rick showered she let Brutus out and retrieved the newspaper. Which she pretended to pore over when Rick appeared.

He halted abruptly as if surprised to find her at his kitchen table reading the newspaper.

They were alone for the first time since Molly's return. She told herself she'd be cool. They'd had a weekend fling. A one night stand. Even as Kaylee thought the thought she winced internally. It made what she and Rick had shared sound cheap and tawdry.

And casual. It hadn't been casual for her. Not at all.

But based on what she read in magazines and the current television shows, a one-night stand was no big deal. She'd be worldly and sophisticated about it. How hard could that be?

Harder than she thought. She glanced up meaning to give Rick a casual greeting, but her heart stopped and her mouth went dry. The breath caught in her throat when her gaze connected with his. Surely his eyes were telling her things, things she ought to be able to figure out. But her brain seemed to have stopped working along with everything else.

He stood there for five seconds at least. Or maybe it was five minutes. Kaylee'd lost all track of the space-time continuum as well.

"You made coffee." He went to the counter and poured a mugful then joined her at the table. "What's the matter? Cat got your tongue?"

Kaylee stared at him. She knew she was staring at him but she couldn't seem to help it. She wasn't being cool and sophisticated. Instead she was gawky and tongue-tied. "I don't know what to say," she finally managed.

"That's a first." The corner of Rick's mouth quirked up in his old half smile.

Somehow Kaylee found that reassuring. Rick was still Rick. Nothing had changed. Maybe if she kept telling herself that, she'd be able to believe it.

Molly appeared at that moment, still in her nightgown, her doll tucked under her arm.

"Hey, Mols." Kaylee held out her arms and Molly stepped into them. Kaylee breathed in the scent of warm, sleepy little girl. She pulled Molly into her lap. "How's my favorite little girl this morning?"

Molly's head swiveled around. "Am I?"

"Are you what?"

"Your favorite little girl?"

Kaylee made a big show of looking around the room, behind her chair and under the table. "I don't see any other little girls here, do you?"

Molly shook her head, her hair swinging to and fro.

"Then I guess you are my favorite."

Molly beamed and snuggled closer, putting her arms around Kaylee as best she could. Kaylee kissed the top of Molly's head. Love seemed to radiate out of Rick's daughter, warming all three of them.

She met Rick's gaze. Was he frowning? No, not exactly, Kaylee decided. He looked confused.

"How about some cereal, squirt?" He pushed his chair back and strode to the pantry.

"I want Kaylee to get it for me."

Kaylee heard Rick sigh and out of the corner of her eye she saw him push his fingers through his hair. He yanked the refrigerator open and withdrew a carton of milk.

Kaylee released Molly and joined Rick in the kitchen.

"I think I've been replaced," he muttered under his breath as he took a spoon out of the drawer.

"Not replaced," Kaylee said. "Added to."

He stopped in mid-motion and his head turned slowly in her direction. Kaylee froze at the same time, realizing how suggestive her words must have sounded. Like she wanted to stay here permanently. Like her presence somehow enhanced the life he'd made for himself and his daughter. She hadn't meant it to sound that way. Or had she?

"I didn't mean—"

"Do we have bananas?"

Both Kaylee and Rick turned to look at Molly. She sat clutching her doll waiting for her breakfast.

"Can I have some cut up on my cereal?"

Rick changed gears faster than Kaylee. "Sure, squirt. I suppose you want Kaylee to cut it up for you." He pulled a banana from the bunch on the counter and bowed before Kaylee comically, swirling the fruit in an elaborate gesture. "I bow to you, Oh Great Banana Slicer. Please accept this humble offering." He straightened and handed her the banana. She bit her lip even as she smiled and accepted it.

Molly giggled. "Daddy, you're being silly."

"That's right, squirt. And I'm out of here." He dropped a kiss on the top of Molly's head, then nodded at Kaylee. "I'll see you later."

Kaylee watched his retreat until the door closed behind him. She loved looking at Rick whether he was coming or going. She blushed at the unbidden image of Rick coming. As he had several times the other night. And so had she. Saturday night had been without a doubt the most passionate, mind-consuming, hottest, wildest— "What are you looking at?"

Kaylee's gaze drifted back to Molly still sitting at the table clutching her doll, her dark brows drawn together in an expression of mystified confusion, much the same way her father's were on occasion. Like the other night, when they'd been in bed together. He'd gazed down at her after the first time as if he couldn't quite believe she was there with him. Although she hadn't admitted it to him, she'd been as surprised as he was to find herself in his bed and that she'd experienced such a mind-boggling sexual encounter.

"Aren't you going to cut up my banana?"

"Hmm? Banana?" Kaylee smiled at Molly.

"On my cereal."

Kaylee stared at the banana in her left hand and the knife in her right.

Molly slid off her chair and placed her doll in an upright position on the seat. She planted herself next to Kaylee and reached for the banana. "Here. I'll do it." She broke the stem and began peeling it while Kaylee watched.

"I better get a different knife, though. I might cut my finger off with that one."

Molly opened the silverware drawer and chose a butter knife. She marched over to the table and laid down the banana and knife then returned for the cereal box, a bowl and a spoon. She frowned for a moment then went back for the milk.

She propped herself on her knees to pour her cereal, scooping up the overflow and returning it to the box. Then she studiously cut the banana into sizable chunks and plunked them into the bowl before carefully dribbling milk over the flakes and fruit.

She settled herself in the chair and began to munch cereal, fixing Kaylee with a curious look. "Maybe you should have some coffee. I don't think you've woked up yet."

"Don't talk with your mouth full," Kaylee said. She and Molly grinned at each other. "I sound like—"

"You sound like—"

"Daddy!" they both exclaimed at once. Cereal crumbs and milk dribbled from Molly's mouth.

Kaylee poured herself some coffee and joined Molly at the table. What had got into her? She was mooning over Rick Braddock like a lovesick girl. She'd never mooned over Bobby Lou Tucker this way. Not in all the years she'd known him.

She'd never experienced mind-blowing sex with him either, she reminded herself. Her encounters with Bobby Lou left her feeling letdown and frustrated more often than not. Never before had she experienced this soul-deep sense of satisfaction and well-being that still lingered more than a day after the fact.

"Why don't you stay here, Kaylee?" Molly asked around a mouthful of banana.

"I am staying here, darlin'," Kaylee reminded her.

"No." Molly shook her head adamantly. "I mean for always. You could be my mommy."

Kaylee nearly choked on her coffee. "Honey, you already have a mommy."

Molly put down her spoon. "But you could be the mommy that lives with me. And Daddy. Couldn't you?"

A lump of emotion swelled in Kaylee's throat. How well she remembered that childhood longing of her own for a regular family with two parents, instead of the makeshift arrangement of living with her mother and grandmother.

She'd only been here in Perrish with Rick and Molly for a week, but this little house felt like home to her. Not only had Molly grown attached to her, but she had started to think of Rick and Molly as her family. What had happened to all those big-city dreams she'd had a week ago? They'd faded, she supposed, to be replaced by the reality that she was a small-town girl. She could go on believing that once she got to Miami she'd somehow magically be transformed, but in her heart she knew it wasn't true. What was the point in trying to be something she was not?

"Sweetie, you know your daddy's letting me stay here and babysit you until he fixes my car. Until you start school. I was on my way to Miami, remember? My cousin Tillie has a beauty salon there where I can work. I have to have a job, Mols."

Molly chomped on another chunk of banana, her brows knit in concentration. She swallowed and her expression cleared. "There's a beauty salon here. Why can't you work there?"

"Here in Perrish? I don't think so."

Molly nodded her head up and down in certainty. "It's by Daddy's work. There's a pink sign. A lady cut my hair there once when I was little."

Kaylee hid her smile at Molly's past-tense reference to her size.

"We can walk there," Molly said. "You can ask if you can work there."

"Oh, Molly, I don't know—"

"We could stop and see Daddy. We could bring him lunch. Like a picnic!"

Clearly taken with the idea, Molly bounced up and down in excitement. "Please, Kaylee. It will be fun."

"But it's so hot out—"

"It's not that far."

"But what if Daddy's, uh, your daddy's real busy? I don't want to bother him."

"We won't bother him."

"Okay, then." Kaylee was fully aware that she'd given in much too easily. Truth was she *wanted* to bother Rick. She wanted to get under his skin the same way he'd gotten under hers. Unexpected contact in the middle of the day might do the trick.

Molly started scooping the rest of her cereal up, cramming it into her mouth. "I'll go brush my teeth and make up my bed.

And put on my clothes. Then I'll help you make sandwiches—"

Molly darted into the kitchen with her empty cereal bowl while Kaylee pondered how she'd let Molly talk her into this adventure. Ridiculously giddy, she tingled at the mere thought of seeing Rick again so soon.

Chapter Eighteen

Kaylee finally convinced Molly that lunchtime was at least three hours away and that they didn't need to pack their picnic yet. Instead she asked Molly to bring out some of her dolls and showed her the bag of fabric remnants. Once Molly understood the material would create new clothes for them, she became caught up in the idea, draping various pieces over her collection of Barbie and baby dolls.

"And with this," Kaylee told her as she pulled out the larger pieces of material at the bottom, "I thought we could make curtains for the windows in your playhouse. And maybe a tablecloth for the little table out there. You can have teddy bear tea parties."

"But what about the dolls? Can't I have doll tea parties, too?"

Kaylee pretended to consider this. "Hmmm. Do your dolls like tea?"

"They like Kool-Aid."

"Oh, I see. Then maybe you should invite them to a KoolAid party," Kaylee told her in a conspiratorial whisper as if the dolls might actually be listening.

"And cookies," Molly whispered back. "They like cookies. The little ones that look like bears."

"Do the bears like doll-shaped cookies?"

Molly giggled. "There's no such thing as doll-shaped cookies! Is there?"

"We could bake some. And let the bears eat them."

"We could?"

"Sure, why not?"

Molly leaned in closer and cupped her hand close to Kaylee's ear. "The dolls and the bears don't eat the cookies. It's just pretend."

"Are you sure about that?" Kaylee grabbed Molly and pretended to nibble on her shoulder. "I'm a bear and I think I've found a tasty little doll!" She made chewing sounds while Molly squealed with laughter.

What kind of sandwiches does Rick like besides peanut butter? Kaylee wondered later as she considered the contents of the refrigerator.

How could she know Rick so well on certain levels and yet know so little about him on others? Because you've only known him for a week, she reminded herself. You can't know everything about a person after only a week.

But knowing Rick this past week had certainly forced her to take a good look at herself. Why, she wondered, was she so set on going to Miami? Because she had nowhere else to go. That was always the answer that came back. But as Rick had asked, was she simply running away from her problems? If so, they would follow her to Miami.

What were her problems, anyway?

No job. Well, working in Tillie's salon would solve that.

A broken-down car. Which Rick would fix. He'd probably have it in tip-top running condition. So that problem was solved. Unless Rick discovered what was hidden in her gas tank, she'd be on her way to her future in Miami. She'd leave Perrish behind. And Rick. And Molly.

Somehow, with Tillie's help, she'd figure out a way to contact the authorities and straighten everything out. She had a sudden urge to hear Tillie's reassuring voice, a voice that reminded her of home, helped her remember who she was.

She picked up the phone and dialed. Since it was Monday, Tillie was home, and from the sound of it, she'd still been asleep.

"Hi, Tillie, it's me. I'm sorry if I woke you up."

"Aw, that's okay, sugar, I was going to get up in another couple of hours anyway. You okay, baby?"

Tillie was seven years older than Kaylee and she'd always had a tendency to mother her. When they'd been younger, Tillie had treated her like her own personal baby doll, dressing her up and taking her for walks in the stroller, accepting compliments on little Kaylee as if it were her due. Kaylee had missed Tillie horribly since she'd moved to Miami. After the stress of the weekend, Kaylee felt close to tears hearing the concern in Tillie's voice. "I'm okay," she replied, hoping she sounded convincing.

"What happened?" Tillie's big-sister-like radar switched on. "It's that guy, isn't it? Something happened with him, didn't it? Are you all right?"

"No. Yes." Kaylee gave a watery chuckle.

"Did he hurt you?" Tillie demanded. "If he did I swear I'll come up there and break him in two."

Kaylee laughed weakly. "No, no, Tillie, nothing like that. It's fine. It's just that—" She glanced into the other room where Molly had lined up her stuffed animals on the sofa and was watching Sesame Street with them, chattering to them as if they could reply.

"What, sugar?"

Kaylee shook her head. No way could she explain what had happened between her and Rick with Molly nearby. "I can't go into it right now. But everything's fine. I guess I'm lonesome is all. How are you?"

"Well, I'll tell you what, sugar, if you're feeling lonesome, I might have the cure."

Had Tillie decided to come and get her after all? "What are you talking about?"

"I'm talking about Bobby Lou Tucker."

A feeling of dread shot through Kaylee. "What about him?"

"He's here, sugar. Showed up looking for you the day after you called."

"Oh, no. He's there in Miami?"

"Acts like he can't wait to see you. Never saw a boy so wound up. I thought you two was through for good after he took up with that Stiller girl. But he sure has a hankering to find you."

"You didn't tell him where I am, did you?" Kaylee panicked at the thought.

"How could I? I don't know where you are. You never did say. Only that you were this side of the Florida State line. You didn't give me a phone number there, either. I been meaning to get caller I.D. Just haven't got around to it."

"Tillie, listen to me, no matter what you do, don't tell Bobby Lou I called. And don't tell him where I am."

"Okay, darlin', I won't. But I thought you'd be pleased as punch he's come after you. You're the best thing that ever happened to that boy and about time he figured it out. Georgia Rose Stiller my eye."

Kaylee's brain was racing, trying to figure out how to extract information from Tillie without telling her everything or making her suspicious. Once she was in Miami, they could figure it out together. But for now, Tillie didn't need to know anything.

"Tillie, what's Bobby Lou doing? Where's he staying? Did you tell him it might be a couple of weeks before I get there?"

"I told him. I don't know where he's staying, one of the motels, I guess. And I don't know what he's doing the rest of the time but he and that no-good cousin of his stop by to pester me at the shop every day askin' if I've heard from you, if I know where you are."

"His cousin Dwayne? Is that who he's with?"

"That Dwayne Holcomb. He may have paid his debt to society, but he still looks like a jailbird to me. Greasy hair and some nasty tattoos. Comes in and gives me the eye, scares my customers. That Dwayne, he's no good for business, I'll tell you that. Bobby Lou, on the other hand, now he's as big a charmer as ever. Has every one of my clients eating out of his hand by the time he leaves. I don't know why he hangs around with Dwayne, that's for sure. But it's always been that way, ever since they was young 'uns."

"Look, Tillie, don't let on that I called you again. You don't know when I'm going to be in Miami."

"A couple of weeks, you told me, by the end of the month. As soon as your car's fixed and that little girl starts school."

"Yes, Tillie. You know that and I know that. But I don't want Bobby Lou and Dwayne to know."

"You don't want to get back together with Bobby Lou? I thought maybe he'd seen the error of his ways and was finally going to ask you to marry him." Tillie sounded wistful. She was a hopeless romantic.

"Still haven't heard from the guy in the bar, huh?" Kaylee asked gently, a smile in her voice.

"Not yet, darlin'. But he's out there, somewhere, I know it. And one of these days we're going to find each other."

"I know you will." As always, it cost Kaylee nothing to play along with Tillie's fantasy.

Tillie's voice dropped. "I'm not crazy, am I, sugar? For thinking Mac and I were meant to be? I know I only met him that one time, but—"

"All kinds of crazy things happen in this world," Kaylee reassured her, thinking of those sparkling gemstones floating in her gas tank. "Sometimes we don't know how or when or why, you know?"

"I know. But you're the only one who never tells me I'm crazy for waitin' and hopin'. Dreamin', I guess."

"So who says dreams don't come true? Who says you can't find what you're looking for? People find it all the time, even when they didn't know they were looking, even when they're not sure exactly what they want. All of a sudden, there it is." Kaylee stared at a photo of Rick and Molly anchored to the refrigerator door with cartoon magnets. It must have been from Molly's last birthday. She was set to blow out the candles on a cake as a smiling Rick looked on.

"Thanks for the pep talk, baby."

Kaylee yanked her thoughts away from the path they were ready to take. "Look, we'll sort everything out when I get there.

Just don't tell Bobby Lou or Dwayne anything."

"All right then, sugar, if that's the way you want it."

"Thanks, Tillie. I love you. I'll see you soon."

Chapter Nineteen

"Who's Bobby Lou?" Kaylee jumped at the sound of Molly's voice coming from right behind her. She turned around holding a hand to her chest to calm her rapid-fire heartbeat. Molly stood looking up at her, clutching one of her bears tightly. "Is he your cousin, too?"

"No, no. He's a—a friend."

"If he's your friend how come you don't want him to know where you are? Are you playing a game? Like hide and seek?"

Kaylee forced a smile. "No, Molly, I, um, want to surprise Bobby Lou when I get to Miami."

"How come?"

Was there ever a six-year-old who asked so many questions? Kaylee wondered. She scrambled for an answer that was the truth but revealed nothing. "Well, Bobby Lou surprised me once. I got a big surprise, as a matter of fact. And now it's my turn to surprise him."

"Oh. Like a surprise on your birthday?"

"Exactly."

Molly's face fell. "I asked Daddy for a surprise on my birthday, but I didn't get it."

"Oh, Molly, I'm sure if your daddy could have got you what you wanted, he would have. Maybe he didn't think you were ready for it yet."

"I wanted a mommy that lives with me. Don't you think I'm ready for that?"

Kaylee gazed down at Molly before she bent and hugged the little girl to her. "I'm sure you're ready to have a mommy that lives with you. Maybe Daddy couldn't find the right one for you in time for your birthday."

Molly nodded and patted Kaylee's shoulder.

A lump swelled in Kaylee's throat as Molly pressed up against her. When she finally let go, Kaylee forced a cheerful note into her voice and turned to once again survey the contents of the refrigerator. She forced her thoughts back to the business at hand. "Does your daddy like tuna fish? Or egg salad?"

Molly scrunched up her nose. "I think he just likes peanut butter. Let's make that."

"Okay." Kaylee closed the refrigerator and opened the pantry door. "Plain peanut butter on white bread. No jelly."

Molly peered up over the edge of the counter as Kaylee made the sandwich. "How do you know what Daddy likes?"

Kaylee blushed, glad that Molly was so much shorter than she was and only six years old. In certain situations, she knew very well what Rick liked. "Um, because, that's how he made his sandwich last night."

"Let's bring cookies, too," Molly suggested. "And drink boxes." She opened the refrigerator and brought three to the counter.

"Potato chips?" Kaylee asked. "And fruit? How about some apples? I could cut them up."

"Okay."

Once the small cooler was packed they set off. The August heat, though still oppressive, was relieved by the shade offered by aged trees which overhung much of the road on which they walked.

Perrish had its own brand of charm, Kaylee noted. The houses were small and neatly kept for the most part. Brightly colored, inflatable swimming pools were standard fare in many of the backyards.

"That's Hannah's house," Molly pointed out as they passed a neat yellow brick home. "She's at her Grandma's up north."

"I bet you miss her," Kaylee commented.

"Yeah. But she'll be back before school starts."

"That's good."

Insects hummed and birds sang periodically to break the stillness. They stepped aside for an occasional car to go by, since there were no sidewalks. The drivers and passengers waved at Kaylee and Molly and they waved back.

Friendly people here, Kaylee thought.

Soon they reached the main street and walked the short distance remaining to the gas station. Kaylee's heart was beating double-time and inside her head a constant refrain repeated itself. *Rick. Rick. Rick.*

She felt light-headed and out of breath as they swung open the door to the station. Blessedly cool air greeted them. Rick, seated behind the desk doing paperwork, looked up at their entrance and offered a full-toothed genuine smile of greeting. Molly ran to him and he grabbed her up in a hug. His gaze met Kaylee's over Molly's shoulder. "Hey, a surprise visit from my two favorite girls. What did I do to deserve this?"

Duh! Kaylee thought. Don't you remember Saturday night? Thank God she didn't blurt that thought out. A peanut butter sandwich hardly seemed an appropriate reward for Rick's efforts anyway. Not after the way he'd made her feel. The way he still made her feel. She hadn't fallen in love with him. Had she? Her tongue glued itself to the top of her mouth.

She couldn't think of a thing to say. Not one word.

"We brought you lunch, Daddy." Molly crossed back to where Kaylee still stood just inside the door and led her closer to the desk. "And then you can tell Kaylee about the lady who cut my hair."

Kaylee opened the cooler and automatically started to unpack it. She felt massively foolish now. If there was a beauty salon in this tiny town, surely there wasn't enough business for two stylists. She didn't want Rick to think she wanted to stay or that she would push her way into their lives.

Rick brought in a couple of stools from the garage and they gathered around the desk. Kaylee had no appetite. Nerves had taken over. She felt shy all of a sudden.

He settled himself back behind the desk and unwrapped his sandwich. "Mmmm. Peanut butter on white bread. Someone knows what I like." His dark eyes twinkled up at Kaylee and then to Molly. "Maybe two someones." He took a bite and chewed.

He took a swig from his juice box. "Now then, what about a lady who cuts hair?" This he addressed to Molly.

"Remember when I was little? The lady who cut my hair? She has a pink sign by her door."

"Oh. You mean Miss Emma. That's Emma Arnold's shop," he explained to Kaylee.

"You mean there is a salon in Perrish?" Kaylee asked.

"There is, but about two years ago Miss Emma's arthritis got pretty bad. She couldn't find anyone to help her out. She's on medication, but when the pain got to be too much, she closed the place up."

"Oh." Kaylee sipped on her juice box trying to figure out why she felt as though the wind had been taken out of her sails.

She hadn't seriously considered staying in Perrish, had she?

"Kaylee can work there then," Molly said.

Rick's eyebrows shot up and his gaze swung to Kaylee.

"You? I thought you were dead set on going to Miami."

"I—I was. I mean I am. I was just—" Kaylee glanced to Molly for help.

"Kaylee says she has to work, Daddy," Molly explained around a mouthful of peanut butter.

"Chew and swallow. Then talk," Rick reminded Molly. "She's going to work. In Miami. Isn't that right?" Rick addressed his question to Kaylee.

"But this way she can stay here and be my new mommy."

"What?" Rick stood so quickly his chair rolled out from beneath him and banged into the wall.

"Kaylee, I think you and me need to have a little talk." He nodded toward the garage. "Molly, we'll be right back."

He ushered Kaylee ahead of him and closed the door behind him once they were through it. She turned to find him crowding her space. "Rick, please, I can explain."

"Well I sure as hell hope so. You've got my daughter thinking she's getting a new mommy? And what does that mean? I'm getting a new wife as well? Too bad no one let me in on the plan since I might have something to say about it."

He moved closer and Kaylee stepped away until her back was against the concrete block wall. "No, I never said I'd be her new mommy. She asked why I couldn't and I told her she already had a mommy. And she said why couldn't I be the mommy who lives with her—her and Daddy," Kaylee stumbled over the words but rushed on, "and I said I had to work and that I was going to Miami and she said there was a salon here and I didn't believe her and she said it's right by Daddy's work and we could bring you lunch and you'd show us where it was. And she was so excited about making you lunch and proving to me there was a beauty salon in Perrish, I—I couldn't tell her no…"

Kaylee's burst of words trailed away and she began to wonder if Rick was still listening. His gaze had dropped from her eyes to her lips as if transfixed. She was nearly panting in her rush to explain everything to him. Then came the surge of heat and excitement she experienced every time he was near. That tingling, heady sensation that raced through her blood and warmed her skin.

Rick kissed her. As if that had been his plan all along. She hadn't expected it but she quickly gave into it. It seemed a lifetime since he'd kissed her though it had been less than two days. She felt the hard length of his body, the soft denim of his shirt, his hot tongue against hers. The silk of his hair brushed her arms as she locked them around his neck.

"God, I've missed you," he whispered roughly as he rained kisses along her jaw and down her throat to her collar bone, his hands buried in her hair.

"Me too," she responded shakily. Her knees felt weak. Her eyes rolled back in her head as his tongue touched a particularly sensitive spot below her ear.

"Are you done talking? Can we have cookies now?" They both turned to see Molly standing in the doorway. Peanut butter smeared one cheek and a blob of grape jelly dribbled down her top.

"Yeah, squirt. We're done, uh, talking. Let's go have some cookies." He took Kaylee's hand and held the door open for her.

"It probably needs a good cleaning," Rick said as they surveyed the front of Mrs. Arnold's shop twenty minutes later.

Kaylee stepped up and peeked through the front window. It was a tiny place. Two hair dryers, two sinks and two chairs. Rick joined her to look inside. "I wonder if there'd be enough business to make it worthwhile."

"Mommy said I need a haircut," Molly said.

Rick glanced down at Molly. "She did, huh?"

"She said I look like a muffin."

Rick and Kaylee looked at each other and then they both turned to Molly who had her hands cupped around her face and was peering in the bottom half of the window.

"A muffin?" Rick asked.

"A raggedy muffin. That's what she said."

156

Rick and Kaylee exchanged grins. "A ragamuffin." He ruffled Molly's hair. "You probably could use a trim, Raggedy Muffin."

Molly giggled as they turned away from the shop for the short stroll back to the station. "I can cut her hair if you want me to," Kaylee informed Rick softly.

Molly, of course, heard every word. "It's okay if Kaylee cuts my hair, right, Daddy?"

"Sure, if she wants to."

"She can cut yours, too. Mommy said you looked like you hadn't had a haircut in months."

"She did, huh?"

"But you're not her 'sponsibility anymore so she wasn't going to remind you."

"Gee, that was nice of her." Rick grinned at Kaylee.

"Anything else Mommy said that I should know about?"

Molly slid a sideways glance in Kaylee's direction. "I forget."

Rick cleared his throat. "We can walk over and say hi to Miss Emma if you want to."

"Let's do that!" Molly jiggled Rick's hand. "She always gives me orange suckers."

Together they made their way down the street, turned the corner and paused before a neat blue house in the middle of the block. After several minutes an older woman in a pale pink housedress answered Rick's knock. The expression of discomfort on her face was immediately replaced by a smile when she recognized her visitors. "Rick Braddock, I do declare." She opened the screen door in welcome. "And this can't be Molly, can it?"

Molly slid her hand into Rick's and smiled up at Miss Emma while she nodded vigorously.

"Well, to what do I owe this pleasure? Come in, come in."

She gestured them forward into a cozy living room. A television set was tuned to a soap opera. Kaylee felt sort of awkward, unsure how she'd come to be here. She had no plans to stay in Perrish, and no money with which to buy the local beauty salon. Why then had she not demurred when Rick suggested a visit to Miss Emma?

"This is a friend of ours, Miss Emma," Rick said. "Kaylee Walsh. Kaylee's a hairstylist. We were admiring your salon."

Miss Emma fixed a keen gaze on Kaylee. "Not much to admire there anymore, I'm afraid. Place has been closed for almost two years."

"It doesn't look too bad," Kaylee assured her. "Except for the dust." Miss Emma's hair was frazzled and untended. How Kaylee wished she could offer to remedy that.

Miss Emma chuckled and waved them to seats. "Yes. Well. I'd hoped to find someone to take it over. But a small town like this." She shrugged. "Though mind you, when I was running it, I turned a pretty penny, if I do say so myself."

She glanced at Kaylee expectantly. Kaylee didn't know what to say. Her gaze slid to Rick for help.

"Kaylee's on her way to Miami," Rick inserted dutifully. "Her cousin has a salon there. She's staying with me and Molly temporarily until I can get her car fixed."

"Oh, oh, I see," Miss Emma said, not bothering to disguise her disappointment.

"Molly here remembers you cutting her hair when she was little." Rick winked at Emma. "She wanted to come and say hello."

"Well, I'm so glad you did." Emma grinned at Molly. "And I remember what a good girl you were that day, and what pretty hair you have."

Rick nudged Molly. "Thank you," she said and giggled. "You gave me a sucker, too. An orange one."

Emma chuckled. "My, what a memory you have." She pushed herself slowly, painfully out of her chair and hobbled past them. "You know, if I'm not mistaken—" She lifted the lid on a covered glass dish on a table nearby, "I have an orange sucker here just for you."

She turned triumphantly and handed Molly the treat.

"Thank you, Miss Emma." She patted Emma's arm. "I'm sorry you can't cut my hair anymore."

Emma stroked a hand along the top of Molly's head. "Oh, me too, sweetheart. Me too. But maybe someday we'll find someone to take over my place and you can come get your hair cut there again."

Her gaze briefly caught Kaylee's, but Kaylee was so touched by the interchange between Molly and Emma, she barely acknowledged it.

Rick stood. "I've got to get back to work. We won't keep you, Miss Emma."

"All right then." She saw them to the door. "Nice to meet you Kaylee."

"You too, Miss Emma."

Rick unlocked the door of the station and removed the *Back in Five Minutes* sign. While Molly and Kaylee packed up the remains of their lunch, a delivery truck arrived and Rick went out to sign for a package.

"That's your new starter," he informed Kaylee when he came back in. "Your car should be up and running by the end of the week."

"Oh. Great." Kaylee pasted a smile on her face. Once Old Blue was operational, she had no reason not to leave Perrish. Except her heart was telling her there were two very good reasons to stay, and they were standing right in front of her.

"Come on, Kaylee. Let's go make doll clothes and cut my hair." Their adventure over, Molly tugged on Kaylee's hand, anxious to move on to the next activity.

Kaylee forced herself to move, to pull away from Rick's gaze. His dark eyes were telling her something, she thought, but what was it? Stay? Go on and go, and let me get on with my life?

"I'll see you girls later." He held the door open for them, ruffling Molly's hair as she went by. Kaylee felt a tug on her own ponytail and she turned in surprise. "Later," Rick told her softly.

Rick watched Molly and Kaylee until they were out of sight. He rearranged the invoices and ledgers on his desk, meaning to finish the paperwork interrupted by the impromptu lunch, but the memory of kissing Kaylee intruded.

He found himself staring at the vending machine on the opposite wall, the snacks a blur as he recalled his most recent encounter with her. He'd been prepared to chew Kaylee out but good for getting Molly's hopes up that she'd stay. Hell, for one crazy moment, he'd allowed himself to hope that she was thinking of staying. But as soon as she'd begun her explanation, her soft Tennessee drawl had washed over him. He knew his daughter well enough to know that she'd let herself get carried away with what could be instead of what was. And halfway through Kaylee's explanation he'd stopped listening. He'd watched her lips form the words, been mesmerized by the sound of her voice and the memories of their previous kisses. Before he knew it he was kissing her. That was all he wanted to do, all he could think about doing. He wanted her. Wanted her to stay. Would like nothing more than for her to be Molly's stepmother and his wife.

For heaven's sake. Four years without a steady woman in his life and in less than a week he'd fallen for the wrong woman.

Idiot, he berated himself. He shoved the unfinished paperwork into a drawer and went out to the garage. He'd fix Kaylee's car, that's what he'd do. He'd give her the opportunity to leave and prove to himself that she'd hightail it out of Perrish as fast as she could, just as he'd expected all along.

So what if she took his heart with her. He couldn't possibly ask her to stay. Could he?

Chapter Twenty

That night Kaylee couldn't sleep. The rest of the day fell into a routine. She'd prepared a meal, the three of them had shared it, Molly's chatter a buffer between her and Rick. But it didn't stop the smoldering looks he sent her across the table, nor, she was sure, did it stop her from returning them.

After some TV and a game of Candyland, Rick bathed Molly. Kaylee read her a story. Together they tucked her in. Kaylee stepped out to the garage to put a load of clothes in the dryer. When she came back in, Rick was dressed in workout clothes, loose- fitting cotton shorts and a baggy sleeveless tee shirt which gave her a nice view of the muscles in his arms.

They both stopped at the same time, staring at each other. Kaylee knew what Rick was thinking and she was sure he knew what direction her thoughts had taken. Molly was in bed. Asleep. Rick's bedroom was down the hall. So convenient. Memories of their one night spent there together raced through her in such a rush she gave an involuntary little cry. Rick took a step toward her.

"I think I'll take a shower," she blurted, dodging around him. No. No way. She wasn't going to sleep with him with a six-year-old down the hall. It was indecent. She couldn't. She wouldn't. But oh how she wanted to.

"I'll be in the garage."

Kaylee took her shower, lingering as long as she could over preparations for bed. When she could delay no longer, she made up the sofa and settled down, knowing she was too keyed up to sleep. She flipped channels on the television, finding nothing of interest. She turned off the light and lay staring up at the ceiling. If only she had a reason to go out to the garage. She needed an excuse. A better excuse than wanting to be in close proximity to Rick. So she could what? Sit there and drool over him?

She punched her pillow and turned on her side. Then flipped to her other side. She could hear the occasional clank of weights, Rick moving around out there.

She repositioned herself on her back. If she went out there—no. She wouldn't. She had no reason. She wouldn't throw herself at him. She turned to her other side, then flipped the covers back as it dawned on her what that other noise was. She had a perfectly legitimate reason to be in the garage. A dryer full of clothes. That needed to be folded.

Immediately. Tonight. Right now.

She grabbed her flimsy robe, tied it around her and padded barefoot to the door. Taking a deep breath, telling herself to act nonchalant, she opened the door as if she had absolutely nothing on her mind but folding clean sheets, towels and underwear into perfect order.

Rick was on his back on the weight bench, shirtless, doing bench presses. A small portable radio was turned low, not to a country station, but classic rock. Aerosmith, Kaylee thought.

"I forgot I had a load of laundry in the dryer," she called by way of explanation. She crossed to the dryer and opened it. The garage was not used as a garage, although it did sport a garage door. It had been converted into a multipurpose area. The walls were paneled, but the floor was concrete. Molly's bike sat next to a lawnmower and other yard tools. The washer and dryer and water heater were lined up against the back wall. Rick had cleared out enough space for a weight bench and a shelf to hold a collection of barbells and other exercise equipment.

Kaylee did her best to concentrate on folding laundry, but the one glance she'd gotten of Rick was burned into her brain. His body glistened with a fine sheen of perspiration. The garage wasn't air-conditioned and even with the window open and a small fan operating on its highest setting, it was quite warm in the small space. Somehow she knew that even though he continued doing bench presses, a hefty dumbbell in each hand, all of his concentration was focused on her. She could sense it, feel it. He was as highly aware of her as she was of him. The knowledge made her tingle inside. A heady rush of anticipation sizzled through her. Even if nothing happened, she could live on this feeling of "what if" indefinitely. Knowing the possibility was there.

From the corner of her eye, she saw him set the weights down and sit up. He began rubbing himself briskly with a towel—chest, shoulders, arms, armpits—drying the perspiration. He scrubbed the towel across his face and over his hair. Then he stood.

She was almost done folding the laundry, had it set in neat stacks on top of the dryer. The air buzzed with electricity, setting every nerve ending on edge. Rick didn't say anything. She closed the dryer door and suddenly he was there, surrounding her. He caged her there with an arm on either side of her, the paneled wall at her back.

She moaned at the sheer deliciousness of his approach. He'd taken the decision out of her hands, determined to give them both exactly what they wanted. His mouth came down on hers. He untied the loose belt of her robe and pushed it aside. His hands were everywhere at once, moving up along her ribcage to caress her breasts, floating down across her back to cup her bottom. All the while, his mouth worked its magic, his tongue and lips mating with hers as if he'd never get enough.

The temperature in the garage seemed to have shot up fifty degrees. Kaylee thought she'd burn up, but she didn't care.

She had to have him, had to be with him, couldn't have stopped what was happening if she'd tried. And she didn't want to try.

She could feel him hard, aroused, which tripled her own excitement. Her robe dropped to the floor. He yanked the thin cotton undershirt over her head and bent to suckle her breasts. Her knees went weak. She whimpered in delight. While he treated her breasts to the pleasure his mouth could give, he worked her boxer shorts down over her hips until they dropped to her ankles.

He straightened, his mouth finding hers again, his hands coming around to cup her from behind, pulling her tight against him. With featherlight motions he swept his hands back around to her breasts, teasing the nipples with a thumb and forefinger before one hand dropped between her legs. His first touch there found her hot and wet and pliant. Kaylee gasped as shock waves rippled through her. She tried to hold onto her sanity, reason, thought, logic, but everything slipped away. She was aware only of him, of what was happening between them, of what he was making her feel.

Blindly, instinctively, she reached for the elastic waistband of his shorts and tugged, pulling it down over his hips, along with his boxers, freeing him. She covered him with her hand, entranced by the length and breadth and steely hardness. Some sort of a male sound emanated from his throat, a grunt of sorts, which sounded like approval, enjoyment. Encouragement? She was panting in excitement as his fingers continued to slide against her hot wet core, egging her on. She closed her fingers around him in a firm grip, mimicking what he was doing to her as best she could.

He moved so fast Kaylee was barely aware he'd lifted her up, somehow able to hold her against the wall and be thickly, deeply inside her in what felt like one motion.

Tiny cries kept coming out of her throat and she couldn't stop them. Bone-deep satisfaction shot through her along with the wish that they could stay like this forever. She opened her eyes, braced against Rick, to find him watching her, barely moving, though what that cost him must have been a lot.

"So good," she whispered.

"Mmmm."

He moved slightly and she gasped, knowing she was close to going over the edge.

His fingers dug into her rear end, the muscles on his arms bulging with the effort of holding her. They were both drenched in sweat, their bodies slick with it, the scent of that and their mating swirling in the air around them.

He moved again, and the torture was exquisite. She braced her hands on his shoulders, her fingers digging into his hot moist flesh.

He made that sound again and moved, out and in. Each time it seemed like he went deeper, hit her harder, there, right there. He lifted her a little bit, slid against *that place* again. And again and again. The tiny cries got louder, bolder, grander. Kaylee fell over the edge, her nails digging into Rick's back, her teeth sunk in his shoulder as he thrust deeper and deeper before he came.

Her entire body turned to jelly. She felt herself melting into a sopping-wet puddle of mind-numbing satisfaction. On some level she knew she should care, that perhaps what had just happened was going to have far-reaching repercussions, but she couldn't think just then.

"Shit," Rick whispered, breathing hard, still holding her upright, although her feet were once again on the floor.

"Hmm?"

"No protection."

"Mmmm. 'Sokay."

He stepped out of his shorts and left them there on the garage floor along with her nightclothes and swept her up in his still-shaking arms.

"Where are we going?" she asked when she realized what he was doing. Somehow he managed to open the door to the house and close it behind him.

"My room. We're going to do this again. This time we're going to do it right."

"No, Rick, put me down." She pushed against his shoulder, but he was already down the hallway, passing Molly's room. "Molly—"

He deposited her on his bed, snapped his fingers at Brutus who slunk out at the unspoken command, then closed and locked the door.

He came back to the bed. "Molly's sound asleep. She's not going to wake up."

"But—"

He covered her lips with a finger. "And if she does, it will be okay. But she's not going to."

Kaylee frowned in the dim light coming in through the half-closed blinds.

He kissed her. "Do you want to go back to the sofa right now?"

She shook her head. "No, but—"

"Shhh." He kissed her again.

She tore her lips away. "I can't do this."

He grinned, his teeth a slash of white in the near darkness.

"Yes, you can."

His body covered hers. The air-conditioning dried their skin and Rick felt big and warm above her. Kaylee wasn't sure, but she thought he was half-aroused again already. Desire sliced through her as his hands and mouth worked their magic, kissing, stroking, suckling, nibbling.

I object. The thought was there, in her brain, but she didn't give voice to it. *This isn't right.* "Rick," she whispered, which he took for encouragement. His head moved lower, from her breasts to her belly, his tongue doing incredibly erotic things on the way. Kaylee felt as if her brain had disconnected from her body, betrayed her in some way.

Her legs parted for him, his mouth connected with the moist flesh between them and she was lost, forgetting that this was something she didn't want to do. How was it he seemed to know her so well when they'd only met a few days ago? How could he know how and when and where to touch her to drive her insane? She came in minutes, covering her mouth with her hands, stifling the scream of pure pleasure that threatened to erupt from her throat because no matter what Rick said, she wasn't a hundred percent convinced Molly wouldn't wake up.

"God, you're incredible," Rick whispered, his voice rough and sexy as he crawled back up, a knee planted on either side of her. He reached into the drawer of the bedside stand and Kaylee heard the crinkle of a foil-wrapped package.

She looped her fingers around his wrist. "It's okay. I take birth-control pills." Rick paused. "Unless you're concerned about—"

"No—no." He kissed her. "I guess we should have discussed this before—"

She giggled. "Talking about it doesn't seem to be a big priority with us, does it?"

"Unh-uh."

He made love to her slowly, powerfully, bringing her on top of him for a while, letting her move at her own pace, making it last as long as possible, as if he were savoring every second of being inside her. Kaylee didn't want it to end, but she knew they couldn't continue indefinitely. What a change from Bobby Lou's technique of waiting until Kaylee was just getting warmed up before finding his own release. Rick seemed to have no particular agenda in mind except to make this as enjoyable as possible for both of them.

She bent over him, kissing him deeply in gratitude for not rushing her, trying to express her pleasure without words. The kiss turned into an erotic attempt for each of them to absorb the other, Rick pulsing deeply inside her until he could hold back no longer. Locked together, he rolled, tucking her beneath him, his thrusts making her think of wild horses, their power unleashed, muscles rippling as they ran free.

They lay together, catching their breath, waiting for the world to settle back around them. She thought that Rick had fallen asleep. Carefully, she disentangled herself from him and crawled to the edge of the bed.

"Where are you going?" he asked, his voice muffled, his hand catching her wrist.

Back where I belong, Kaylee thought. "I'm going to go get my robe and stuff."

"Why? You don't need it." His voice was stronger now that he'd turned his head away from the pillow.

"I'm not staying in here with you."

"Why? Because of Molly? I told you she—"

"I know. She won't wake up. It doesn't matter. This doesn't feel right to me. I know it doesn't make sense. But it's how I feel."

She leaned over and kissed his cheek. He kept his fingers circled around her wrist. "How about a shower?"

"Rick—"

"I'm going to take one. Come on. We're hot and sticky. Perfect way to cool off."

Kaylee hated to admit how much she wanted to join him. She had vivid memories of their other night together, which had included some interesting shower maneuvers.

"Okay. A quick one. And just a shower. No funny stuff." He squeezed her wrist. "I don't know if you've noticed.

But no one's been laughing."

His tone of voice gave her pause. He sounded so serious. Was it even remotely possible that he'd been as affected as she by their lovemaking? She tugged her hand away. "I'll go get my things."

He had the shower running when she got back inside the house. She closed and locked the bathroom door behind her. Kaylee clipped her hair up and Rick held the curtain back so she could step under the spray first. Then he joined her there.

The water was a few degrees above tepid, refreshing but not jarringly cold or hot.

She tilted her head back and let the water run over her. Rick stepped up close behind, running a bar of soap over her bare skin. First the front, then turning her to repeat the movement to her back side. Then she did the same to him. As good as his word, he didn't take the opportunity to attempt another sexual encounter. Kaylee didn't know about Rick, but she was barely functioning as it was. Her bones were hardly able to support her body.

When they were both clean and rinsed, Rick turned off the shower and they toweled each other dry. Kaylee leaned her head against his chest, breathing in the scent of pure male laced with soap. He tilted her head back and kissed her, a kiss full of meaning.

She didn't want it to stop. Didn't want to stop kissing Rick, didn't want to be away from him. Her nipples tingled where they rubbed against his chest. She felt that slow liquid feeling start to run through her again, as if her blood had become too hot and was melting her bones.

Rick was into it as much as she was. His hands seemed to roam everywhere at once and the kiss got deeper and hotter, like it was never going to end.

He was aroused. Again. Rick's hands slid down over her bottom and splayed against the backs of her thighs, spreading them apart. She made a sound in her throat, of encouragement, excitement, no longer caring how or where it happened. He lifted her a little, and she tried to assist, locking her arms around his neck, going up on her tiptoes, rubbing against him.

He let go of the kiss, like a drowning victim coming up for air, looking around him in a daze. Kaylee's arms were still around his neck, her head tilted back. She struggled to open her eyes when she felt him move, taking her with him.

"Where going?" she mumbled, easing her grip on him.

"Right here." He lowered the lid on the toilet seat and sat, tugging on her hand.

Kaylee gave him a skeptical look. The toilet was wedged between the tub and the vanity. There was barely enough room for the toilet-paper hanger. "This won't work."

He gave her hand another tug. "Oh, I think it will. I think we'll make it work. Come here," he invited.

Carefully, she lowered herself on top of him, sucking in a breath as she eased down, sheathing him inside her inch by inch. Her whole body was alive with sensation, every nerve ending stretched taut in anticipation of what would come next.

It was awkward, that was the only word for it, trying to make love to such a hunk of man in a tiny bathroom, but Kaylee hung on for the ride, barely noticing when her knees hit the back of the tank, or when the toilet paper dislodged from its moorings and unraveled across the floor.

Every ounce of attention she had centered itself on Rick, their gazes locked together just as their bodies were before they found the rhythm of a slow sensual dance that unnerved them both by the time it ended. When it did, Kaylee dropped her head to his shoulder, sinking her teeth into her lip, willing herself not to get emotional, not to say the words that were on the tip of her tongue. Words that would probably send Rick running in the other direction so he'd be lost to her forever. *I love you. I'm in love with you.* A slow deep shudder ran through her at the thought of losing him for all time.

When her breathing had slowed she disentangled herself from him.

Her knees were shaking, but she somehow managed to stand and dress herself before she opened the door. There stood Molly, her doll clutched in one arm, her fist rubbing her eye. Kaylee took a step back and bumped into Rick, stepping on his foot in the process. She heard his "Oof" of surprise, but she couldn't take her eyes off Molly.

"What're you guys doing?" Molly asked. She yawned hugely and tried to squeeze past them. "Daddy, move please. I need a drink."

Thank God Rick had wrapped a towel around his waist before she'd opened the door. Kaylee felt her skin heat in embarrassment as Molly eyed her in the mirror while Rick filled a cup with water from the tap. "You've got your shirt on wrong-side-out again, Kaylee."

Kaylee glanced down to see that Molly was correct. "Oops." Her color deepened tenfold if possible. "Well, I'll fix that later. Night, sweetheart."

"Good night," both Rick and Molly said in unison. Rick winked at her in the mirror before he bent to retrieve the fallen toilet paper. Kaylee scooted up the hall to the living room and dived under the covers on the couch, yanking them to her chin.

Chapter Twenty-One

The aroma of roasting meat greeted Rick as soon as he opened the front door the following evening. His mouth watered. Brutus padded over, tail wagging, and Rick rubbed the big dog behind the ears. Molly appeared clutching one of her dolls. Her hair had been freshly washed and obviously recently trimmed. Her bangs hung in a neat line above her eyebrows.

"Look at Josie's new dress." She held the doll out for Rick's inspection. "Kaylee made it. But I helped." Molly was beaming from ear to ear. Rick tried to remember when he'd ever seen Molly so happy and couldn't. He put an arm around her while he made admiring noises about the doll dress, all the while fighting down the dread. How would Molly react when Kaylee left? *How will you?* he asked himself. He already knew the answer to that. Not well. He'd miss Kaylee desperately.

He headed for the kitchen. This is how it's supposed to be, he thought. How different it was to come home these past few nights to a hot meal already prepared, Kaylee and Molly waiting for him. How had he managed all this time, picking Molly up from the babysitter's and coming home to an empty house, except for Brutus? Preparing some simple meal for the two of them? He'd made a life with Molly, done the best he could. But he hadn't realized how lonely and empty it truly was until Kaylee arrived.

Stay, he wanted to tell her. Stay and I'll do everything I can to make you happy. I'll be good to you. I'll never leave you.

He stopped on the other side of the counter and Kaylee looked up from the potatoes she was mashing.

The potato masher stilled. Her gaze met his. "Hi," she breathed. He could see a light sheen of perspiration on her upper lip. Tiny sprigs of damp curls framed her face and trailed along her neckline. The kitchen was warmer than the rest of the house due to the stove and oven in action.

"Smells good." Great line, Rick, he told himself. Very smooth. How can she keep from falling all over you?

"It's roast beef. Mashed potatoes. Gravy. Vegetables." "And biscuits. We made biscuits, Daddy. Not from a can. And I helped." Molly edged up close to Kaylee, stuck her finger in the potatoes and popped it in her mouth.

"Mmmm. Good. Go wash your hands, Daddy, so we can eat."

Nothing like a six-year-old to put a grown man in his place. "Yes, ma'am!"

In the bathroom he berated himself some more. Now he couldn't even walk into his own bathroom without being assailed by memories of being there with Kaylee. He splashed water over his face and ran his damp hands through his hair, then stared at himself in the mirror. He had to stop with the fantasies about this perfect family which included Kaylee. Might as well start now.

Each and every one of Rick's intentions flew out the window by the time dinner was over. Like a lovesick teenager, he'd covertly watched Kaylee's every move, from the way she buttered a biscuit, to her knife sliding through the roast beef. He counted each bite she took, all the while pretending that he wasn't affected by her presence.

Somehow it was decided that he was next in line for a haircut. He might as well get a free haircut out of the deal before Kaylee disappeared from his life, right?

First he walked Brutus. Then he got Molly ready for bed and read her a story. He offered her an extra drink of water which she declined. Then he showered because Kaylee preferred to cut wet hair. And he left his shirt off because what was the point of getting hair all over a clean shirt?

He noticed Molly was sound asleep as he padded down the hall barefoot, wearing his favorite pair of well-worn and faded jeans. Kaylee was at the kitchen table sewing another doll dress. She glanced up when he entered and blew a big purple bubble in his direction, then sucked it back into her mouth and popped it.

She rose abruptly. "Ready?" She indicated the chair she'd set in the middle of the kitchen.

"More than ready," Rick answered. She wasn't the only one who could throw out those double entendres.

If Kaylee picked up on the hidden meaning of his words she gave no indication. She draped a towel over his shoulders and picked up the comb and shears she'd left on the counter.

"How do you like it?" she asked.

She was standing in front of him, combing his hair over his forehead which put him at about eye level with her bustline.

"I like it. Very much."

She glanced down as he grinned up at her. She was blushing. She blushed more than any woman he'd ever known.

She moved behind him. "I meant your hair."

"Any way you like it."

"Not too short, I suppose."

"No one's ever complained that it's too short."

"It's pretty thick."

"You're the expert."

"How long has it been?"

"About twenty-four hours."

"Since your last haircut?"

"Oh. Couple of months, I guess."

"It grows fast."

"Under the right circumstances."

"Rick…" There was a definite strain in Kaylee's tone.

"Don't make this harder than it is."

Rick squirmed uncomfortably, not sure if it was Kaylee's close proximity or his own double entendres, but he was definitely turned on. "I think it's too late."

"I'm cutting now. Sit still and stop talking."

Could there be anything more intimate than having a lover's hands in your hair, Rick wondered. Well, of course, there could be, but Kaylee's hands in his hair were conjuring up all sorts of images of her hands elsewhere on his body. It was exquisite torture to have her so close, yet hardly touching him. He followed her movements as best he could while he kept his head still. He gazed at her elbow, her breasts where they strained against the cotton of her sleeveless top.

Snip. Snip. Snip. Wisps of his hair floated to the floor as she worked in a silence broken only by the low hum of country music from the radio which sat on top of the refrigerator.

She moved around him from side to side, concentrating on the haircut. Then she moved in front of him and bent closer, combing his hair, visually examining it on either side of his head until her gaze met his.

"Could you, uh, spread your legs?"

"Gladly."

Rick did so and she straightened and stepped between them. She raised her arm and the hem of her top rose with the movement of her shoulder, revealing her tiny waist and her navel. How much torture could one man take?

Snip.

Rick couldn't help himself. He placed his hands around her waist beneath her top. Her skin felt like warm satin. How well he remembered the feel of her skin against his.

178

He breathed in her scent along with the faint aroma of grape-flavored bubble gum. "Kaylee…"

Snip.

He leaned forward, lifted her top and skimmed his lips across her stomach.

Snip.

"Oops."

Rick froze. He looked up. "What's 'oops'?"

She gulped audibly. "I told you to sit still," she scolded.

"What did you do?" He reached up to feel the top of his head. He felt a row of rather short spikes.

"It might be a little shorter than you expected."

"Kaylee—"

"Well you grabbed me, and it distracted me!"

And he wanted to do it again. He suddenly didn't care if he ended up bald from this encounter with Kaylee. It would be well worth it. He pulled her closer and nuzzled her again. "Shave my head. I don't give a damn." He pulled her down to his lap and kissed her properly.

She still held the scissors and comb, but her arms came around his neck in welcome.

"Rick," she mumbled between kisses.

She tasted faintly of grape. "Where's your gum?"

He slid his hands up to cup her breasts through her bra.

"Swallowed it," she gasped before he took her mouth in a deep searching kiss.

She straddled him and he held her close so she could feel how much he wanted her. "Kaylee."

She squirmed against him. Rick held on until she turned her head away. He thought he heard her utter a breathless,

"No."

He was on fire and rock hard for her. How could she tell him no?

"Stop it. I promised myself I wouldn't do this," she whispered.

"Do what?"

She shook her head and slid out of his arms. He let her go even though he didn't want to.

She took a deep, steadying breath. "Please don't make this any harder than it is."

"I can't—"

"Stop doing that. Stop turning everything I say into something about sex."

"Sorry. I didn't mean to." Not that time, anyway.

Were there tears in her eyes? Why?

"Kaylee, I—"

She shook her head. "Don't. Please. Let me finish with your hair. I'm sorry, it's going to be shorter than you expected. But then we're done."

She sniffed and started cutting his hair. Rick crossed his arms over his chest and kept his mouth shut. Which was, he now knew, what he should have done in the first place.

Chapter Twenty-Two

Kaylee had no idea how she managed to finish cutting Rick's hair without either bursting into tears or crawling back into his lap and giving in to the fierce desire that gnawed at her.

She wanted him. For all time. Forever. But that would mean staying in Perrish. She could turn this little house into a home for the three of them. Be a mother to Molly and a wife to Rick. Maybe there'd be brothers and sisters for Molly later on.

She could have a whole different life than the one she'd expected to create in Miami. When she left Bertie Springs, she'd thought she had no choice. But she had lots of choices. It was her life. She could go to Miami. She could stay in Perrish. It didn't have to be one or the other. She could go anywhere she chose, live wherever she wanted.

After Rick's reaction to the very idea that she might not leave, he'd never believe she'd stay in Perrish permanently. And he'd never ask her to. What if she told him she wanted to stay? That she was in love with him? The very thought that the sentiment wouldn't be returned was enough to keep her silent.

Sure, Rick wanted her in his bed. He'd made that clear enough. But she couldn't be sure he wanted anything more than that. And she wasn't going to set herself up for disappointment. *If you don't like the answer then you oughtn't to have asked the question.* She could hear another of Granny Daisy's admonitions in her head. It had taken her years to realize that all those little sayings of Granny's held a ring of truth.

Besides, if Rick wanted her to stay, he ought to be able to say so, right? If he couldn't put his heart on the line, she wouldn't dangle hers out there for him. If he was ever going to find another wife, he'd have to risk it.

The following few days were strained. Kaylee thanked God every day for Molly's presence. She sewed her heart out, finishing up the doll clothes and the playhouse decorations.

They cut out cookies using Molly's paper dolls as an outline and spent an afternoon decorating them with colored frosting. Molly glowed at her accomplishments and never failed to give Rick a rundown of their daily activities.

On Thursday, Rick had a softball game, the last game of the season. Kaylee tagged along to get out of the house, but also because she wanted one more memory of Rick's physique outlined in his baseball uniform.

Friday evening Rick arrived home with the announcement she'd been both anticipating and dreading. "Your car's fixed."

"Great!" she responded brightly.

"School starts on Monday, you know."

Was he watching her for a reaction? Was he hoping she'd beg to stay? Even though that's what she wanted to do, she refused to give in to the urge. She smiled even bigger.

"Wonderful. I'll be out of your hair then, won't I?"

She blushed and looked away. Her smile faded. She had unintentionally reminded them both of the other night when she'd cut his hair and he'd kissed her. His hair was much shorter than she'd intended. It stuck up in fashionable spikes on top of his head. The back and sides were trimmed smooth and short.

He looked better than ever as far as Kaylee was concerned. The haircut made him look more open and approachable. Less intimidating.

After their pizza dinner, Molly and Rick settled in the living room to watch *A Bug's Life,* which Rick had rented from the small selection at the convenience store. Kaylee kept one eye on the movie while she put the finishing touches on the curtains for Molly's playhouse. The little tablecloth was already done.

Tears pricked her eyes as she came closer with every stitch to finishing them. She'd hang the curtains and cover the table. Molly would hold tea parties with her teddy bears and dolls. But Kaylee wouldn't be there to share them. She wouldn't mix the cherry Kool-Aid that the dolls were so fond of and put it in Molly's plastic tea pot. She wouldn't be there to help her pour or to wipe up the spills when the little cups overturned.

Kaylee made a strangled sound in her throat and blinked rapidly, pretending she had something in her eye when Rick glanced her way.

She tried to imagine Rick perched on one of the little chairs, conversing with Molly's dolls, sipping Kool-Aid and nibbling bear-shaped cookies. He'd do it, of course, if Molly asked him to. But tea parties were a girl sort of thing. Meant to be shared with another female. Maybe Molly's friend Hannah would be there. And maybe Hannah's mother.

But I won't be, Kaylee thought to herself, as she knotted the last stitch and broke the thread between her teeth.

Gently she smoothed the material between her fingers, her gaze going to Molly and Rick who were cuddled together in the recliner, chuckling over a bit of amusing dialogue in the movie.

Abruptly she stood. "All done," she said. "I'm going to go hang these up."

She escaped the living room through the sliding doors to the lanai and crossed the yard to the playhouse. It would be dark soon. Frogs croaked and insects hummed. A hard rain earlier in the day had temporarily lifted the humidity, so it was almost pleasant outside.

Kaylee ducked inside the playhouse to find it was even dimmer, the only light coming in the two small windows and the tiny door.

She'd already installed brackets for the curtain rods. All she had to do was thread the curtains on the rods and hang them. She sat on one of the little chairs and picked up a rod. In minutes she had both the curtains on the rods and was ready to hang them.

She knelt on the floor in front of the window and fitted the ends of the rod to the brackets.

"Need any help?"

Kaylee jumped at the sound of Rick's voice, and turned to find him hunched over in order to peek in the door. She squelched her immediate reaction which was to grab him and haul him inside with her. Instead she somehow managed to maintain her cool. "No thanks. I've about got it. Besides, there's hardly room for both of us in here."

As if to prove her wrong, Rick edged his way through the door, a feat requiring some interesting maneuvering and flexibility on his part, until he was inside, crowding her.

The temperature in the small space shot up. Kaylee tried to move back to give him room, to keep from touching him, but there was nowhere for her to go.

She stared at him, her hands still holding the curtain rod, every instinct she possessed longing to reach out and touch him where he knelt next to her.

"Here, let me do that," he told her softly. He took the unattached end of the curtain rod from her. At the brush of his hand against hers, she gasped. As if that was all the encouragement he needed, he dropped the rod. His fingers closed around her wrist and pulled her to him. His mouth came down on hers and Kaylee was lost. Lost in the rough caress of his lips, the heat of his tongue as it tangled with hers.

She pressed herself against him, her breasts smashed against his chest, her arms locked around his neck. His arms tightened around her. Tiny sounds bubbled up in the back of her throat. Sounds of want and need and all the words she couldn't say. All the words she was sure he didn't want to hear.

They tumbled to the floor mindless of the child-sized furniture that got pushed aside and out of the way.

Kaylee was trapped beneath Rick's weight, but she felt no discomfort. She felt more alive than she had in days.

Rick's mouth traveled beneath her jawline to her ear. He tugged on her earlobe with his teeth. His tongue darted out to touch that sensitive area below and behind her lobe and Kaylee arched against him in reaction.

His hands tangled in her hair and his mouth found hers again.

How was she going to survive without him? she thought wildly. How was she going to live without this? This sense of *aliveness*? This all-consuming awareness of this particular man.

She did her best to communicate her feelings to him in her response. When his hands cupped her breasts through her clothes she welcomed his touch. He teased her nipples, rubbing the hard erect tips until she moaned. He raked his teeth across one and she nearly went through the ceiling.

Kaylee knew he was as excited as she was. He yanked her close, fitted her body to his even though they were both still fully dressed. Memories of their lovemaking flooded through her mind. Oh, how she wanted a repeat of those nights. How she wanted the feel of Rick's skin next to hers, complete access to every part of him.

Rick had one arm around her back and the other lower, his palm splayed across her bottom, while he kissed her deeply, making love to her mouth, as their bodies mimicked the motion.

His hand slid down to her bare thigh and back up beneath her shorts, his fingers delving into the cushion of flesh he found there before exploring even further.

Kaylee tore her mouth from his. "I—I can't breathe," she choked out. She was covered with perspiration. Her clothes were hot and damp and so were Rick's.

"Me either," Rick whispered back, before he took her mouth again.

"Daddy?"

Kaylee braced her hands on Rick's shoulders and stilled.

Their mouths popped apart.

"Kaylee?" came Molly's plaintive voice from the lanai. "Daddy?" She sounded as if she were on the verge of tears. "Where are you guys?"

"Right here, honey," Kaylee called. She tried to scramble away from Rick, but there was no place to go. "We're almost done."

Rick stared down at her, his eyes sparking fire, even in the dim light. "Are you kidding?" he whispered. "We were only getting started." He grinned, a full-mouth smile, his teeth slashing white in the near darkness. "Be right there, Molly," he called through the window.

"The movie's over," Molly informed him.

"Okay. Go brush your teeth and pick out a book for me to read. I'll be in in a minute."

"Can Kaylee read to me tonight?"

Rick sighed and rolled his eyes. "See? I told you. I've been replaced," he whispered to Kaylee.

"Maybe we can all read the story together," Kaylee called back to Molly, her gaze on Rick. "How about that?"

"Goodie," Molly answered. They heard the sliding door click back into place behind her. They were alone again.

Kaylee scrambled up. She picked up the dangling curtain rod and snapped it into place, achingly aware of Rick radiating body heat and desire as he watched her.

She picked up the other rod and hung it, fussing briefly to straighten the material. She had to get out of here. Now. Before Molly decided to come out and see exactly what was keeping them.

"We're done here," she informed Rick.

She edged closer to where he blocked the door. He didn't move for a minute. She could hardly see his face in what was now almost total darkness, but she knew he was watching her.

"If you say so," he answered softly. He backed out of the playhouse, leaving her room to follow. They went back inside both aware of the effort they made not to touch each other.

Chapter Twenty-Three

Molly had chosen P.S. Eastman's *Are You My Mother?* Kaylee found it hard to believe she'd picked that particular book at random. She and Rick took turns reading the pages aloud. Kaylee did her best to disguise her emotional turmoil, but she knew her voice was huskier than usual and she cleared her throat more than once after she read. She thought maybe Rick too was affected by the book's message, as the little bird tried to figure out who its mother was. Was it a reflection of Molly's internal struggle? Of her desire to have a "mommy who lived with her"?

Kaylee had no answers. She held herself together until they'd finished reading and turned out the light. She gathered Molly close in the glow of the nightlight and kissed the top of her head as she said her good nights. She knew Rick was watching from the doorway. Did he have any idea how precious his daughter had become to her? Did he know how much she would miss his little girl when he gave her no choice but to leave?

On Sunday afternoon Rick's softball team hosted their annual barbeque and pool party. This was a chance for all the team members and their families to get together and socialize.

Kaylee would have gladly bowed out but Rick, and especially Molly, counted on her attending. Her car was fixed. There'd been no reason for her to stay through the weekend, except her own foolish agreement to attend the party. Her reluctance to disappoint Rick's daughter. The plain fact that she didn't want to leave at all.

She got to meet a few of the other team members and their significant others she'd seen attending the games. She was not immune to the admiring male gazes directed her way, including Rick's when she donned a swimsuit at Molly's request. She refused to cower or hide because the suit didn't fit her perfectly. Eat your heart out, she told Rick silently. If you want me to stay, you better say something pretty damn soon or this is the last you'll be seeing of me.

By bedtime, her bravado had deflated. Tomorrow, whether she wanted to or not, she'd finish packing her things, climb in Old Blue and head for Miami. She'd tell Tillie about the package in her gas tank and together they'd figure out what to do.

She kissed Molly good night, holding her a little longer than she usually did. How she'd miss this little girl. Rick studiously avoided her gaze, which somehow hurt more than she thought possible.

She made up her bed on the couch for the last time and pulled the sheet up to her chin. He doesn't want me. That thought played over and over in her head. He'll never ask me to stay. *Idiot!* she chided herself. Why'd you have to go and fall in love on the way to Miami? Why couldn't you wait until you got there?

Tears seeped from beneath her lashes. She tried to stop them, but the harder she tried the more insistent they became. At least she could cry quietly. Sort of. Except now her nose was running. She brushed at the tears with the backs of her hands, but she needed tissues.

Annoyed with herself, she threw the covers back and padded down the hall toward the bathroom. In the dark she groped for the box of tissues on the counter, grabbed several and mopped at her face and drippy nose. She sniffed loudly and stepped back into the hall and collided with Rick.

She yelped in alarm.

"Rick?"

"Kaylee? What are you doing?"

"Getting some tissues."

"Why didn't you turn the light on?"

"Because I didn't need a light to find the tissues."

"What's wrong with your voice?"

"Nothing."

"Are you sick?"

"No. Excuse me."

Kaylee made to step around Rick, but he reached for her in the dark. His arm grazed her breast through the thin camisole she wore.

"Kaylee, what's wrong?"

"Nothing."

"Are you crying?"

"No." Technically true. She had been crying. And she probably would cry some more. But at the moment she was not crying.

Rick cupped her cheek, his fingers sliding back into her hair, his thumb grazing her jaw. His lips touched her eyelids in a gentle kiss, then her cheek, her lips. "Why are you crying, sweetheart? Don't cry."

"I'm not," she whispered determinedly.

His kiss became more insistent. Cursing herself, Kaylee gave in to it. Their bodies melded together, triggered by instinct and memory. Kaylee could feel every muscle, could remember every nuance of Rick's lovemaking.

"I've missed you," he whispered. As if she'd been doused with icy water, Kaylee broke the embrace. He missed her, but did he miss *her*? Or did he miss having sex with her?

If he didn't know what he wanted by now, she wasn't going to help him figure it out.

"I've missed you too." She extricated herself from his embrace and walked away, back to the living room, to her makeshift bed. She knew without a doubt she wasn't going to cry anymore. At least not tonight.

Chapter Twenty-Four

Morning dawned too bright and too early, but Kaylee surprised herself with her buoyant mood. She made breakfast, chattering with Molly about the fun she'd have in first grade. Rick sat morosely silent staring into his coffee, shoving scrambled eggs and toast around on his plate without eating.

Listen, buddy boy, Kaylee told him silently, you better figure some stuff out pretty quick or it's going to be too late. He didn't look like he'd slept too well. Good. Kaylee hid her smile of satisfaction. If she'd shed tears, then he ought to be losing some sleep.

When it was time to leave for school, Kaylee knelt down next to Molly, straightened her collar and adjusted the straps of her Miss Kitty backpack.

"Now you know I'm leaving for Miami today, right? I won't be here when you get home."

Molly nodded. "Yes you will."

"No, Molly, I won't. I have a job in Miami. Remember? We talked about this."

Molly nodded again. "I remember. But you won't leave. I don't think Bobby Lou will care if you don't surprise him."

"Bobby Lou?" Rick echoed. "Your boyfriend? The guy who dumped you? He's waiting for you in Miami?"

193

Kaylee glanced up at Rick. "It's not what you think."

He didn't look like he believed her. "Huh," was all he said.

Kaylee couldn't explain Bobby Lou's presence to Rick, not without telling him about what was in her gas tank, which she had no intention of doing. Besides, what difference would it make? He wasn't going to ask her to stay anyway. Kaylee fixed her attention on Molly once more. "Mols, you know I'd stay if I could. But I can't." *Your daddy doesn't want me to.*

Molly put her arms around Kaylee and hugged her tight. "I asked God for a new mommy. And Miss Tiffany says God always answers prayers. Especially ones from little kids."

Kaylee had no argument for that one. "Okay, sweetie. You have a good day at school, now. I love you."

"I love you too."

Molly loped off toward the truck.

Rick hesitated as Kaylee straightened. Finally he looked right at her. Say something, Kaylee screamed silently. *Ask me to stay.*

"I'll be back with your car as soon as I drop her off."

"Thanks!" She gave him her fake smile. She got a whiff of his clean male scent as he followed Molly out the door. She refused to call him back, hang on, beg to stay. Like a typical male, Rick didn't recognize a good thing when it was staring him in the face.

Kaylee cleaned up the kitchen. She packed the remainder of her belongings. She took Brutus for a short walk down the street. Rick's neighbors, Kevin and Irv, were working in their garden. She waved and they waved back.

She loaded the washing machine with the linens she had used and left Rick a note to put the load in the dryer later.

Where was Rick? It shouldn't take him that long to drop Molly off at school and stop by the station to pick up her car. The plan was that he'd help her load her things and she'd drop him back off on her way out of town. But it was taking him forever to get here and it was making Kaylee antsy, giving her too much time to think, making her wish for what could be instead of what was.

Somehow it would all come out in the wash, as Granny Daisy used to say. Maybe Rick would come to his senses and arrive suddenly in Miami and sweep her off her feet and tell her he couldn't live without her. Why not? She'd expected to meet the man of her dreams in Miami. Was it her fault it happened before she'd even arrived?

The phone rang and Kaylee picked it up cautiously on the second ring. It was Rick.

"Hey, it's me. I've got a problem with your car."

Kaylee bit her lip. "I thought it was all fixed with the new starter and all."

Rick gave one of his humorless laughs. "Yeah, me too. I'm pretty sure it's your fuel pump, but I want to make sure. I'm going to be here for a while."

"The fuel pump. That's not in the gas tank, is it?"

Rick chuckled for real this time. "Uh, yeah, they sorta have to put the fuel pump where the fuel is."

"Um, Rick—" What? What was she going to say? How was she going to explain? There's a stash of stolen jewels in my gas tank? I know because I accidentally dropped them in there the day I met you?

"I'll be back as soon as I can, okay? I just wanted to let you know."

Kaylee sighed in resignation. At some point, those stolen jewels were going to have to come out of her gas tank. She supposed it might as well be now. By the time Rick arrived perhaps she'd have thought of a way to explain their presence.

"Okay."

Kaylee had finished the load of laundry, changed the sheets on Rick's bed, taken Brutus for another walk and cleaned Molly's room by the time she heard the front door open and Rick's familiar stride across the terrazzo floor. She looked up from her seat at the kitchen table where she'd been halfheartedly doing the newspaper's crossword puzzle, unable to squelch her welcoming smile as Rick appeared in the kitchen. His scowl was deeper than she'd ever seen it and he didn't return her greeting. Instead he yanked out the chair across from her and opened a bundle wrapped in a blue shop rag to reveal a familiar plastic-wrapped package that smelled of gasoline. Carefully he removed the three glass vials and poured their contents out into three neat piles on the tabletop. Deep dark blue, clear sparkling green and blood red stones winked up at her.

Kaylee stared at them while Rick sat back, arms crossed, clearly waiting for her reaction.

"I had a feeling you might find those."

"You didn't think I would, huh? You think I'm some ignorant grease monkey from the sticks that you could con."

Kaylee shook her head. "I never thought that."

"Jig's up, Kay Lee," Rick said, emphasizing her two separate names. "You want me to call the cops or you want to take a ride with me and turn yourself in?"

"What are you talking about?" Kaylee asked aghast, so shocked by Rick's attitude and insinuating tone she wanted to slap him. Where was her lover of the other night, the man she'd convinced herself she was in love with? Who was this sneering stranger speaking a language she could barely understand?

"Drop the Miss Innocent act, okay, Kay Lee. I found your stash. I don't know for sure where you got it, but I sort of vaguely recall something on the news a couple of weeks ago about a jewel heist in Knoxville, Tennessee. I'm pretty sure you didn't come by these honestly or you wouldn't have hidden them where you did. Doesn't matter if you fess up to me, or you wait to let the cops get it out of you. Hell, I probably wouldn't believe anything you said now anyway."

Tears stung Kaylee's eyes at that statement, but she willed them back. "Rick, please. Whether you believe me or not, I honestly, honestly, had nothing to do with the robbery. I never saw this," she pointed to the package, "until I found it the day my car died."

"Oh? How can that be when I found it in the gas tank of your car? Attached to a cord which I'm guessing might have been connected at one time to the base of your gas cap. Too bad it came loose and got sucked into the fuel pump. No wonder your car was acting up."

Kaylee shook her head, her thoughts whirling. How could she explain someone else had hidden the package in her gas tank? Even though she knew who had done it, she doubted Rick would believe such a wild story. Of course he'd think she was in on it.

He'd made that much clear already.

She looked up into Rick's disgusted expression.

"Is this why you're meeting your lover-boy Bobby Lou in Miami? Is this his surprise?"

Kaylee stared at Rick, trying to follow his train of thought. "Rick, honestly, I can explain. Bobby Lou's waiting for me, but I didn't know he'd be there. Not until Tillie told me. And his cousin Dwayne—"

"Yeah, yeah, and I bet his nephew Jim Bob was in on it and probably his uncle T-Rex, too," Rick cut in sarcastically. "So what's it going to be? You want me to call the cops or haul you on down there so you can turn yourself in?"

Kaylee shook her head. "Rick, you don't understand—"

"Oh, I think I do. You waltz in here with your broken down car and your sob story about your poor granny and your cousin in Miami and I buy it hook, line and sinker, fix your car for free, let you move into my house, allow my daughter to fall in love with you—" Rick slammed his fist down on the table, scattering the gemstones across its well-scrubbed surface.

"God, how could I have been so stupid?"

Kaylee put a hand out toward him. "Rick, I didn't—"

He glared at her. "Don't. Don't lie to me anymore. Don't touch me."

Kaylee pulled her hand back as if she'd been burned. A slow seething anger started to build at Rick's bull-headed summation of the facts as he saw them. He wasn't going to let her explain. He wanted nothing more to do with her and that hurt, but she'd be damned if she'd let him see how much. She encouraged the anger because it could cover the hurt for now. "I'm packed. And I want to leave," she told him through a clenched jaw. "I'm telling you I never saw these before the day I met you. I wish I could pretend I never did see them. Most of all I wish you believed me." Kaylee stood, her chest heaving with anger, hurt and frustration. "Did you fix my car or didn't you? Because one way or another, I'm getting out of this town and never coming back. We're done here."

She moved past him into the living room. All of her things were stacked near the front door. She hoped like hell he'd put her car back together and that it was waiting for her outside. Otherwise, her grand exit was about to blow up in her face.

"Oh, no you don't." Rick was a step behind her and his fingers curled around her upper arm to stop her.

She whirled on him, yanking her elbow from his grasp. "Get your hands off me. You've got no right. You think you've got it all figured out how that package ended up in my gas tank. I'm telling you, I had nothing to do with it. You do whatever you have to do, but I'm leaving right now. And I'm never coming back here."

She took two more steps before Rick caught up with her. The doorbell rang and they both froze. Kaylee could hear her own panting breaths, her heart pounding in her throat. The doorbell rang again. Rick let go of her arm and stepped in front of her. He peered out through the side window and glanced back at Kaylee. He swore softly before he opened the door.

Two men in suits and sunglasses stood on the small porch, perspiring profusely in the August sun. "Rick Braddock?" At Rick's nod, one of them held out some identification to Rick.

"I'm Special Agent Joel Billings with the FBI. This is Agent Max Ferguson. I wonder if we might ask you a few questions?"

Rick's shoulders visibly sagged and he glanced back at Kaylee once more, giving her what she took to be a rather apologetic look. He stepped back allowing the two agents to enter.

Chapter Twenty-Five

The two stepped inside, removing their sunglasses as they did so. Rick closed the door behind them. They nodded at Kaylee. She swallowed her gum.

Brutus darted out from the kitchen, whining in inquiry as he snuffled the newcomers. Rick snapped his fingers. "Brutus. Enough." He pointed to the kitchen. As if satisfied with his inspection, Brutus trotted off.

"We're here because you recently requested a starter for a certain make and model of vehicle from a salvage-parts dealer. We believe that vehicle was used in connection with a crime in Knoxville a couple of weeks ago. We'd like to ask you a few questions about the car and the owner."

Rick's gaze slid uneasily to Kaylee. "Sure. You want to have a seat?" He indicated the sofa and chairs.

The two sat side by side on the edge of the sofa. One of them, Rick wasn't sure if it was Ferguson or Billings, took out a small notebook and a pen.

Rick sat hunched forward on the edge of the recliner and Kaylee, clearly resigned to her fate, lowered a hip to the arm of the chair nearest her.

"Now then," began the younger agent, "the vehicle in question—" he rattled off the year, make, model and serial number, "—is jointly registered to one Daisy Blue Walsh of Bertie Springs, Tennessee, now deceased, and one Kay Lee Walsh of the same address. We have reason to believe that Kay Lee Walsh may be in possession of the vehicle."

"I'm Kay Lee Walsh," Kaylee said before Rick could beat her to it. Each of the male heads swiveled in her direction. "It's my car. I asked Rick to fix it for me when it broke down here a couple of weeks ago."

"I see," said the one Rick had decided was Ferguson.

"We'd like to search the vehicle, if you have no objection."

Kaylee shook her head. "No, no objection, but I know what you're looking for. I already found it."

The two agents traded looks with one another before refocusing their attention on Kaylee. "And what was it you *found*, Ms. Walsh? What is it you believe we're looking for?"

"A bunch of gemstones. Rubies, sapphires and emeralds, I think. They were stolen from a jewelry store in Knoxville on August third."

"Uh-huh." The agents stood. "Ms. Walsh, we'd like you to come with us." Billings removed a pair of handcuffs from his pocket. "We'll be taking you into custody and impounding your vehicle."

Rick stood also, moving between the agents and Kaylee. "On what charge?"

"Aiding and abetting a known felon in a robbery. Withholding evidence. Those are just for starters."

"But you don't even know if she was involved," Rick pointed out exactly as Kaylee had pointed out to him earlier.

"If you don't step aside, sir, it's my duty to inform you that you can be charged with obstruction of justice and interfering with a federal agent in the line of duty."

Rick thought about this for a moment. He couldn't afford to get arrested. He had Molly to think of. But for all his earlier threats, he wasn't quite ready to see Kaylee handcuffed and hauled out of his house by the FBI before she'd had a say. Maybe her Little Miss Innocent act wasn't an act after all. And if it wasn't, if he'd been wrong in jumping to conclusions, he wanted to be one of the first to know. "Okay, look. Could you ask her some questions before you go hauling her off to jail?"

He looked at Kaylee, and in his gut he knew. She'd been telling him the truth earlier. Had he been so desperate for a reason not to ask her to stay, for a way to protect himself from future hurt, that he'd latched onto her supposed guilt, made himself believe she wasn't what she seemed? Pathetic. "Just ask her. You won't be sorry." Not as sorry as I am, he thought.

That same feeling he'd had when his marriage to Brenda was falling apart washed over him. Brenda had wanted more—more money, more material trappings and a man who could provide them. When he found those gemstones, he'd thought the same was true of Kaylee; she was simply going about it a different way. Kaylee wasn't Brenda, but he should have remembered that before he confronted her. Now it was too late.

He'd probably ruined any hope of a future with her by his earlier accusations.

To Rick's surprise, the agents backed off a bit. They looked past him to Kaylee. "Ms. Walsh? Is there something you'd like to tell us? You're entitled to legal counsel before you make any kind of a confession."

Kaylee's chin came up. She spoke to the agents but she looked at Rick. "I don't have anything to confess. I didn't do anything wrong. But I'll be happy to tell you everything I know or suspect and I don't need a lawyer holding my hand to do it."

She started at the beginning—how she found the package dangling inside her gas tank, and had accidentally dropped it in, then to her conclusion that Dwayne, and possibly Bobby Lou, had been in on the robbery and used her car in the process.

"I didn't know what to do. I didn't want to make trouble for Rick and Molly. I decided I'd deal with it when I got to

Miami. I knew my cousin would help me. We could contact the authorities then."

The agents asked more questions; Ferguson took more notes. "So the stolen gemstones. They're still in your gas tank?" He paused, pen poised in his hand as he looked at her.

Kaylee's gaze connected with Rick's. "Uh, no, actually. They got caught in the fuel pump and Rick had to take my car apart this morning. He found them and brought them here. They're in the kitchen. On the table." She stood. "Come on. I'll show you."

She took the few steps into the kitchen and stopped dead in her tracks. Agent Billings bumped into her from behind, but she hardly noticed or acknowledged his mumbled apology.

"Oh, no." The table was empty. There was no trace of the small piles of gemstones that had been there minutes ago. Brutus lay next to the table, looking quite pleased with himself. He gazed up at Kaylee with his soulful brown eyes, licked his chops, adjusted his position slightly and belched a satisfied doggy burp.

Kaylee stared at the dog. She knew it wasn't funny, but for some reason she felt a smile tug at her lips. "Um, I think we might have a little bit of trouble recovering the, uh, evidence," she informed the two agents.

Chapter Twenty-Six

"We'll have to take the dog into custody," Agent Billings decided. "Monitor his, er, activities."

"Hold on a minute here. Let's not be hasty," Ferguson said. He lowered his voice even though he could still be heard clearly. "We don't even know if she's telling the truth. If either one of them are telling the truth. What proof do we have that the dog ate the evidence?"

Billings surveyed the tabletop and the surrounding area, as if making note of the overturned glass bottles missing their caps, the wad of gasoline-soaked plastic that had fallen to the floor, and finally to the satisfied-looking mongrel panting happily nearby.

"We don't." He turned to Kaylee and Rick. "Who does the dog belong to?"

"He's mine," said Rick. "I can almost guarantee you he's, um, in possession of your evidence. He'll eat anything—and I do mean anything—that's left on the table."

"We'll see about that. Is there a veterinarian here locally? We'll have him examined and X-rayed, at department expense, of course. If we determine he's consumed the evidence, we'll go from there."

"Doc Walters in Jannings Point has been seeing him since he was a pup," Rick said.

"Very well. Let's get in touch and see if the good doctor will see us this afternoon. You two will have to come along, of course. We can't allow you to move freely until we've determined the truth of your earlier statements.

Rick glanced at his watch. "That's fine, but I have to pick up my daughter from school in about twenty minutes."

Ferguson barely suppressed a groan indicating that this case wasn't going at all the way he'd expected it to. "Fine. Let's make that call. We'll stop and retrieve your daughter on the way."

Kaylee focused on the large black clock on the wall of Doctor Walters's waiting room. Rick and Billings had taken Brutus back to the examining room. Agent Ferguson was babysitting her and Molly. Molly had discovered a book filled with pictures of cats and was contentedly poring over it in the chair next to Kaylee.

She'd been delighted to discover that Kaylee hadn't left, just as she'd predicted that morning. Kaylee worried that it would only add to her belief that she'd soon have a mommy who lived with her. No way was that going to happen, not with the revelation of Rick's suspicious mind. Kaylee was still emotionally reeling from the realization that Rick actually believed her to be a jewel thief. That she'd somehow used him, manipulated him for her own purposes and could walk away and never look back.

Look before you leap. She'd heard that phrase many times when Granny Daisy warned her against making ill-advised choices without thinking them through. The lessons hadn't sunk in very well. She'd fooled herself into believing she knew everything she needed to know about Rick after only a couple of weeks. She thought he knew her in the same way. She thought they'd connected. Bonded. Not only physically.

Emotionally. But for Rick to jump to such inaccurate conclusions about her meant he didn't know her. He didn't know her at all. And she didn't know him.

Kaylee saw no reason to hide the fact that Rick's earlier words stung. She'd barely said two words to him once the FBI had arrived. She had nothing to say to him, she'd decided, if he thought so little of her. Anger simmered inside her every time she thought of it, but she couldn't manage to think of much else.

Even in her current state of mind, Kaylee hadn't missed the few curious glances Agent Ferguson sent her way. He'd opened his mouth twice as if preparing to speak, but he hadn't. No doubt he'd picked up on her silent fuming and thought better of starting a conversation with her.

She could hear Granny Daisy's voice in her head telling her to mind her manners. She couldn't think of a way to give him an opening under such awkward and unusual circumstances, so she simply smiled at him, forcing her unpleasant thoughts out of her mind.

"So you grew up in Bertie Springs?" he asked her.

Kaylee nodded. "Born and raised."

"My mama had cousins up around that way. Every now and again we'd go visit them, but I doubt you'd know who they were."

"Oh, I don't know," Kaylee replied. "My Grandma Daisy, she knew everyone for miles. Either went to school with them or sold eggs to them or was somehow kin to them. Try me."

"Well, let me think," Ferguson said, leaning back in his chair and looking up at the white speckled ceiling tiles. "Russell and Ernestine Bricker are two I remember. I think they'd be Mama's cousins on her daddy's side. They had a big old place out north of Bertie Springs, probably closer to Strawberry Plains."

"Rusty Bricker? Now did he own the tractor dealership there in Calder Cove?"

"Yep, that's him. He had about seven or eight kids, I never could keep track."

"I think Tommy Johnston married one of his girls. I went to school with Tommy. He was our star quarterback my freshman year."

"Could be. Gosh, let me see who else. Mama had a big family."

"What's your mama's name? Maiden name, I mean."

"Southworth. Eleanor Southworth. She was born in Wildwood."

"I bet if we talked long enough we'd find somebody we knew in common," Kaylee told him with a smile. He grinned back at her and she couldn't help noticing he had perfect teeth and soft hazel eyes fringed with dark lashes.

He nodded. "Six degrees of separation."

"What's that?"

"A sort of theory, that everyone is separated only by a few degrees, that if you knew everyone's history you'd find they had someone in common that they knew."

"Hmm." Kaylee glanced at the clock again. The minute hand had hardly moved. Abandoning her book, Molly climbed into Kaylee's lap. She was uncharacteristically quiet. Kaylee smoothed her dark hair back and kissed her forehead. "You okay, darlin'?" Molly nodded, her fingers clutching a handful of Kaylee's shirt.

Max smiled at Molly before his gaze snagged Kaylee's once again. "You wouldn't by any chance have any friends or relatives by the first name of Jill, would you?"

Kaylee thought for a moment. "No, I'm pretty sure I don't. Who's Jill?"

The agent gave her a sheepish grin. "Aw, she's a girl I met a long time ago that I can't seem to forget."

Kaylee smiled. "That sounds like someone else I know who has the same problem."

"Hearing your accent reminded me of her. Thought she might be from the same area as you. I met her in a bar. And before you say anything, I know bars are not the best places to meet women. At least not the kind of woman you'd want to settle down with. But this girl, we clicked—you know what I mean? She was with a couple of her friends. I was on my way back to the Academy with a couple of my buddies. We spent an hour or so together before I had to get on the road." He shook his head. "I never forgot her."

"So?" Kaylee asked, her curiosity piqued. "You never saw her again? You never called her?"

Ferguson ducked his head. "You'll think I'm an idiot."

"No, I won't. Why would I think that?"

"She wrote down her phone number for me on a cocktail napkin and I stuck it in my pocket." He scrunched up his face as if even now the memory pained him. "We got a flat tire on our way back to the Academy. In, of course, pouring rain."

Thinking she knew what was coming, Kaylee whispered, "Oh, no."

"I got soaked. We all did."

"And the cocktail napkin?"

"A soggy mess of paper fiber and dribbles of blue ink. No way to reconstruct that number."

"Oh, no. That's so sad. Jill could be the love of your life."

"Well, I don't know about that, but I sure would have liked to know her better, see where it went. I can still picture her. Big blue eyes. Long, dark hair. And a grin that lit up the room."

"Maybe you'll meet her again."

He shrugged. "I keep hoping. Every time I'm in the area, I stop in at that bar, just in case. But so far, no luck."

"That's weird. My cousin, well, she's not my cousin, but anyway, she's sort of in the same boat you are. Met a guy she never forgot even though she never heard from him again. She keeps dreaming of finding him again."

"So me and your cousin, we're both crazy, huh?"

"Don't you think everyone dreams of finding what they want? Maybe we're all crazy."

He tilted his head in acknowledgment. "So tell me about this Bobby Lou Tucker and his cousin Dwayne."

Kaylee launched into past history which quickly put Molly to sleep. Ferguson, however, hung on her every word, leaning forward in his chair, making eye contact often, asking leading questions. Kaylee didn't care. She had nothing to hide. Her whole history with Bobby Lou was common knowledge in Bertie Springs, and so was Bobby Lou's history with Dwayne.

If Max Ferguson and his buddy Billings could make the nightmare of the stolen gems in her gas tank go away without anybody getting too badly hurt, that was fine with Kaylee. Although she was still having a hard time believing Bobby Lou had been partners in crime with his cousin.

"So what's with you and Braddock?" Max asked. In the car, when he'd met Molly, he'd told her she could call him Max. Then he'd looked at Kaylee and pointedly told her she could, too. No such invitation had been extended to Rick, and Kaylee was sure he'd noticed. He'd ridden in the front of the vehicle with Agent Billings and Brutus. She and Max shared the back with Molly between them.

"Nothing. He's just a friend." She winced as she said it and hoped Max didn't notice. Rick was, could be, should be, so much more than a friend. "He offered to fix my car if I stayed to babysit Molly until school started. I was supposed to leave for Miami today."

"I see," Max said, in a tone that made Kaylee think he saw way more than she wanted him to. He sat back in his chair, though, and fell silent for the duration of the wait.

The first thing Rick saw when he returned to the waiting room was Kaylee holding a sleeping Molly in her lap. The second thing he saw was the appreciative gleam in Max Ferguson's eyes as he gazed at Kaylee.

The thought of Kaylee and Max Ferguson, Kaylee and another man, any man, made him sick. Please God, there had to be some way to salvage the mess he'd made of things.

Ignoring Ferguson, Rick crossed the waiting room and hunkered down in front of Kaylee. He covered her hand with his, where it was curled around Molly. "How you doing?" he asked.

The look in her eyes said it all. The warmth he used to see there, the delight in her expression was gone. "I'm fine." Her voice was neutral, with a note of dismissive chill. He wanted to get down on his knees, beg her forgiveness, bury his face in her lap and hope she'd comfort him the way she did Molly. But now was not the time or the place. Instead he stood and reached for his daughter. "I'll take Molly."

Molly woke up, objecting as he shifted her from Kaylee's lap to his arms, but she snuggled her head down on his shoulder with a sleepy sigh.

Rick hid his satisfied smirk as the seating arrangements were switched on the ride back to Perrish. The consultation and subsequent X-rays had confirmed that Brutus had swallowed the stolen gems as well as the three bottle caps. Doc Walters had suggested the simplest method of recovery was simply to let nature take its course. "He's a big dog and those stones are small. Add some canned dog food to his kibble. That'll probably move things along," he'd told Rick. He'd also suggested feeding Brutus cotton balls soaked in milk.

Since Rick was holding Molly, he took the backseat next to Ferguson while Kaylee rode in front with Billings and Brutus. Rick buckled Molly into a seatbelt, crossed his arms over his chest and kept his mouth shut. He wasn't the only one. The tension inside the vehicle was butter thick.

It was decided that one of the agents should stay with the dog at all times. It was the only reasonable way to recover the stolen gems, other than taking Brutus into custody, which meant a trip to their field office in Jacksonville. Doc Walters hadn't thought it would take more than a day or two for the gems to reappear, so Billings had informed Rick that Agent Ferguson would be watching over Brutus full-time in his own environment starting tonight. Meanwhile Billings would be coordinating the surveillance on the two suspects in Miami, and setting up the operation to apprehend them.

"I'll take the couch," Max happily informed Rick and Kaylee after Kaylee had thrown together a simple meal and Molly had been bathed and put to bed.

Kaylee looked at Rick, Rick looked at her. Max watched the exchange with undisguised interest. "That'll be f—" Rick began, but Kaylee cut him off.

"Actually, Max, I sleep on the couch. Maybe you and Rick can bunk together." Her tone was syrupy sweet, her smile a mile wide. Rick ground his teeth together.

"Oh, I'm sorry," Max said with such feigned innocence Rick wanted to punch him. "I guess I thought—"

"Thought what?" Rick barked.

"Nothing. I'll uh—sure. If you've got a sleeping bag or an extra pillow and blanket that'd be great. No problem." He got up off the couch and started down the hall to the bedroom. "Back here, right?" He nodded at Rick and disappeared.

Kaylee began making up the couch as she'd done almost every night for the past couple of weeks. Except one.

"You know, you could have gone along with me. Slept in my bed instead of making me share a room with him."

Kaylee didn't turn around. Surely Rick knew how impossible that was for her. "I don't think so," she said quietly.

"Kaylee, I'm sorry."

"For what?" She kept her voice light. But what exactly was he apologizing for?

He dropped into the chair with a defeated air. "Damned if I know. Being me, I guess. That ought to cover it, huh?"

Kaylee slid him a sideways glance and continued fussing with the sheets and blanket. She could feel the anger she'd pushed down all evening bubble up close to the surface. She remembered all the times Bobby Lou had let her down or hurt her in small ways over the years. How he'd always managed to charm and sweet-talk her with meaningless apologies and false remorse. How she'd let him do it time after time. She wasn't going to let a man, any man, get away with it any more. "Not good enough," she told him. "Not even close."

Rick sighed but didn't seem surprised. "I know. I screwed up. I was looking for a way out, I think, and jumping to conclusions about you, making accusations without giving you a chance to explain seemed as good a way as any. Then. It doesn't now."

Kaylee's browed furrowed. She turned to look at him. "A way out of what?"

"Of wanting you to stay."

"You were going to ask me to stay?" She started to smile, but Rick's answer wiped it right off her face.

"No. But I wanted to."

"Oh." That hurt. More than what had happened earlier. Kaylee could feel herself deflating inside.

"I didn't *want* to want to. Understand?"

Kaylee stared into Rick's dark eyes. "You hated that you wanted me to stay. And you were too afraid to ask me. Afraid I'll walk away like Brenda did."

"Yeah, that about sums it up."

The anger was there again and Kaylee welcomed it because it pushed the hurt aside. "Then why are you apologizing? You got what you wanted, Rick. You still have it. Knowing how little you think of me, I wouldn't stay here in a million years. Not if you got down on your hands and knees and begged me I wouldn't."

"I know. I know I got what I thought I wanted. I know it's my own fault. But the thing is, Kaylee, I feel like I've got nothing. Nothing at all."

Kaylee refused to feel one ounce of sympathy for him. "I thought we'd gotten to know each other pretty well these past couple of weeks, but I was wrong. You don't know me. And you don't owe me anything. So let's forget it."

He stood and took a step toward her. "I'm not going to forget it. And neither are you."

Kaylee froze, not sure what she'd do if he touched her. Give in? Push him away? Melt like she always did whenever he touched her?

But he didn't touch her. "I'm sorry. That's all. I'm just...sorry." He turned and walked away down the hall to his room. She heard the door click softly and she let out the breath she hadn't even realized she was holding.

Chapter Twenty-Seven

Kaylee tossed and turned, her thoughts whirring round and round in her head. Anger warred with hurt which fought with sadness. She'd jumped to conclusions about who Rick was and what they had together and she'd been wrong. So wrong. No matter what he said now about his earlier accusations, she couldn't let it go. His willingness to think the worst of her had come a bit too easily to him. Which only proved he didn't know the first thing about her. Everything between them had happened too fast. They could have taken the time to gradually build a relationship, to find out what they needed to know about each other. But now it was time they didn't have.

It seemed especially cruel that she'd found Rick now, before he was ready to make a commitment to another woman. Four years was a long time, but Brenda's betrayal had scarred him, and Kaylee supposed she understood. She'd been crushed when Bobby Lou had dumped her for Georgia Rose. But she hadn't been married to Bobby Lou and she didn't have a child by him. Although she'd sort of assumed they'd be together forever, there'd never been a formal commitment, no engagement ring, no real plan for the future.

She and Bobby Lou drifted along, the same way they'd done since high school.

It wasn't a grownup relationship, Kaylee thought now. She'd been crushed at the breakup, but the wounds were more to her pride than to her heart. If she were truly honest with herself, she had to admit she didn't miss Bobby Lou all that much. She missed the idea of Bobby Lou. The possibility of a future with a man, a family, growing old together. But the truth was, she could no longer envision a future with Bobby Lou Tucker. Yet much too quickly and easily she'd envisioned the possibility of one with Rick Braddock. And Molly.

Kaylee refused to shed tears over Rick, she was still too angry, but her eyes welled up when she thought of Molly. That darling, darling, little girl deserved a mother. One who lived with her like she wanted. *She deserves me.* Oh, Lord, she realized, she'd created the same problem for herself that Rick had. In order to be Molly's mother, she'd have to marry Rick. Which had been the same objection he'd voiced not long ago. In order to give Molly a full-time mother, he'd have to get married again. He admitted then he was gun-shy. Why had she let herself fall for him? Why had she let herself dream what now seemed to be an impossible dream?

There's no fool like an old fool. How many times had Granny Daisy uttered those words? Too many to count. Granny'd had no patience with people who didn't learn from their past mistakes.

That's it, Kaylee decided, as she fell into an uneasy sleep. There was no future for her with Rick Braddock. And the sooner she admitted it and dealt with it, the sooner she could move on with her life.

"You're a putz, you know that?"

Max Ferguson's voice floated up from the floor in Rick's bedroom. Rick knew the agent wasn't asleep, just as Max surely knew he wasn't. They'd both been tossing and turning for at least a half hour, ever since Rick had left Kaylee in the living room and crawled into bed. He knew Ferguson couldn't be very comfortable lying on the hard floor with an old comforter as padding beneath him and Rick's extra pillow to cushion his head, but he was having a hard time working up sympathy for the other man who seemed intent on goading him.

Rick wanted to be angry. Earlier he'd have liked nothing better than to smash Ferguson's smug face into the nearest wall. Preferably a brick one. But after his conversation with Kaylee, the fight had gone out of him. "Yeah. I think that's the general consensus around here."

"She's in love with you," Max said wistfully.

"You think?" Even that comment failed to lift Rick's spirits. He'd blown it and he knew it.

"Oh, yeah. You must have majorly screwed up. She is pissed."

"She scares the hell out of me."

"Yeah, well, like I said, you're a putz."

"I'm a putz," Rick chimed in at the same time.

"None of my business if you don't hang on to her. I hear there's an opening in the Miami field office."

Rick went on full alert. "Is that some kind of threat?"

"Nah. Just a statement of fact. Night."

He heard Ferguson roll over and settle down. If not for the agent's interest in Kaylee, he could almost like the guy.

Chapter Twenty-Eight

Rick was in a black mood the next morning which didn't surprise Kaylee at all. When she came into the kitchen he was putting together a lunch for Molly, a half-finished cup of coffee on the counter nearby. Molly was just finishing her cereal.

"Hi, darlin'," Kaylee greeted her, dropping a kiss on top of her head.

"Hi, Kaylee." Even Molly seemed subdued for once. Her glance slid uneasily to Rick as she slid off her chair and moved past him to put her bowl in the sink. "I'll go brush my teeth now, okay, Daddy?"

Rick grunted his approval. He slid a peanut butter and jelly sandwich into a small plastic bag and tucked it into her lunch box. Kaylee noticed a juice box was already there along with a tiny box of raisins and two cellophane-wrapped cookies.

Kaylee poured herself a cup of coffee and leaned against the counter. He made a point of putting as much distance as possible between himself and her as he returned the jelly to the refrigerator. So far he hadn't acknowledged her presence with so much as a glance, which pissed Kaylee off all over again.

"Good morning, Rick," she said with exaggerated syrupy sweetness in her tone. "How are you today?"

He cut his gaze in her direction, his eyes like dark laser beams cutting across her. She was reminded of her first encounter with him, how she'd found his tough-guy persona a bit intimidating. But she knew too much about him, now. Knew for all his outward toughness, he could be wounded just as easily as anyone else.

He didn't answer her right away, and when he did, it was in a slightly sarcastic sneering tone she didn't particularly care for. "Why, I'm just fine, Kay Lee," he said, mimicking her southern drawl. "And how are y'all doin?'" He gave her a smile that was a lie if she'd ever seen one.

Ooh, Kaylee wanted nothing more than to wipe the pretense of all is well out of his voice and off his face. She set her cup down so hard on the counter coffee sloshed over the edge. She took a step toward him.

He raised one eyebrow but stood his ground as if waiting to see what she'd do next. Their gazes locked, and it occurred to Kaylee that she could disarm him in about two seconds. All she had to do was press up against him, twine her arms around his neck and touch her lips to his. He'd be undone, he'd forget how hurt and angry at himself he was. He'd melt.

But then so would she, and she wasn't quite ready to let go of her anger. She wasn't going to be the one to give in, smooth things over, make it all right. Because the bottom line was, even if she did, it would change nothing between them. Rick wasn't ready for any kind of commitment. And she couldn't stay here without one.

Her past and her present clashed head-on at that moment. She'd thought she and Bobby Lou would eventually marry and settle down together, but he'd given her no choice when he found someone else and she hadn't seen it coming. She'd decided on a life in Miami, but the detour into Rick and Molly's life now made her question that choice.

So they stood frozen, three feet apart, until Molly returned, licking a smear of toothpaste off her bottom lip. "I made my bed, too, Daddy." She reached up on the counter for her lunchbox and marched to the table to stow it in her backpack which sat ready to go on one of the chairs. She hoisted the pack over her shoulder and stuck her arms through the straps. "Ready!" she announced.

Rick jumped as if she'd startled him with her announcement and tore his gaze away from Kaylee's. She wondered what he'd been thinking, if his thoughts had paralleled hers, if he'd thought of bridging the distance between them, of taking her in his arms and kissing her until she forgave him. The sad thing was, she was pretty sure it would have worked. He picked up his keys from the counter and stepped over to Molly, ruffling her hair. "Good going, squirt. Tell Kaylee good-bye."

Molly shot across the kitchen and grabbed Kaylee around the thighs tilting her head back and grinning. "Bye, Kaylee."

Kaylee kissed her forehead. "Bye, darlin'. Have fun at school today."

She watched the two of them retreat, each taking a piece of her heart with them.

Molly was a big part of the equation. She couldn't stay here and allow Molly to become even more attached to her.

Max appeared almost as soon as the door closed. "Is the coast clear?" He grinned at her when she held up a mug to him, and he nodded, indicating his desire for coffee.

"Rick and Molly are gone, if that's what you mean," she informed him as she poured him a cup and took a seat across from him at the table.

"So tell me about this cousin of yours," Max suggested after taking the first sip.

"Tillie?"

"If that's her name. Any chance she could be involved in the heist? Could she have aided and abetted the two men?"

Kaylee choked on her coffee and had to grab a napkin quick to catch the dribble down her chin. "No. No way."

"How can you be so sure? It happens all the time." He glanced down at the small notebook he'd set on the table in front of him. He opened it and ruffled through a few pages before continuing. "You said this Bobby Lou Tucker is a charmer. A sweet-talker. How do you know he didn't talk your cousin into helping him and his cousin? Maybe she knows about the gems in your gas tank and is just waiting for you to show up?"

Kaylee shook her head at the ludicrous idea. "No. I'm telling you, Max, Tillie has no idea what's going on. She certainly wouldn't help Dwayne Holcumb any more than I would."

Max looked as if he didn't quite believe her. "We've got a surveillance team staking out your cousin's salon. I want visual confirmation of the suspects. I want to keep an eye on them until we recover the evidence. We have to be very careful about procedure since our perp isn't actually in possession of the stolen goods. Our case will be much stronger if we can physically connect him with the gems."

"How are you going to do that?"

Max shrugged. "We'll use your car as bait. He thinks the stones are still in your gas tank. He's waiting for you to arrive in Miami so he can retrieve them. We keep an eye on him and an eye on your car. Before you leave here we'll install a package similar to the one you found in your tank. When he makes his move to retrieve what he believes are the real stones we'll move in.

"In the meantime, the Miami team will be sending me photos of your cousin, Tucker and Holcumb later this morning. I'll need you to identify them."

"Okay, sure. No problem."

Max picked up his coffee mug and regarded Kaylee over the top of it as he took a sip. "So how are you doing today?"

"Fine. I'm fine." Kaylee knew her response came too quickly. Her automatic reassurances were not to be believed.

Max grinned at her as he set his mug down. "For what it's worth, last night I informed your boyfriend that he's a putz."

Kaylee didn't even bother to deny her relationship with Rick. Although categorizing him as her boyfriend in light of his behavior this morning might be pushing it. "Why would you say that?"

Max shrugged. "Because it's true. You're crazy about him and he's making you miserable. Making himself miserable, too, if you ask me. That makes him a putz in my book."

"You said that to him? I bet he didn't like that one bit."

"You wouldn't think so, would you? But he actually agreed with me."

"Maybe that's why he was in such a foul mood this morning," Kaylee observed.

Max shrugged. "I don't think he slept too well. But maybe there's hope for him yet."

"How so?"

"According to pop psychology, acknowledging the problem is the first step toward doing something about it."

Kaylee rubbed at the wood grain running through the tabletop. "I don't know what he can do about it, Max. His first wife, Molly's mother, left him for a rich guy, a more glamorous life in Atlanta. He's afraid of that happening again. That's why—that's why—"

To her horror, Kaylee's eyes filled with tears and her vocal chords refused to cooperate further in her explanation. Except this time, instead of feeling hurt for herself, she felt Rick's pain. As if the crushing blow Brenda had delivered to him had hit her instead.

"That's why he's screwing things up with you. He's doing it on purpose so he won't get hurt again."

Kaylee nodded, sniffed and blinked back the tears. "That's almost exactly what he told me last night. He knows he's doing it, but he doesn't seem to want to change it, either."

"Maybe he's not in enough pain, yet."

Kaylee rose to retrieve the coffee pot and refilled their cups. "What do you mean?"

Max waited until she was seated again. "You've heard of addicts and alcoholics not reforming until they hit bottom. Often, there's a point where not changing is simply too painful. The pain acts as a catalyst forcing a change in behavior. Rick hasn't hit bottom yet, but based on what I observed between the two of you yesterday, I'd say he's well on his way. Give it some time. Give *him* some time. You might be pleasantly surprised."

"You know, you sort of sound like one of those pop psychologists yourself."

"Well, I did major in psychology. And I have spent a lot of time working with the FBI's profiling unit. Human behavior can be fascinating. I didn't mean to put you through psychoanalysis this morning, though. Sorry if I overstepped some boundaries."

Kaylee shook her head. "No, no, it's okay. A lot of this is my fault. You talk about giving him time. That's what I should have done in the first place. I should have given us both time to get to know each other before I—before we—" Kaylee cleared her throat. Max didn't need to know any of the details. "We don't know each very well. I've only been here a couple of weeks." She sighed and gazed out the window to the unrelenting green landscape.

"It doesn't matter anyway. I can't stick around to see what might happen. I can't wait for Rick to figure out he wants me here. I promised Tillie I'd come to Miami. She's holding a place for me in her salon. I need an income. So the sooner we can put everything into motion, the better."

Max nodded his understanding. He reached across the table and patted her hand. "It should only be a day or two. Three at the most before we have everything we need. Hang in there, okay?"

Kaylee dredged up a smile for Max. What other choice did she have but to hang in there?

Later that morning, Max set up his laptop and asked Kaylee to look at the photos the Miami surveillance team had sent.

The first one was of Tillie, her dark hair cut in a sleek style that clung to her head, her eyes obscured by designer sunglasses as she unlocked the door to her salon. "That's Tillie," Kaylee confirmed. The picture of her closest friend made her long to be in Miami. Anywhere but here.

Max studied the picture for a moment as if memorizing Tillie's features then brought up the next one. It showed a slender man in a short-sleeved blue shirt, jeans and cowboy boots, one foot up and braced against a storefront behind him, arms crossed over his chest as if he were waiting for someone.

"That's Bobby Lou."

Funny, Kaylee thought, how the picture of Bobby Lou stirred virtually nothing inside her.

Max nodded and brought up another photo. Kaylee watched as it downloaded onto the screen. The camera had caught Dwayne exiting Tillie's salon, his brow furrowed, an angry grimace clouding his features. His fists were clenched as if he were spoiling for a fight. Kaylee could almost imagine passersby giving him a wide berth as he barreled down the sidewalk. A chill crept down her spine. "And that's Dwayne," she confirmed.

"Okay, good." He took the chair across from her. "I think I need to interview your cousin. Away from the salon. Do you know her daily schedule?"

Kaylee shrugged. "I know she usually closes the salon around five, but she stays open later on Thursdays if she has appointments."

"So she's home most evenings?"

"I guess. I don't think she's going out much right now. She just broke up with the last guy she was dating."

Max made a few notes in his notebook. "Okay. I'll talk to Joel. I might fly down there later today. We may need her cooperation if we're going to set a trap for Holcumb and Tucker."

"I hope Bobby Lou isn't involved."

"Right now there's no way to know that. He's keeping Holcumb company, which isn't a good sign."

"I know. But I know Bobby Lou well. At least I thought I did. I just can't believe he'd knowingly rob anyone. He's a good guy. It'd be totally out of character for him."

"We'll get to the bottom of this. Maybe you're right. Maybe Tucker isn't involved in perpetrating the crime at all. Maybe he's just along for the ride."

Joel Billings arrived to relieve his partner's dog-sitting duties. Max left to fly to Miami to interview Tillie.

Unlike Max, Joel seemed to have no interest in socializing whatsoever. He was perfunctory, polite, but all business, spending most of his time either on his cell phone or his laptop computer.

Kaylee didn't envy either agent the task of taking Brutus out to do his duty. Doc Walters had provided them with a handled container to "catch" Brutus's leavings. Then the agents washed the contents of the container with the garden hose using a fine mesh sieve to retrieve any of the stones that appeared.

Joel returned with a couple on his first time out. That seemed to cheer him immensely. Brutus gave Kaylee a soulful look as he reentered the house with his new handler. He seemed baffled by the excessive interest in his droppings. Kaylee chuckled at the dog's woebegone expression and offered him a treat from the jar Rick kept on the counter. Brutus wolfed it down in one bite, tentatively wagging his tail in a plea for more. Instead Kaylee scratched him behind the ears, ready to make a comment to Joel. But Joel was already on his cell phone, speaking in a low tone to someone Kaylee imagined to be his superior at command central.

Without Max for company, she was bored and restless. With Molly in school, there was little to occupy her time. She knew very few people in town other than Rick and Molly. There was only one person she knew of who might welcome a visit. On a whim, she slipped on her old flip-flops and escaped the house.

Miss Emma answered her knock dressed in a pink flowered housedress, her hair looking as if she hadn't touched it yet this morning.

"Hi, Miss Emma. Remember me? Kaylee Walsh."

"Of course I remember, Kaylee, what a lovely surprise. Come on in and have a cup of coffee with me."

Emma moved somewhat stiffly toward the back of the house to a sunny yellow kitchen. Mugs were already lined up on the counter and she slid two toward the coffeemaker. Kaylee saw her rub the knuckles of her right hand before she reached for the coffee pot.

"Why don't you let me pour," Kaylee said. "You sit."

"Thank you, dear. The stiffness is the worst in the mornings." Emma took a seat at the small round table and rubbed at her knuckles, each in its turn. Kaylee put the coffee on the table and sat next to her, drawing Emma's hands into her own. Gently she massaged each finger, up to the top and along the backs of Emma's swollen hands, the way she'd learned to do in nail tech class.

"Oh, that feels so good." Emma's eyes moistened. "Hal used to do that for me before he died last year." She sniffed. "I guess it's just nice to be touched." She gave Kaylee a weak smile.

"Better now?" Kaylee asked.

Emma nodded. "Once my medicine kicks in, it's not so bad. But I move pretty slow most mornings. The hands are the worst, but I've got a touch in my knees and my shoulders, too."

Kaylee took a sip of coffee, eyeing Miss Emma's hair, unsure how to begin. Perhaps she'd been wrong in coming here.

Just say your piece, she could hear Granny Daisy admonishing her. Spit it out.

"Miss Emma, why don't you let me fix your hair for you?"

For a moment Miss Emma seemed taken aback by the offer, but she recovered quickly. "Oh, that'd be wonderful, dear. If you're sure you wouldn't mind."

"No, not at all," Kaylee assured her. "I've missed working."

"Well, you've got your work cut out for you with this rat's nest up here." She gestured at her head of unruly hair. "You see what you can do with it."

"I'm an excellent stylist," Kaylee assured her, retrieving her pouch of styling tools from her purse. "I can give you references from the salon back in Tennessee."

"Oh, that's not necessary, dear. I'll be able to tell by what I look like when you get done with me."

Emma directed her to a nearby bathroom where she found towels, a curling iron and mirror. Kaylee plugged the curling iron in then draped a towel around Emma's shoulders and began to work through the snarls in her hair.

"It makes me so sad to see my shop sit empty," Emma said. "Why, when I was running it, it was sort of the town hub, for the ladies anyway. They'd come in even if they didn't need to, just to chat, have a cup of coffee, hear the latest news. It can be that way again, I know it can. People warm up to you real fast, don't they, dear?"

Kaylee thought of Rick, of the wariness she'd seen in his gaze when they'd first met, how he'd kept his distance. But then he had warmed up. Quite nicely, as a matter of fact. Warm, ha! That didn't even begin to cover the amount of heat the two of them generated every time they touched. Even last night, as hurt and angry as she was, the heat between them was still there.

"Kaylee?"

Kaylee yanked her thoughts back into place. She needed to stick to the business at hand for now. "I'd love to buy a salon like yours, Miss Emma. I've always wanted a place of my own, but I don't have any money. None. I've got a job at my cousin's salon in Miami. I hope I can work for her and save some money, and maybe someday…" Kaylee trailed off. Her dreams were running away with her. And she was dreaming the impossible.

"Well, you never know, dear. Maybe we could work out some sort of arrangement if you're interested in taking over my salon."

Kaylee shook her head as she continued to work on Emma's hair. She'd worked out the snarls and began to apply the curling iron. "I couldn't pay you anything until I got going and started to turn a profit. And, um, there's another problem. If I stay in Perrish, I won't have anywhere to live."

"But I thought you lived with Rick and Molly?"

"That was only temporary, until school started. I'll be leaving in a couple of days."

Carefully, Emma picked up her mug and took a sip. A gleam came into her eye.

A half hour later, Kaylee held the mirror in front of Emma. She'd combed and teased, curled, styled and sprayed. Emma looked like a different person than the one who had answered the door earlier.

Emma stared at her reflection. "Oh, my. It's just the way I used to do it. But it's been forever since I could manage it." She looked Kaylee squarely in the eyes. "Let me make you an offer just in case you ever decide to come back to Perrish."

Emma offered to finance the start-up costs. She had a neighbor who would print up flyers on her computer to advertise the shop's re-opening. "If you need a place to stay, I've got a perfectly good extra bedroom. You can help out around here, and we'll call it even."

"Miss Emma, this is all so kind of you. I'll think about it, I will. But please don't count on it." Kaylee gave Emma a gentle hug and started for home. Well, Rick's house. It wasn't her home. She had to remember that.

All afternoon and evening, through dinner preparation and Molly and Rick's return, the idea of owning Miss Emma's salon was never very far from Kaylee's thoughts. As often as she told herself not to dream that Rick would ask her to stay, that she could live and work in this little town, make a life here, she couldn't help it. Rick was quiet to the point of brooding, which luckily Molly's chatter about her day at school covered. Kaylee chatted with Joel, trying to draw him out, ignoring the fact that Rick had little to say to anyone.

Especially her.

Chapter Twenty-Nine

Kaylee had almost drifted off to sleep when she heard the phone ring in the kitchen and a more muffled duplicate coming from Rick's bedroom. She heard the low murmur of Rick's voice when he answered before it rang a second time, although the words were not clear. His bedroom door opened and she heard the familiar pad of his feet in the hallway. She propped herself up on an elbow, although he probably couldn't see her in the dark.

"Kaylee?" he whispered as he came closer.

"I'm awake," she told him.

"Phone for you. It's your cousin."

"Tillie?" Kaylee flipped back the covers and grabbed for her robe. "Why is she calling at this hour?"

"I don't know. She already apologized for waking me up. Which she didn't, by the way." His tone was full of meaning, but Kaylee was too distracted to decipher it just then.

She hurried into the kitchen and picked up the receiver.

"Tillie? What's wrong? What happened?"

"Nothing's wrong, sugar. Matter of fact, everything is right as rain." Tillie giggled. Kaylee frowned, trying to remember the last time she'd heard that lighthearted laugh from her cousin. "I wanted to thank you for sending the FBI after me."

Max's earlier question about Tillie's possible involvement with Bobby Lou and Dwayne reared its ugly head. She'd adamantly denied it then, but what if she'd been wrong? "Oh, no, Tillie, you're not—you're not in trouble, are you? You didn't—"

"It's him, Kay Lee, darlin'. It's Mac."

"Who's Mac? Mac from the bar? What are you talking about?"

"The FBI guy. It's Mac!"

Kaylee sat hard in a chair, her mind trying to catch up with Tillie's revelation. "You mean Max?"

"Is Mac!" Tillie's excitement sent her voice to a new crescendo. "It's him, it's him, it's him! My guy. The guy from the bar."

"Is Max?" Kaylee asked again.

"Can you believe it? After all these years. And it's all because of you, my baby cousin. Well, you, I guess and Bobby Lou. And that damned Dwayne. He showed up at the door, Max, not Dwayne, and I thought it was him, but I kept telling myself it couldn't be. And he kept looking at me sort of funny like the whole time he was asking his questions—"

"But—but, wait. Tillie, his name is Max. Maxwell, I think is his given name. Not Mac."

Tillie giggled again, her joy radiating through the phone line. "I know, isn't it crazy? You want to hear something crazier? He thought my name was Jillie. You know, like a nickname for Jill. All this time he's been looking for somebody named Jill."

Kaylee sat back in the chair, trying to absorb what Tillie was saying. "He told me a story about meeting a girl named Jill in a bar, and how he lost her phone number—"

"In a rainstorm."

"Yes. And I told him about you, about the guy in the bar you'd never forgotten, but the names—"

"I'm telling you, it's crazy. The only thing we can figure is it was so darned loud in that honky-tonk we misunderstood each other's names."

"But didn't you write your name down when you gave him your number?"

"Sure I did, sugar. But my name got washed away with the numbers in the rain."

"Of course it did." Duh, Kaylee thought to herself. "So Max is Mac. And you're—"

"I'm over the moon, that's what I am. It's still there, whatever it was that was between us that night. Like the last ten years never happened."

"Is he still there with you? Max?"

"No, he said he had to get back to Perrish. But we're going to get together real soon. *Real* soon."

"Tillie, this is so—so—"

"Unbelievable, I know. Except I always believed. And you did, too."

Did I? Kaylee wondered. Or was I just paying lip service to Tillie's pipe dream?

They chatted a few minutes longer and hung up with a promise to talk again in a day or two. In the near dark Kaylee padded back to the couch. Too keyed up to lie back down and try to sleep, she mulled over everything Tillie had said. She remembered Max's comment about six degrees of separation, that if they'd examined everyone they knew, they'd come across a common acquaintance. But never in a million years had she dreamed that individual would be Tillie. So maybe dreams do come true.

"Everything okay?"

Rick's voice startled her and she jumped. She hadn't heard him approach this time. "Your cousin," Rick prompted, when she didn't answer right away. "Is she okay?"

"Oh, yes, sorry. She's fine. Better than fine, actually. She just called to say—" *that she found the man of her dreams.* Kaylee choked on the words. It hurt too much just then, to admit that the man of Tillie's dreams wanted her, while the man of her own dreams, who was standing about three feet away, did not. She cleared her throat. "It doesn't matter. She's fine. Everything's fine."

Rick waited a beat. She heard him draw a breath as if he were going to make some sort of announcement. But when he spoke all he said was, "Okay, then. Well, good night."

"Good night," she called softly after him as he retreated back down the hall to his room. His black cloud of the other day had cleared up at least. He didn't act angry any more. He acted *resigned,* Kaylee thought. As if he'd given up whatever internal struggle had brought it on in the first place. He'd given up on *them,* then. He'd leave her no choice but to go to Miami. He was making it clear. There was nothing for her here.

Rick awoke the next morning decidedly sick of having FBI agents in his house around the clock. Max Ferguson's smug assertions about his poor handling of his relationship with Kaylee were bad enough. At least the guy had a personality. And Rick found it hard to be too annoyed with him when Max was so aggravatingly right in his assessment. Joel Billings, aside from the fact that he had almost zero social or conversational skills, *snored.* Loudly and continuously. Rick had been tempted more than once during the night to escape to the living room and see if he could cuddle up next to Kaylee. Except the way Kaylee was behaving around him these days, he'd probably have more luck cuddling up to a block of ice.

From sheer exhaustion, he'd finally dropped off to sleep in the wee hours of the morning, Joel's exhalations still thundering in his ears.

He was groggier than usual and the sight of Kaylee up and dressed and stirring some delightful-smelling concoction in a skillet only added to his grumpiness. Her continued presence was a constant reminder of what he couldn't have, of what he'd lost or backed away from on his own. His feelings about her, about a future with her were so jumbled he hadn't begun to sort them out. Not that he'd had much downtime anyway with Joel and Max coming and going, fussing over poor Brutus.

Molly was seated at the table with a glass of orange juice in front of her. "Hi, Daddy."

Rick dredged up a smile for her and ruffled her hair as he went by. Returning her perky greeting was completely beyond him. He poured himself coffee and glanced in the skillet to see some sort of scrambled egg and potato mixture that looked like it was ready to be dished up. His stomach growled in anticipation.

Kaylee turned and smiled at him. "Hungry?"

Oh God, Rick thought wildly, let's not start that again. The memory of their early verbal encounters, the meaningful glances, the double entendres was almost enough to make him wince. Conversation was definitely beyond him this morning. He grunted, which she could take to mean whatever she wanted.

Toast popped out of the toaster just as he retreated to the table and sat next to Molly. In seconds a plate appeared in front of each of them. Kaylee sat across from them with a cup of coffee. She reached across to Molly's plate and picked up her toast and buttered it for her. Molly was stuffing eggs into her mouth by the forkful. "Can I have grape jelly, too?" she asked.

"Don't talk with your mouth full," Kaylee and Rick admonished her at the same time. Kaylee and Molly giggled and Rick felt a corner of his mouth lift. Again came the thought, this is how it could be. All the time. If you'd let it. And right behind the thought came the panic. The fear that Kaylee would walk away from him. Him and Molly. He might survive it, but Molly would be crushed. He had to be sure. But he was afraid he'd never be sure enough.

He watched Kaylee spread jelly on Molly's toast and set it back on her plate. He ate his eggs and drank his coffee and kept his mouth shut, for he'd learned this was the wisest course for a man in his position.

It was enough to listen to Kaylee and Molly banter back and forth. Kaylee'd put onions and cheese in the eggs along with potatoes and tiny bits of ham and some other indefinable seasoning that had him savoring every bite. Molly shared tidbits about her teacher and school, the class pet, which was a black rabbit, and a new girl who'd begun to cry when she realized she'd forgotten to bring her lunch.

Joel made an appearance, looking scrubbed, shaved and efficient as ever. As soon as Brutus saw the leash in his hand he stopped waiting for tidbits to fall from the table and scrambled out from underneath it, ready for a walk. A mild commotion at the front of the house signaled Max's arrival. Kaylee got up for coffee refills when Max skidded to a stop in front of her. He picked her up in a bear hug and swung her around in the limited space available before setting her on her feet. "Thank you, thank you, thank you, Kaylee Walsh. You saved my life!"

Kaylee laughed self-consciously and stepped back, putting distance between herself and Max. He held onto her hands and looked down into her face, a goofy expression on his face.

"What are you talking about, Max? I haven't done anything."

"Oh, but that's where you're wrong," Max assured her, finally releasing her hands. "You're the key that unlocked a door I was afraid had been closed to me years ago. A door I never thought I'd find."

Rick sat back in his chair, crossed his arms over his chest and frowned. He hadn't considered Max as serious competition for Kaylee's affection, but now he wasn't so sure. Maybe he'd have to assault a federal officer after all.

"Max, are you okay?" Kaylee asked. "Can I get you some coffee? Maybe you need to sit. You don't seem quite yourself."

"I found her, Kaylee," he said as she poured coffee for him. "I found Jillie. I mean Tillie."

"Of course you found Tillie. I gave you her address. That's why you went to Miami, remember? To interview her."

Max nodded. "That's what I'm trying to tell you. Jillie, my Jillie, is your cousin. Tillie."

"I know, Max. Tillie called me last night. I think it's great."

Rick couldn't miss the wistful note that had crept into Kaylee's voice, even though he had no idea what they were talking about.

"The girl, the one I told you about, the one I met in the bar in Knoxville all those years ago that I never forgot—"

"And you lost her phone number and you couldn't find her."

"Right. All this time I thought her name was Jillie, but it wasn't. Her name is Tillie. Your cousin. Tillie."

"I know. And I guess that means you're Mac, huh?"

Max grinned, his eyes sparkling. "Crazy, isn't it? All this time, I was looking for someone named Jillian, and she was waiting to hear from someone named Mac. When I saw her picture yesterday, I thought it was her. Even though it's been such a long time, there was something about her that made me think maybe. And when I arrived for the interview, the longer I talked to her, the more convinced I became, until finally, I just outright asked her. She'd been looking at me in an odd sort of way, too, like she remembered me. It's her, Kaylee. Your cousin Tillie's the woman I've been waiting ten years to find."

Kaylee leaned against the counter smiling softly, her gaze on Max. "Wow."

Molly scooted off her chair and marched her plate into the kitchen and set it in the sink. "I'm going to watch TV," she announced to no one in particular.

Even though he didn't have all the details, it didn't take a genius to put two and two together. Max wasn't after Kaylee. It was her cousin he'd evidently known in the past and lost track of that had him acting like a lovesick moron. Rick breathed an internal sigh of relief, shoved his chair back and picked up his empty plate. "No TV until you brush your teeth, Molly. And we've only got about five minutes before we have to leave so make sure your backpack is ready to go."

He set his dishes in the sink and cut his gaze to Max. "Sounds like that opening in the Miami office will come in handy after all."

"Daddy, I'm ready," Molly called.

He gave Kaylee and Max a wink. "You two have fun today."

Chapter Thirty

By mid-morning Max and Joel had set up command central at the kitchen table. They were either talking on cell phones or tapping keys on their laptops. Kaylee did her best to stay out of their way, for her presence was clearly not needed or wanted. From the bits and pieces of conversation she heard, she gathered that they were planning to set a trap for Bobby Lou just as Max had suggested.

Early in the afternoon, nearly driven crazy with boredom, Kaylee stopped by Emma's once again and borrowed the keys to the shop. She told herself she just wanted to have a closer look, that it didn't mean she would stay and take Miss Emma up on her offer, but she couldn't resist.

Under the shade of a live oak, Kaylee sat in Old Blue for a few minutes thinking about nothing in particular. She'd parked in front of the undeveloped lot next to Emma's salon and regarded the little shop thoughtfully. Squinting her eyes, she envisioned it open for business, the small front stoop swept, the plate-glass window shining, lights on inside. She imagined the small-town comings and goings, young mothers bringing their toddlers in for a first haircut, senior citizens making Saturday appointments for a wash and curl, teen girls wanting updos for prom or homecoming.

Kaylee allowed herself to do the unthinkable. In her mind's eye she saw herself behind the counter, answering the phone, welcoming clients, becoming a part of this small community the same way she'd once been part of life in Bertie Springs. She saw her name over the door instead of Miss Emma's. Most of all she saw herself fitting in, here in Perrish, Florida, saw it becoming home, the same way she'd fit in and felt at home with Rick and Molly, and yes, she could admit it now, even Brutus.

Her expression clouded, as she reminded herself that Rick was doing everything he possibly could to make sure she didn't fit too neatly into his life. He'd grabbed the first opportunity to get rid of her. She sighed. Okay, so that wasn't going so well. She could still enjoy her temporary fantasy. She could still explore the inside of Emma's shop and let herself play "what if" games until darkness fell.

Palming the key Emma had given her, she exited Old Blue and climbed the three steps to the door. She left the door open, letting the screen door fall back in place. The air inside was thick and stale with the humid heat. She moved slowly through the shop, running her hand along the back of one of the two stylist's chairs, peeking into the tiny bathroom and the combination laundry and storeroom. A combined washer-and-dryer unit was framed by shelves for supplies and towels. A broom and handled dustpan sat in the corner.

With nothing better to do, Kaylee began sweeping, mopping and scrubbing. After two years of sitting empty, dust had accumulated in every corner. Kaylee hummed along to the portable radio as she worked.

She could imagine the salon bustling with business, the dryers humming, the laughter and chatter of her clients.

A small counter held a coffeemaker. She'd bring in cookies or coffee cake every day. Mini muffins or date-nut loaf, she thought. She loved to bake.

Word of mouth would spread. As soon as she could, she'd somehow locate another stylist. Or maybe a barber. In a conventional small town such as Perrish, some men weren't too keen on having their hair cut in a unisex salon.

She and Emma had even gone so far as to discuss a name for the business. They both liked Kaylee's Kuts. *I still have my new name*, Kaylee thought to herself. Even if she didn't have the big-city glamour and sophistication she'd hoped to acquire along with it.

I could be happy here. The thought skimmed across her mind, and she knew it was true. She beamed at her reflection in the now-spotless mirror.

But maybe she could be happy in Miami, too. She'd been dreaming of beaches and nightclubs and stores for months. Even if she couldn't afford to go out often or spend much, she could enjoy the atmosphere of the city. She could window shop, save her money, splurge on one item at a time. It would be an adventure and so different from the small-town life she'd always known.

The screen door opened on a slow, groaning squeak. Kaylee whirled. A man entered, easing the door shut behind him. He regarded her from where he stood, framed by the dim late afternoon light behind him. "Well, well, Kay Lee Walsh, as I live and breathe."

He held his arms loose at his sides while he looked her up and down. Kaylee clenched her gum between her teeth, her knuckles whitening as she gripped the handle of the broom.

He took a couple of steps toward her and stopped. "I think you and me got some business we need to discuss."

Kaylee's heartbeat revved up. For the first time, it occurred to her that Dwayne Holcumb was not just Bobby Lou Tucker's no-account jailbird cousin. He was a dangerous criminal, a thief and a liar, possibly armed and dangerous. And she was alone with him. Completely, utterly alone with no phone and no one to help her.

Somehow she knew that the worst thing she could do was show Dwayne that she was afraid or intimidated by him. He'd enjoy that and it would give him some sort of power over her. She refused to give him the satisfaction. Pretending a nonchalance she was far from feeling, she eased her grip on the broom, neatened the small pile of dirt and dead bugs she'd swept up and blew a bubble. "What's up, Dwayne?"

She reached for the handled dustpan and swept the dirt into it all the while wondering how he had found her, could she use the broom as a weapon, should she try to run? The only door was behind him, so running, at the moment anyway, was not an option. She'd have to brazen it out, hopefully outwit him or charm him into a false sense of security so she could escape.

If Dwayne was surprised by her casual question and stance, he didn't show it. "What's up, darlin', is I think you have something that belongs to me. Give it up and I'll be on my way."

Finished sweeping the dirt into the dustpan, Kaylee set the dustpan aside but held the broom in front of her, forcing herself to look relaxed. "I don't know what you're talking about," she stalled. "What could I possibly have that belongs to you?"

She blew another bubble and gave Dwayne her best wide-eyed innocent look. Bad move. That seemed to piss him off. He crossed to her in three angry strides, his fingers curling around her upper arm in a painful grip. "Don't play games with me, girl. I already checked your car. It's gone and I want it back."

"Those jewels don't belong to you," Kaylee informed him. She blew a big bubble in his direction, popped it and yanked the gum back in her mouth.

As though genuinely amused by her statement, he smiled, exposing a tiny dimple at the corner of his mouth as well as teeth stained from tobacco. "Haven't you heard, darlin'? Possession is nine-tenths of the law."

She glared up at him. "Then I guess you're SOL, aren't you, Dwayne? Cuz you're not in possession of those gems you stole."

"No, but I soon will be because you're going to give them back to me before I have to hurt you." So quickly Kaylee didn't see it coming and had barely registered the click in the still air, he had a switchblade at her throat. He drew her closer to him, his hot fetid breath in her face, his dark gaze boring into hers. "All you have to do," he told her in a soft, deadly drawl, "is give them back. Cuz, frankly, darlin', I'd hate to cut up that pretty face of yours."

Like a ticker tape, thoughts and ideas swept through Kaylee's head. Go along with him. Tell him you'll get the jewels, but they're not here. Get him to go outside with you. You'll have a better chance to escape. But what came out of her mouth was the question that somehow had been utmost in her mind since he'd walked in the door. "How did you find me?" Was that breathless voice hers? What had happened to her earlier false courage?

Dwayne's nasty smile deepened. He gave a reluctant chuckle. "Small towns, darlin'. Best way in the world to get information. Bobby Lou got it straight from his cousin Anna Mae. Woman's got a memory, I'll say that for her.

Remembered she got a call from some fella in Perrish, Florida, lookin' for a babysitter. Heck, as soon as I heard that, I hightailed it up here. Wasn't too hard to find that old car of yours. Too bad you didn't leave what you found where it was. Otherwise, I wouldn't have had to come looking for you. I'd be on my way and you'd never know the difference."

"Where's—where's Bobby Lou?" Surely Dwayne hadn't hurt his favorite cousin? Kaylee wouldn't have thought so before now. But the ruthless look in Dwayne's gaze made her think twice.

"Still hung up on my little cuz, huh?" To her revulsion he tugged her even closer to him, letting her feel every muscle and sinew. "He ran home. Home to his job at the poultry plant. Home to that bitch, Georgia Rose. Georgia Rose don't

like me much. Afraid I'll get my poor little cuz in trouble. But
you like me, doncha, Kay Lee?" He rubbed up against her
hip. "I'll make you forget all about Bobby Lou. Whaddya say,
darlin'?"

Ick! she thought, but Kaylee knew better than to voice
that reaction. She had to get out of the shop, out into the
open, and somehow get away from Dwayne. Get home, get
Max, get Rick, someone, anyone to help her. Home, she
thought. When she thought of home, she thought of Rick's
house. Safety. Security. *Love.* That thought scampered
through her head, before practicality resumed its march.

"I think," she said with a breathlessness she didn't have
to fake, fear and loathing made it real, "I should get those
jewels you stole and give them back to you. That's what you
want, right, Dwayne?"

Dwayne had clearly been sidetracked by his earlier
suggestions and his close proximity to her. She could almost
see the wheels turning in his sluggish brain as he recalled
what had brought him here in the first place. "Yeah. Yeah,
that's right. Them stones is gonna make me rich. Better than
pure gold. All them stones came from North Carolina, did
you know that? That's what makes 'em so special. 'Specially
the emeralds. Rare and special. Just like you, huh, darlin'? See,
Bobby Lou ain't the only one can talk pretty to the ladies."
His gaze swept over her, pausing at her heaving chest before
slowly refocusing on her face. "You'd like me better if I was
rich, wouldn't ya, darlin.' I'd show you a real good time."

Kaylee could feel her stomach roll at Dwayne's
suggestion. She swallowed back the nausea, her gum going
with it. "We can talk about it after—after you get what you
came for.

"They're at—they're at the house I've been staying at. I'll
take you there." Max was there, too. Or maybe Joel.
Somebody would be there. What time was it, anyway, Kaylee
wondered. She hoped Rick wasn't home with Molly yet. She
hoped she'd run Dwayne right into the arms of one of the
FBI agents and no one got hurt.

Dwayne eased his grip on her arm and slid around behind her, grasping her other elbow, keeping the knife at her throat. "You'll have to pardon me, but I'm not exactly the trusting type any more. I'm goin' ta keep my knife right here as insurance until I get what I want, okay, darlin'?"

Chapter Thirty-One

Rick slowed the truck as he came down the street past Emma's salon, surprised to see Kaylee's car parked in front of the vacant lot next to it and a car he didn't recognize parked close behind hers.

Alerted by his interest, Molly gazed out the window of the truck. "Look, Daddy, there's Old Blue." "I see, honey," he replied absently.

"Where's Kaylee?" she asked, scanning the area through the window. "Is she at Miss Emma's?"

"I don't know." Rick cruised slowly past the salon. The screen door was closed but the inside door stood ajar. Was Kaylee inside? Doing what? An errand for Miss Emma?

He U-turned and pulled in behind the second car and killed the engine. The car behind Kaylee's had Dade County license plates. Rick got an uneasy feeling in his gut. He lowered the windows in the truck halfway, debating about what to do. It seemed logical to investigate, see if Kaylee was inside the shop, and if so whether she was alone or with someone. Someone like Bobby Lou. Or his loser cousin Dwayne. If either or both were in there with her, it could only mean one thing. They'd come for the loot they'd stolen.

Calm down, he told himself. It could also be her cousin. Perhaps Tillie had shown up unexpectedly. Maybe Kaylee had called her and begged her to come. And when she arrived they'd decided to tour Miss Emma's salon.

"Stay here, squirt," he told Molly. "I'll be right back."

"I want to come see Kaylee, too," Molly insisted, using both hands to release her seatbelt buckle.

"Molly, listen to me." Rick's tone got her attention. She stared at him. "Let me go see if Kaylee's here first, okay? Then I'll come back and get you."

"But why can't I come?"

"Because I said so." Rick's tone grew sterner as the unease in his gut increased. "You stay here, doors locked. I'll be right back."

"But, Daddy—"

Rick cut her off with a look. "Molly, don't argue. Just do what I tell you."

Molly crossed her arms over her chest and threw her body back against the seat, her lower lip protruding.

Rick approached the steps to the salon from the side, ready to take them both in one stride when voices inside brought him up short. Kaylee's voice asking a question. *"Where's Bobby Lou?"* And a man's voice answering in a southern drawl underscored with a sort of threatening contempt.

He heard the man say Bobby Lou had gone back to Tennessee, back to the woman he'd hooked up with there. Bobby Lou Tucker had no intention of resuming his relationship with Kaylee.

The exchange continued, the words easily overheard through the open screen. Kaylee was offering to lead her male visitor to the stolen gems. There was no mistaking the nervous fear underlying her tone. And no wonder. Rick momentarily froze when he heard the man assure Kaylee he'd keep a knife close to her side until he had what he came for.

Carefully, Rick moved away from the steps, around to the side of the building. He pulled his cell phone from his pocket and stared hard at the truck where Molly was surely watching his every move. He put his hand up in a warning for her to stay put then put his finger to his lips hoping she got the message to stay quiet as well. He sidled farther back along the side of the building and dialed Ferguson's number. In a whisper he explained the situation and gave directions to the salon. He snapped the phone shut and moved forward a few steps where he could keep an eye on his truck, Kaylee's car and any movement between them and the salon door.

He heard the creak of the screen door opening and footsteps shuffling along the cement stoop and down the steps. He heard a clatter. Something dropped and fell to the sidewalk, but he couldn't see what it was. Rick swore beneath his breath. Kaylee was being held hostage and there was no guarantee that Ferguson would arrive before Dwayne Holcumb got her into a vehicle. She'd have no choice but to take him to the house, and what? She could only stall some more because the majority, if not all, of the stolen gemstones were in FBI custody. Ferguson had been keeping count as they appeared and matching the stones to a color printout with diagrams and exact dimensions of each provided by the gem dealer they'd been stolen from. Based on Brutus' recent activity, he expected to collect the last few stones today.

But perhaps Ferguson would contact Billings and have him remain at the house, hidden, just in case Kaylee and Dwayne returned there. That would be excellent insurance. They'd catch him one way or another, and hopefully no one would get hurt. Especially not Kaylee. Please, God, not Kaylee, who'd been innocent from the get-go. If she got hurt in the process of trying to do the right thing he'd never forgive himself for accusing her of being involved. Idiot, he cursed himself for the thousandth time. What had he been thinking?

Partially concealed behind a cluster of overgrown ixora, he watched as Kaylee and Dwayne began to move toward the parked cars. Dwayne was about Kaylee's height, maybe a little taller, thin as a cord, but Rick wasn't fooled. During high school he'd tangled a time or two with guys who had that muscular, wiry build. What they lacked in bulk they made up for in strength and agility. Rick itched to attack, to yank Kaylee away from Dwayne and his knife, but common sense prevailed. He was unarmed, for one thing. And he had Molly to think about. He wasn't fool enough to believe that if she saw him fighting with another man his daughter wouldn't come to his aid. The last thing he needed was a six-year-old in the midst of a knife fight.

Dwayne swiveled his head as he forced Kaylee to move slowly and deliberately toward the cars, but he never once looked behind him. Moron, Rick thought contemptuously, as he carefully moved behind a clump of palmettos in the vacant lot where he could see but wouldn't be seen should Dwayne decide to look over his shoulder.

Dwayne stopped suddenly, clearly perplexed as he studied the parked vehicles. He'd obviously planned to use the car he'd been driving as opposed to Old Blue, but Rick had parked close enough behind him that he would now have to do some maneuvering to get out.

He seemed to be debating. He said something to Kaylee that Rick couldn't hear. They started to move in the direction of Old Blue when a voice from the truck startled them.

"Kaylee!" Molly squealed in delight.

Before Rick could move or think or react, she'd unlocked the truck door, opened it and slid to the ground, nearly falling out in her rush to get to Kaylee.

She ran to Kaylee, intent on wrapping herself around her, but Dwayne's arm blocked her. He got a grip on her upper arm and growled. "Get outta here, kid."

Molly glared at him defiantly. "No. I want Kaylee." She squirmed in his grasp.

"Molly, it's okay," Kaylee tried to reassure her, but Molly was having none of it. She wiggled for all she was worth trying to escape Dwayne's hold. He gave a disgusted sort of strangled sound from the back of his throat, eased the knife away from Kaylee as he lifted Molly up and shook her off.

Molly landed flat on her back on the ground with a surprised "Oomph".

It seemed to happen in slow motion and yet so quickly that Rick wondered what had kept him rooted to his spot for so long. Seeing his daughter tossed aside, hearing the wind getting knocked out of her, sent rage surging through him.

He raced toward Dwayne and Kaylee with a bellow. Dwayne shoved Kaylee away from him and turned holding the knife out in front of him.

Hardly realizing what he was doing, seeing the flash of the knife, Rick went in low, his old football instincts coming back. He took Dwayne down with a tackle around the knees, but Dwayne was ready. He fell and lunged at the same time, the knife catching Rick in the side, snagging in his shirt before Dwayne pulled it free.

Rick grunted in surprise, distracted by the slice of pain. Dwayne kicked out, freeing himself from Rick. He got to his feet, eyes flashing, knife at the ready. He glanced at Kaylee, who had sprinted back to the steps of the salon and grabbed the broom she'd dropped there. She advanced on him, holding it by the bristle end, the handle pointed in his direction.

She glanced nervously at Rick, who was hauling himself to his feet, blood dripping down his side. She fixed her gaze on Bobby Lou's cousin. "Drop the knife, Dwayne," she warned him in a low voice. "It's over. I lied. I don't have those gems. The FBI has them. Or most of them anyway."

Dwayne smiled, an evil leer, clearly not believing her.

"Come on now, darlin.' You and me. We can make a deal."

Kaylee shook her head, her gaze cutting briefly to Rick then to something behind Dwayne. She shook her head slightly in warning. Dwayne stared at her, puzzled.

"Molly, no!" she shouted. She rushed Dwayne with the broom handle. At the same time, Molly's small, sneaker-clad foot made determined contact with the back of his knee, buckling him. Kaylee brought the broom handle down on the hand holding the knife at the same time Rick tackled him again. A car screeched to a halt in the middle of the road just a few feet away. A door opened and gun drawn, Max Ferguson yelled, "Halt. FBI."

An excited barking began and the next thing Dwayne Holcumb knew he was being kicked in the shin by a little girl while a broom handle hovered above his eye socket. A large brown dog with drooling jowls emitted furious growls while tugging on his pants cuff. Drops of blood stained his shirt where a knee with a whole lot of weight behind it pinned him flat to the ground. Agent Maxwell Ferguson of the FBI informed him of his rights while holding a gun to his head.

Chapter Thirty-Two

Rick looked up from the examining table in the emergency room as the curtain slid back. Kaylee and Molly stood there holding hands with identical anxious expressions.

He waved. "Hey, girls."

"Daddy!" Molly dropped Kaylee's hand and rushed toward him. She paused to stare at the line of stitches the ER doctor had just installed in the gash in his side. "Does it hurt?" she asked in awe. "Can I touch it?"

"Sure, go ahead. Doesn't hurt a bit." Molly tentatively touched the sutures with her fingers. "What's that brown stuff?"

Rick twisted his head to look at the wound. "I don't know, squirt. Probably something to kill germs."

"Billy Hunsacker got stitches in his chin when he fell off the monkey bars. But he only had three. You have way more than three."

"Yep, pretty impressive, huh?" Rick grinned and ruffled Molly's hair. His gaze caught Kaylee's. She looked like she was about ready to burst into tears.

"You okay?" he asked.

She nodded. "I'm so, so sorry."

"Hey, it's okay. It's a scratch."

She shook her head. "It's all my fault. You could have been—" her gaze shifted to Molly and she shut up.

"So could you," he reminded her. The memory of Dwayne with his knife in Kaylee's side would be with him for a while.

She shook her head, blinking back her tears. A nurse appeared with a large bandage which she proceeded to unwrap from its sealed package and place over Rick's wound. "Now, Mr. Braddock, you need to take it easy for a couple of days. No heavy lifting, no strenuous activity or you'll pull the sutures out." She produced a small bottle. "Doctor's sending you home with something for the pain. Take one every four hours if you need it tonight and tomorrow. After that, you can take ibuprofen or acetaminophen." She continued to go over a page of instructions.

Rick tuned her out. He was glad to be alive. Glad neither Molly nor Kaylee had been hurt. Dwayne was in custody. Billings and a couple of state troopers were transporting him to Jacksonville where he'd be processed and transferred to Tennessee. Ferguson had stayed behind to take their statements as soon as they were able to give them. Then he too would disappear. The whole episode would be behind them. Life would go on as normal.

The nurse had finished. She helped Rick to a sitting position. His torn and bloodied shirt was in a plastic bag. She offered him the top half of a set of scrubs and helped slip it over his head. "You're free to go," she informed him. She smiled at Molly. "Looks like you've got a couple of nurses here to take care of you at home."

"Come on, Daddy." Molly tugged on his hand as he slid off the hospital cot. "I missed Rugrats. And I'm hungry. Can we have grilled cheese for dinner?"

Kaylee stepped forward. "Do you need help?"

Rick knew he could walk out of the hospital under his own steam. But the chance to get close to Kaylee one more time was too good to pass up. "Yeah," he said, "yeah, I think I do, if you don't mind." She moved close to his uninjured side and he draped an arm around her neck. He could smell the scent of her shampoo and the barest hint of grape bubble gum on her breath. It was almost more than he could do not to bury his face in her hair, hold her close, and tell her, tell her what? That he was sorry? That he wanted her to stay? That he'd completely screwed up? His mind shied away from the possibilities.

The three of them walked out together. He'd figure out what needed to be said later.

For now, this was enough.

They were in the bathroom together once again. It was late. Molly was asleep. There was an injured party. But this time it was Rick. After a long-overdue meal of grilled cheese sandwiches and tomato soup, it hadn't taken much to get Molly into bed. He'd showered then which ruined the bandage the nurse had so carefully applied. Luckily, she'd sent them home with some extras and Kaylee was carefully taping one in place over his stitches.

His side ached and he was tired. The pain medication they'd given him in the emergency room had worn off and he was eyeing the bottle of pills on the top shelf of the medicine cabinet. One of those and he'd probably be out like a light. Which wouldn't be a bad idea.

Kaylee straightened. "Do you think you'll be okay tonight? Um, I mean…" She trailed off as if not certain what she was asking.

Rick moved a fraction of an inch closer to her. "I hope so. I'm going to take one of those pills they gave me which will probably knock me out. But it wouldn't hurt if I had my own private nurse nearby." He settled his hands on her waist. "You know, just in case."

"Just in case what?" Kaylee challenged him. She had dark circles under her eyes but she was trying not to smile.

"Just in case, I, uh, take a turn for the worse. You could cool my fevered brow or something." He grinned.

"You'd only get a fever if you develop an infection. Frankly, you seem pretty darn chipper to me. I don't think you need a nurse by your side."

"No, but it'd be nice to have you there anyway." He waited, but when she didn't react, he stepped back, dropping his hands to his sides. He stepped to the cabinet, opened the bottle and downed one of the pills. "I'll be in a drug-induced sleep anyway, if you change your mind."

He left the bathroom and called to Brutus. They both disappeared into his bedroom.

Kaylee turned on the shower wanting to wash away the day, glad it was over. She was so tired she could hardly think. When she left the bathroom she went into the living room and stared at the couch. The last thing she wanted to do was make it up so she could sleep there tonight. On tiptoe she went back down the hall and pushed open the door to Rick's bedroom. As he'd said, he was out like a light, lying on his back, one arm drawn up to protect his injured side, the other thrown back over his head. Brutus snored on the floor beside him.

There was an entire side of the bed not in use. They wouldn't even be touching each other. And she'd be close by, just in case he needed her, she reminded herself. Kaylee retrieved her pillow.

Rick woke the next morning to find Kaylee next to him. He blinked to make sure he wasn't dreaming or having a painkiller-induced hallucination. She was practically hugging the edge of the bed, her back to him. He reached over and lifted a curly strand of dark hair and let it fall back to her pillow. A painful realization struck. He was going to have to let her go. Even if he wanted her to stay, even if *she* thought she wanted to stay here in Perrish, even if they both were interested in seeing if what was between them could develop into a permanent relationship. He wouldn't, couldn't make the same mistake twice.

If Brenda'd had a chance to be on her own, explore her options before they'd married, maybe they could have avoided a painful divorce. Most likely they'd never have married in the first place. He couldn't entirely regret their union because it had produced Molly and he couldn't imagine life without his little girl. But both he and Molly had suffered when Brenda had decided she wanted something entirely different, something she probably hadn't known existed before she'd married Rick.

Kaylee was a small-town girl, but she'd told him the day he'd met her she dreamt of a life in Miami. A bigger city, a different environment, a life unlike the one she'd left behind. If she stayed in Perrish she'd simply be duplicating the life she'd known in Bertie Springs. Wouldn't she always wonder "what if"? What if she had gone to Miami? What if she'd met someone else there? What if she ended up hating herself and him for not taking that opportunity when she had the chance?

No. No way. Whether Kaylee realized it or not, she *needed* to go to Miami and find out for herself what a future there might hold. And if she decided to come back, at least she'd come back with no illusions. She'd know what she'd chosen. And if she didn't come back? Then I'll just have to survive, Rick told himself. Somehow.

Carefully he eased himself to a sitting position, wincing as his side protested the movement. He slid out of bed, the better to remove himself from temptation. He didn't want to do anything to upset Kaylee. And he didn't want to create more memories to torture himself with after she was gone.

Chapter Thirty-Three

Kaylee came awake slowly, trying to discern exactly where she was before her decision last night came flooding back to her. She knew before she glanced over her shoulder that Rick was no longer in bed. Sunlight poked through the edges of the blinds, which meant she'd slept later than usual. She sat up, shoving her hair out of her eyes, feeling groggy and listless.

Today she'd leave for Miami. She had no choice. Her enthusiasm for the journey which had her bubbling over in excitement a few weeks ago had drained away. She looked around Rick's bedroom. A pair of jeans and a white tee shirt had been tossed over the back of the only chair. His closet door was ajar and she glimpsed his clothes and shoes, boxes on the upper shelves, a baseball bat leaning against the doorjamb. His nightstand held a couple of magazines focusing on sports and automobiles. Curiously, Kaylee moved the top two aside to find a parenting magazine beneath.

She bit her lip, blinking back threatening tears. She tilted her head back and sighed. Rick didn't need magazines filled with so-called expert advice to tell him how to parent.

He probably didn't need expert advice on much of anything. Except how to trust a woman again.

I'm not Brenda. She'd told him that. Thought he understood it. But it didn't make any difference. Rick wasn't ready to have her in his life.

Kaylee pulled on her robe, made a bathroom stop and went out to the kitchen.

"Hi, Kaylee!" Molly greeted her. "Daddy's making me a chocolate-chip waffle."

"Is he? That sounds yummy." She kissed the top of Molly's head, putting off looking into Rick's eyes as long as possible.

She straightened and moved to the counter for coffee. Rick extracted a round, no-longer-frozen waffle from the toaster oven. "Watch closely," he told her with a sheepish grin. "I don't share my culinary secrets with just anyone."

Feeling dangerously close to tears again, Kaylee watched as Rick arranged chocolate chips in a smiley face on top of the waffle. "Now for the piece de resistance." He picked up a can of ready-made whipped topping and filled in eyebrows, a nose and a moustache.

"Impressive, huh?" he glanced her way and grinned. Then his smile faded.

Kaylee forced herself to smile back. She looked into his eyes. "Yeah. Impressive."

He cleared his throat and turned away with the plate in his hand. "Madam." He set it in front of Molly continuing his French chef farce for her benefit. "Would Madam care for some maple syrup this morning?" He held the bottle as if it were a fine wine, and Molly a discerning diner who wished to see the label. "It's a fine vintage," he informed her. "From the vineyards of Mrs. Butterworth. 2006. An extraordinarily good year for the sap."

Molly giggled. "Yes, please, monsieur. But don't dribble it on the chocolate chips this time."

"As you wish, madam." Rick poured a thin stream of syrup on top of Molly's waffle and capped the bottle. "Does madam require help in cutting up her meal?"

Molly shook her head. "I can do it myself."

"Very good, madam."

He gave her a bow and retreated, syrup bottle in hand.

"And for you, madam?" He asked as he neared the counter where she'd been watching the entire scene. "Would you care for one of our fine chocolate-chip waffles this morning?"

"Have one, Kaylee," Molly entreated around a mouthful. "They're good."

"Don't talk with your mouth full," Rick reminded her. He turned back to Kaylee. "So how about it?"

"Would you excuse me?" Setting her cup on the counter, she hightailed it back to the bathroom just in the nick of time. Burying her face in a bath towel, she turned the water on in the shower, dropped the lid on the toilet seat and sank down on top of it. She let the tears flow along with great racking sobs that seemed to come from a well of grief inside of her and sadness so great it temporarily overwhelmed her.

She thought of all her years in Bertie Springs, especially the last few when it was just her and Granny Daisy. She thought of Bobby Lou's desertion, how humiliated she'd been at the time but how little she'd missed him. She thought of her mother taking up with Russ, the chicken-feed salesman, deciding to leave for good with him. How abandoned she'd felt then, unworthy of her mother's commitment.

That's probably how Rick felt, she realized now, after Brenda left. It was probably why she identified so strongly with Molly, whose mother had abandoned her as well. But Molly was lucky. She had Rick. And I had Granny, she reminded herself. But now she had no one. And that's the way it's going to be. So get used to it.

Tears spent, Kaylee felt hollow but relieved. She could get on with what she had to do. Say her good-byes and be on her way. She turned off the shower and splashed her face with cold water. She waited a few minutes for the redness in her eyes to dissipate. Then she opened the door and crossed the hall to Molly's room.

She could hear Rick and Molly in the kitchen. It sounded like they were cleaning up from breakfast.

Quickly she donned some clothes. Back in the bathroom she fixed her hair, did a quick makeup job and brushed her teeth. When she opened the bathroom door, Molly was waiting outside.

"I have to brush my teeth," she informed Kaylee.

"Sure, darlin'. Sorry I took so long."

She went back out to the kitchen. Rick was leaning against the counter reading the sports page, a cup of coffee nearby. He looked up, raking her with an intense gaze. "You okay?"

"Sure. I'm fine." The weird thing was, she was fine. Sometimes all you need is a good cry. Another of Granny Daisy's wisdoms. Resigned to her fate, having dealt with her emotions, Kaylee was ready to do what she had to do.

Molly reappeared, teeth brushed, hair combed, backpack in place. "Ready, Dad?"

"Ready, squirt." He took another gulp of coffee.

She looked up at Kaylee. "Bye, Kaylee."

Kaylee dropped down to her level. "Bye, sweetheart. You be a good girl."

Molly patted Kaylee's shoulder. "You too."

Kaylee couldn't help but give a sad chuckle at that.

She straightened. Rick was looking at her. "I guess this is good-bye, then."

She made herself smile. "I guess so."

He stepped close and hugged her. She hugged him back. Neither seemed inclined to let go.

"Da-ad. Are you taking me to school or not?" Molly asked.

"Yes, ma'am." His face was still pressed into Kaylee's hair, voice muffled. He broke the embrace, gave her a quick kiss on the cheek, his gaze not meeting hers this time. "Bye."

"Bye," she whispered as she watched the life she wanted walk out the door. Brutus lumbered in and sat by the table giving her a piteous look. Then he gave a doggy sigh of resignation and slid down, resting his head on his paws and gazing at her with that sad, hopeful expression.

Kaylee wondered if she'd been wearing that same look on her face. Reaching down she rubbed the top of his head.

"We're both pathetic, you know that?"

Then she marched into Molly's room to survey the contents of her suitcase. Time to finish packing.

On the way to school Rick tried once again to reinforce the idea that Kaylee would be gone for good after today, but Molly would have none of it. She was convinced Kaylee would be at home just as she had been the past few weeks. Plus, Kaylee hadn't left when she was supposed to the first time, so Molly refused to believe she would this time either.

Rick finally gave up. He stopped in the school office to explain Molly's tardiness and kissed her good-bye. He knew Molly was in for a big disappointment come this afternoon. But then so was he.

And it's your own damn fault, he told himself. You could still ask her to stay. Get down on your hands and knees and beg her. Why don't you?

He knew the answer to that. Because deep down inside he was afraid Kaylee would leave the way Brenda had. Afraid his little house and his simple life in a small town wouldn't be enough for Kaylee because it hadn't been enough for Brenda.

He told himself Kaylee was nothing like Brenda. She'd proven that over and over again. In the way she took care of Molly, the way she delighted in simple pleasures, like going to the beach or sewing doll clothes. She gave without counting the cost. Brenda always kept score.

But he had to let her go.

At a stop sign, he glanced down to adjust the radio dial and noticed the edge of a small pink paper bag sticking out of the dashboard holder where he kept receipts, pens, maps and other miscellany. "Damn!" Rick accelerated as he reached the main road.

Kaylee was putting a bag in Old Blue's trunk when he pulled into the driveway and parked next to her.

"Forget something?" she asked.

"Sort of."

He opened his door and got out. "I forgot to give you these." He held up the pink bag. She took it and peered down into it giving him a quizzical look. She removed the small box and opened it.

"Those earrings," she said, her astonishment clear.

"I bought them for you that day at the mall. I was waiting...for the right time to give them to you."

"Oh." Disappointment replaced astonishment. "Thank you."

Her gaze met his. "I'm glad you came back. I, um, forgot to tell you something."

Rick nodded. He'd forgotten to tell her something too. Several somethings. Suddenly it didn't seem so important to make her say it first.

"I don't want to leave."

"I can't ask you to stay."

"What?" they asked each other in unison.

Rick slid his arms around Kaylee's waist. "I can't ask you to stay."

"Yes, you can," Kaylee assured him. "Ask me."

Rick shook his head. Surely this was the hardest thing he'd ever had to do. At the back of his mind was the memory of Brenda's disillusionment with him, with their marriage. He never wanted to see that same look in Kaylee's eyes when she looked at him. He never wanted to be the one responsible for taking her dreams away from her. "No. You need to go to Miami. I *want* you to go to Miami."

"Liar," she breathed.

"Kaylee—ah, hell." He stepped back, shoved his fingers through his hair and leaned against his truck. "You have to go. This isn't about what I want. This is about what you want."

"I know what I want."

He shook his head. "You don't. You only think you do."

"How can you say—"

He silenced her with a finger over her lips. "You think you know because you've got nothing to compare it to. You think you can settle for life in a small town, with me and Molly, even though you've done nothing since you got here but talk about going to Miami."

"But that was before—"

"I know. But I can't ask you to stay and have you always wondering if you made the right choice."

"I wouldn't. I won't."

Rick shook his head. "I can't take that chance. I won't risk my heart or Molly's. And I can't take your dream away from you. I tried it with Brenda. It doesn't work."

"I'm not Brenda."

"I know that. Believe me, I know that. But I still want you to go to Miami. I want you to be sure of what you want. I don't want you to settle for anything less."

What if Rick was right? Kaylee didn't want to believe that he might be. Everything between them had happened so quickly. Maybe they both needed some distance to put it into perspective. Maybe Rick needed time, too. To decide what *he* wanted. She wasn't going to force him into a decision he wasn't ready to make.

"Okay. It's a deal."

"You could have argued with me more." He gave her his lopsided grin.

"When I come back—"

"*If* you come back."

"Okay. *If* I come back, I'll argue with you all night if that's what you want."

"*If* you come back, I won't spend the nights arguing with you, that's for sure." He bent and kissed her, hard and fierce. Kaylee wrapped her arms around his neck, never wanting to let go. But eventually he set her away from him. She got behind the wheel of Old Blue and he closed the door. She turned to rummage in her purse for a pen and paper. She scribbled Tillie's phone number on an old grocery-store receipt and handed it to him.

"Here's where I'll be."

Rick glanced at the paper and nodded. "Okay. Drive safe."

She looked up at him. "I will." She grabbed her sunglasses and jammed them on. Rick's last memory of her shouldn't be of her eyes filled with tears.

She took one last look at Rick's house. She sighed and started the engine, which turned over smoothly and purred like a satisfied kitten. She backed out of the driveway and headed for the interstate and her future in Miami.

Chapter Thirty-Four

Kaylee arrived in Miami to find that Max had finagled the weekend off and he planned to whisk Tillie away on Friday night almost as soon as she finished at the salon. When Tillie expressed regret at the timing, Kaylee assured Tillie she'd be fine on her own. She couldn't expect Tillie to choose her over Max, the recently rediscovered love of her life.

So instead of plunging into work on Saturday, she went to the beach alone. She meandered along the shore, watching the families with small children, fathers helping the kids build sandcastles, mothers slathering the toddlers with sunscreen. She watched the couples strolling hand in hand or jogging together through the sand. The beach had been a lot more fun the day she'd gone with Rick.

She set up Tillie's beach chair and set to work on her tan. Before long a couple of guys struck up conversation with her, and invited her to a nearby outdoor bar for a drink. She slowly sipped a frozen strawberry margarita, smiled and chatted but she couldn't work up any enthusiasm to return their interest. Compared to Rick, she found them lacking. She went back to Tillie's place and showered and watched old movies before she finally fell asleep.

Sunday she went to the nearest mall, not because she had any money to spend, but it cost nothing to browse or try on clothes. Everywhere she looked it seemed there were mothers with little girls, in the changing rooms, in the food court, sitting on the benches. Kaylee thought of Molly and wondered what she was doing now. Had Rick taken her shopping for new school clothes? Did he even realize that she might need some new outfits? Or did Brenda do that on a weekend when she came to pick Molly up? It would be such fun to shop with Molly, Kaylee thought. Maybe they could go for ice cream after.

Kaylee turned away from watching a mother and daughter licking ice-cream cones and giggling across the table from each other. She blinked rapidly, assuring herself that she couldn't possibly be tearing up over such a normal, everyday occurrence. She'd had enough of the mall, but where else could she go? The thought of returning to Tillie's for another lonely evening depressed her further. She wandered through Lincoln Road which was filled with shops and restaurants. She could stop somewhere, have a drink, but the idea held little appeal. She had very little cash. Sitting at a bar by herself could only make her even more sharply aware of how much she missed Rick.

Eventually, she went back to Tillie's and took a long bubble bath. Tillie had a stack of magazines and Kaylee kept herself company with several of them while she soaked and sipped from a glass of wine. She went to bed early, willing herself to go to sleep and stop wondering what Rick and Molly were doing, whether they missed her, how they were getting along without her.

She woke up so early that Monday stretched endlessly in front of her. She made herself go walk along the beach, figuring she was in Miami now, exactly where she'd dreamed of being. It would be silly not to take advantage of it. If she kept walking as much as she had this weekend, soon her one-size-too-small swimsuit would actually fit her.

The beach was virtually deserted at such an early hour on a weekday. A few joggers and strollers like herself, but there was nothing there to distract her from her thoughts.

When she returned to Tillie's, one glance at the clock told her that Rick and Molly were probably at the kitchen table by now, Molly with a bowl of cereal and Rick with his coffee. She smiled as she recalled Rick reading the comics to Molly, the murmur of their voices, the slice-of-life look at their morning routine.

She picked up the receiver of Tillie's phone and pressed the number one and the area code. She wanted so desperately to hear their voices. Slowly she hung up the phone. This time when the tears filled her eyes she let them come. She pulled out a chair at Tillie's small kitchen table, laid her head on her arms and sobbed her heart out.

Ever since she'd left the tiny, safe world of Bertie Springs her life had taken twists and turns she hadn't anticipated. A month ago she'd been so sure a new life awaited her in Miami, certain that she could change, adapt, fit in, exactly as Tillie had. But since her stop-off in Perrish, she wasn't sure of anything anymore.

She'd thought she knew who she was and what she wanted. But living with Rick and Molly made her question everything about herself. Maybe *that's* what scared Rick. Maybe it wasn't so much that he didn't know her. He was afraid she didn't know herself as well as she should.

Of course he'd think that. One minute she was dead set on leaving small-town life behind forever. The next she was begging to stay in a tiny town like the one she'd left.

One thing was clear to her now. She couldn't contemplate a return to Perrish until she'd given Miami a chance. Rick would accept nothing less. He was right. She needed to figure out what she wanted and be sure, really sure, before she stepped back into his life.

Dreams. Ha! she thought. This was her big dream, she thought, to be by herself.

Walking a practically deserted beach alone. Although she had to admit, the beach was soothing and beautiful in the early morning. She liked being in such close proximity to it that she could go whenever she wanted.

Roaming the mall and wishing she had a little girl to shop for. Even if it was just window-shopping, it was refreshing to have such a variety of goods to wander through, to touch or try on. Back home the nearest mall was twenty miles away and it wasn't much of a mall.

Deflecting interest, conversation and free drinks from handsome, available men. Even though she wasn't interested at the moment, discovering that other guys were interested in her soothed the wounds created by Bobby Lou and Rick's behavior.

If she stayed in Miami she could have her own salon, her own place to live. But at the moment her heart was still stuck in small-town Perrish with Rick and Molly.

Somehow she made it through the rest of the day, cleaning Tillie's nearly spotless condo, doing her laundry, mindlessly flipping through more magazines. Tomorrow would be better. Tillie would be back. They'd go to work together. Maybe that's why she was in such a funk, she tried to tell herself. She just needed to work.

Tillie finally breezed in around ten that night. Kaylee had the TV on but she hadn't been concentrating on the program. She'd given up trying to concentrate on anything other than thoughts of Rick and Molly and the future she might have had if Rick had asked her to stay. Her mind kept straying back to Emma Arnold's offer to sell her the salon and give her a place to stay in her home until she got on her feet. She wouldn't have stayed in Rick's house in any case, not unless they were married. She couldn't shake the feeling that she'd found everything she wanted right there in Perrish and she'd somehow lost it.

Tillie's joy was hard to watch in the face of her own dismal thoughts, but Kaylee did her best to share it.

"Darlin,' I feel just terrible about leaving you alone here," Tillie said as she came into the room.

Kaylee straightened her spine and forced a smile to her face. "It's okay, Tillie. You know I understand. There's so much to do here, I hardly missed you at all," she lied. "I went to the beach and I window-shopped. A couple of guys bought me a margarita. It was fun."

"I brought you something." She waved a white paper bag. "Baskin Robbins chocolate peanut butter." When Kaylee didn't react right away, Tillie nudged her. "What are you waiting for? Come on, girl. Get a spoon and let's get to it."

Kaylee trailed after Tillie and sat across from her, spoon in hand. Tillie lifted the lid on the pint-size container and scooped up a bit of the ice cream which had softened during her trip home. "Mmm. This ice cream is sure to cure all ills."

Kaylee took a tiny taste, trying to work up an appetite as well as some enthusiasm for a conversation about Tillie's weekend. "You sure don't look like you've got any ills, Til. Or that you need ice cream to cure them."

Tillie grinned and took another huge bite. "I wasn't talking about me. I was talking about you."

"Me? Nothing wrong with me. I'm fine." There it was again. That unconvincing phrase. It hadn't fooled Max a few days ago and it sure wouldn't fool Tillie.

"So you didn't spend all weekend moping around missing that mechanic and his daughter?"

"No!" The denial sprang to Kaylee's lips automatically, but she caught the knowing look in Tillie's eye. "Not all weekend." She smiled helplessly at her cousin. "Just most of it."

"Mmhmm. I thought so. Did you call him?"

Kaylee shook her head. "I thought about it. But I didn't. He has the number here. If he wanted to call, he would."

"You planning on going back there?"

Kaylee put her spoon down. She didn't want ice cream at all. And eating it certainly wasn't going to cure what was wrong with her. She shook her head. "I don't know, Tillie. I don't think so. Rick didn't ask me to stay. Even if he wanted to, he didn't. I don't think I can go back and just sort of insinuate myself into his life. He doesn't want me there."

The truth of those words sent annoying tears into her eyes. She blinked them back and tried to smile at Tillie. Tillie reached across the table and squeezed Kaylee's wrist. "Oh, hon. I'm so sorry. It doesn't seem quite fair that we both found the men of our dreams and only one of them is cooperating."

Kaylee chuckled wetly at Tillie's summation and changed the subject. "So Max is, ahem, cooperating?"

Tillie sat back and licked her lips like a cat who'd swallowed an especially tasty canary. "Darlin,' if the man *cooperated* any better, I'd be dead. I'm still pinching myself to make sure this has happened. After all these years." She shook her head. Her gaze connected with Kaylee's. "I'm in love. The giddy, heart-pounding-when-he-walks-in-the-room, romance novel, fairy-tale, sickeningly sweet kind of in love."

"And he is too? For real, Til?"

Tillie nodded. "He's worse than me, I think. I could barely get him on the plane. He was ready to chuck it all and stay here. His whole career, everything he's worked for, he was ready to walk away from it rather than leave without me. But I finally convinced him that was a bad idea. I need a husband with a steady job to support all the kids I plan on having with him."

"You talked marriage? Already?"

"You better believe it, hon. I know it sounds crazy. I know it's only been a couple of days. Ten years and a couple of days," she acknowledged. She hesitated. "So I've got a business proposition for you, kiddo. I want you to buy my salon."

"Tillie, you know I can't afford to do that—"

"I'll make the terms so easy, you won't be able to say no. I'll even sell you this condo at a reasonable price. Or rent it to you cheap, if you'd rather. Kaylee, I'm moving back to Knoxville."

Kaylee felt as if someone had just pulled a plug and deflated her. She sagged in her seat and stared at Tillie. "You're leaving? For good? But I just got here."

Tillie squeezed her wrist again. "I know, sugar. I know. But Max is with the Bureau in Knoxville. His family's all around there, and so's mine, what's left of it. It just makes more sense for me to relocate than for him right now."

"But—but..." Kaylee couldn't think of a reasonable argument. Her cousin had finally found Max. Who could blame her for wanting to start her life with him as soon as she possibly could. Just like that, Kaylee's future, the one she'd planned on in Miami seemed to be evaporating right before her eyes. Because in all of her dreamt-up scenarios, Tillie was a part of it.

"Sugar, you been telling me you want a salon of your own someday. Now you've got that chance. You can buy mine. It's a good business, good steady clientele, great location. You'd do fine running it, I know you would, or else I wouldn't offer to sell it to you. I'll help you every step of the way, whatever you need."

"It's just so sudden," Kaylee said. She couldn't absorb Tillie's offer. Couldn't quite picture herself in a big city all alone, not knowing a soul once Tillie left. Owning and running her own business to boot. It seemed too big somehow. Too much. Too soon.

But in the back of her mind she began to see the possibilities. She'd have the life she dreamed of. Her own salon, her own home. Beaches. Shopping. Nightclubs and restaurants. Men who weren't afraid to admit they were interested in her.

"Well, look, we don't have to decide anything tonight. Tomorrow we'll go in, introduce you around, you can have a look at the operation, see what you think. I'm not leaving for a few weeks. You can think about it."

"Okay. I will. I appreciate your faith in me. It's just that I'll miss you. I always pictured the two of us together once I got here."

"I know, sugar." Tillie gave her a sideways hug as she got up to put the ice cream in the freezer. "But it will all work out. You'll see."

The phone rang then and Tillie answered it on her way to the refrigerator. "Hi, darlin.' I know. I miss you, too."

It had to be Max. Kaylee waved good night and escaped the kitchen, resisting the urge to cover her ears as Tillie launched into a syrupy conversation with Max.

She tried to imagine Rick calling to say he missed her. She punched her pillow down as she got into bed. *That,* she told herself crossly, was never going to happen.

Chapter Thirty-Five

"Kay Lee Walsh, I've never known you to be a moper, but I swear you've done nothing but since you got here," Tillie stated the moment she walked in the door. She set her keys and purse on the table near the door and toed off her shoes.

Gripping the handled bag filled with Chinese take-out she advanced into the living room and stood halfway between the television and the sofa where Kaylee was curled up pretending to watch a rerun of *Bewitched*. If only she could be like Samantha, twitch her nose and make things the way she wanted them to be.

"Earth to Kay Lee, earth to Kay Lee," Tillie chanted before snapping her fingers in front of her cousin. "Come in, Kay Lee."

Kaylee snapped out of her TV-induced stupor. "I'm sorry, Tillie. I was a million miles away." She got up.

"Or at least a couple hundred," Tillie muttered.

"Here, let me take that." Kaylee relieved Tillie of the food and went into the kitchen. She pulled plates and utensils out of cupboards and drawers and set the table. Tillie opened a bottle of wine and poured two glasses. She took a seat at the table and watched while Kaylee set the food out, opened each of the containers and then seated herself.

In silence they each helped themselves to moo goo gai pan and fried rice. Kaylee took a couple of bites then did nothing more than push the food around on her plate, her chin in her hand as she stared at it. She sighed, oblivious to Tillie's thoughtful gaze.

"Why don't you call him, hon?" she asked.

Kaylee's head came up. "Who?"

Tillie snorted. "Who? Rick, that's who. You've been moping around here for two weeks. It's obvious he's the reason why."

Kaylee shook her head then took a sip of the wine. She pushed her plate away. "I can't call him."

"Why?"

"You know why." She'd told Tillie everything that had happened from the moment she'd met Rick to the morning he'd practically pushed her out of Perrish and insisted she go to Miami.

"So what? He told you to give the big city a try and come back when you realized it wasn't what you want. He didn't put a time limit on it, did he? He didn't say give it six months or a year. He told you to come back when you were ready. Girl, in case you haven't figured it out yet, you're ready."

"I can't go back after only two weeks!"

"Why not? You did what he asked you to do," Tillie pointed out practically. She took a bite of food and chewed, waiting for Kaylee's response. "If you ask me, you never should have left in the first place."

"Didn't you want me here?" Kaylee asked.

Tillie reached across the table and covered Kaylee's hands with hers for a moment. "Oh, girl, of course I did. You don't know how much I wanted everything to go just like we planned. There's no one I'd rather work with or have as a roommate. Or eventually take on as a business partner. But baby, life doesn't always work out the way we think it will. You've been here for a couple of weeks. You're a great stylist and you'll get even better the longer you work at it. My clients love you. I love having you here. But Kay Lee, face it. Your heart's not in it. You don't want to be here. You're making yourself miserable."

Kaylee nodded. Tillie was right, but where did that leave them?

Tillie's salon was a funky little place in a South Beach shopping area. Her clients were a mix of trend-setting twentysomethings and wealthy older women looking for cutting-edge hairstyles to ward off the natural toll age was taking on them. This time of year, the shop had its share of walk-in tourist types as well. Kaylee had already established herself with a few new clients.

No doubt about it, the salon was successful and would provide a steady income if Kaylee took it over. But Kaylee wasn't sure she could ever feel at home there. If she'd ever get used to the snobby sophistication of many of the customers, the attitude of the wealthy and privileged that allowed them to treat a hairstylist, not as an equal, but as a servant of some sort.

While Tillie seemed to take it in stride, and find it secretly funny as she collected her sizable tips, Kaylee found herself resenting such behavior, no matter how monetarily generous her clients were.

One thing she never tired of was the beach. She was even getting used to being hit on by preening men with too-tanned bodies and excessive egos. Maybe if she dug beneath the tan, she'd find a real man inside one of them.

"I bet he's just as miserable as you are."

Kaylee wanted to believe that might be true, but she was afraid to hope. Maybe Rick and Molly had closed up the gap left by her absence. They'd been on their own for four years before she showed up and she'd been a part of their lives for less than a month.

Why then did it feel as if she had a gaping hole where her heart should be? Why did she lay awake at night wondering how they were, what they were doing, if they missed her? At the back of her mind was the thought that maybe Rick would never be ready to have a woman in his life permanently.

Maybe his experience with Brenda had scarred him so severely he couldn't move past it. If that were the case, Kaylee wasn't sure she wanted to find out. If she stayed in Miami she had hope. If she went back to Perrish and confronted Rick, all hope of a future with him might die.

"I'm afraid," she whispered to Tillie.

"Of what, darlin'?"

"That if I go back, he still won't want me to stay." Tears threatened at speaking the truth out loud, but Kaylee blinked them back. She took another sip of her wine and gazed at her older, wiser cousin.

Once again Tillie reached across the table and squeezed her hand. "Well, darlin', if that's the case, wouldn't it be better to find out sooner than later?"

Kaylee shrugged. "Probably. But maybe if I stay here, I might meet someone else. Someone great and I'll forget all about Rick."

Tillie gave an unlady-like snort of laughter. "Sure, darlin'. That could happen to you just like it happened to me. For ten years I met a lot of someone elses. And I forgot all about Max, didn't I?" She held Kaylee's gaze with her own. "You might want to think about that."

"Do you think maybe Rick doesn't know me well enough to trust what he feels? We didn't have much time together."

"Neither did Max and I." Tillie grinned, then turned serious. "So go back and show him who you are."

"I thought I already did that. I was in his house. Taking care of his little girl. Being me. I don't know how everything got so confused. How I got all turned around about myself."

Tillie sat back and propped her chin in her hands. "You know, when I first moved here, I felt a little of what you feel with some of the salon clients. I'd think they were stuck-up snobs looking down on me based on nothing more than the way they were dressed or an off-hand comment. And don't get me wrong, there are more than a few people in this town who are snobs. But a lot of them aren't. It took me a while to stop making a judgment based on appearance or what I think I know about someone. People are who they are, and it doesn't take very long to figure out where they're coming from.

"I don't know Rick, but I'm guessing he knows all he needs to know about you. He knows what's in your heart and he knows what's in his. He knows if this relationship is the right one. He might be afraid to admit it, he's a guy after all, and they can be a little slow on the uptake sometimes, but I think he's going to figure it out. You're the real deal, Kay Lee. You don't know how to be something you're not. So don't forget that."

Long after they'd finished watching the movie Tillie had rented, as she lay in the twin bed in Tillie's guest bedroom, she thought about Tillie's words, knowing there was a grain of truth in them. Either Rick was as miserable as she was or he didn't want anything more to do with her. Maybe he was glad she was gone, out of his life and hoped never to see her again. And as Tillie said, if that was so, wouldn't she be better off knowing now rather than living in this self-imposed limbo?

She'd been herself the whole time she'd been in Perrish. Well, except when she'd attempted to put on airs for Brenda's benefit. And look how well that had turned out. She'd learned that particular lesson quickly.

Now that she thought about it, she'd been freer to be herself those few weeks with Rick and Molly than she'd ever been. They were strangers and she an unknown quantity to them. She wasn't Daisy Walsh's granddaughter or the girl that no-good Bobby Lou Tucker dumped. She wasn't the girl whose mother ran off with the chicken-feed salesman. The only change she'd made was a slight adjustment to her name.

She'd had no thought of impressing Rick and Molly and no reason to do so. They were an unplanned, temporary stop on her way to Miami. But they'd become so much more.

Kaylee couldn't get over the irony of how her life had changed since she'd arrived in Florida. She'd dreamed of a life in a big city, joining forces with Tillie, meeting the man of her dreams and one day owning her own salon. But before she'd even arrived in Miami, she'd found a place very much like the one she'd just left. She'd found the man of her dreams, and the possibility of owning her own salon there, too. What she thought she wanted had changed on the way to Miami.

Kaylee planned to make one phone call first thing tomorrow. And depending on the outcome of that, she had a choice to make. She might leave the dream of a life in Miami behind forever.

Chapter Thirty-Six

Rick unlocked the door to his house and Molly followed him inside. Only Brutus was there to greet them. What did you expect, he asked himself. You told her to go to Miami. You didn't ask her to stay. Now she's gone.

Molly stopped in the middle of the living room, her head cocked as though listening, her gaze darting all around. Her backpack slid to the floor and she turned back to Rick. "She's not here."

"Who?" Rick asked even though he knew exactly who. He didn't want to be the one to say her name aloud.

"Kaylee, Daddy. Where is she?"

Rick hunkered down in front of his daughter. "Come on, squirt. You knew she was leaving today. She went to Miami."

Molly's eyes filled with tears. "I didn't think she'd leave, though. I've been saying my prayers."

She bent her head to Rick's shoulder and started to cry in earnest. Rick closed his eyes and mentally kicked himself for every reason he could think of. Inviting Kaylee into his home. Falling in love with her. Letting her go.

"Daddy, what's wrong with me? Why can't I have a mommy?"

He rubbed her back appalled at the track her thoughts were taking. "Molly. There's nothing wrong with you. You do have a mommy."

"Not one that lives with me," she pointed out with the pure logic of a child.

"I know. But it isn't because there's something wrong with you." Maybe there's something wrong with me, he thought. No. He knew. He lived in fear of repeating his first marital disaster. He couldn't stand the thought of another woman walking away from him and Molly. So he never got involved. Never asked for what he wanted. That way no one could break his heart. Or his daughter's.

Except Molly's heart was clearly broken by Kaylee's departure. And he might as well admit it to himself, even if he couldn't admit it to anyone else. He was pretty broken up about it, too.

His house seemed dismally empty in a way it never had before Kaylee's arrival. It no longer seemed like a home. There wasn't the same kind of light and laughter that had been here up until this morning. It was now just the place he and Molly ate and slept. And mourned.

Molly quieted and Rick stood with her in his arms. He felt rotten. Disappointed in himself and sad for Molly. Kaylee would have stayed. She'd wanted to stay. But he'd been so intent on setting her free, he hadn't realized what it would mean to be here without her.

He opened the refrigerator and looked at the contents. After Kaylee's home cooking, his simple meals, always adequate in the past, held no appeal whatsoever.

"Are you hungry, squirt?" he asked as he reviewed the possibilities.

"I guess." Molly kept her head on his shoulder.

"How about cheeseburgers? There's tater tots in here. You like those, right?"

"I guess."

"You can have a cherry popsicle for dessert, too." He tried to coax some enthusiasm into his voice, hoping it would transmit itself to Molly.

"Okay."

He set her down and started working on the meal. She sat at the table, laid her head on her arms and stared out of the window. He heard her sigh like she had the weight of the world on her shoulders.

A month later, Rick lay in bed doing what he did every night since Kaylee left. Staring up at the ceiling. The paddle fan whirred, making a gentle clicking sound every few seconds. The mildly hypnotic rhythm of the fan had not helped him come up with a solution to his dilemma no matter how long he stared at it.

He couldn't believe the hole Kaylee's absence left in his life. He'd known her less than a month but he missed her more than he'd ever missed Brenda after their years together. He ached for Kaylee in a way he'd never ached for Brenda. What he felt when Brenda left was disappointment. In her. In himself. In the fact that the marriage he'd thought was a lifetime deal had crashed and burned so quickly.

He kept thinking about Kaylee's comments about how they hardly knew each other. But Molly had taken to Kaylee instantly, as if she knew Kaylee was the one. Molly wanted a mother who lived with her, but Rick had seen no indication that Molly wanted Brenda in that position. Molly tolerated Brenda, just as Brenda seemed to tolerate the fact that she'd given birth to Molly and was her biological mother. But Molly loved Kaylee. And Kaylee hadn't been afraid to return Molly's love.

Maybe Molly's instincts were sharper than his own. Or maybe hers were simply untarnished by the experiences that made him cautious. Too cautious? He'd known in his gut from the moment Kaylee walked into his garage that she was something special. Even in the short time they'd been together, he'd felt like the king of the world.

She complimented him on his parenting skills, an area he wasn't especially confident in. He smiled when he was around her, something he hadn't been doing much of lately. Kaylee made him feel good about himself, about his choices. She hadn't judged. She *got* him. She got what he was about after spending just days with him.

And he'd thrown it away.

Clearly, the only solution was to get Kaylee to come back to Perrish. Ask her, no, beg her to marry him. Promise to do whatever he could to make her dreams come true. He hoped she didn't ask him to move to Miami. But if that's what it took, he'd do it. It'd be worth it if it meant having her in his life, having a family again.

First he'd have to find her. Miami was a big place. He'd been so sure that sending her on her way was the right thing to do, that he could live with leaving the decision to come back entirely up to her, he'd torn up the paper with Tillie's phone number on it and dropped the bits into the garbage can at the curb. A can that had been emptied by the time he got home that day.

He didn't even know the name of her cousin's salon. Tillie. That's all he had to go on. A salon owned by someone named Tillie. That was probably a nickname. But for what? Matilda? What was Matilda's last name? Not Walsh, surely. Kaylee said she and Tillie weren't even cousins.

Finding Kaylee in Miami would be like searching for a needle in a haystack. Had anyone ever actually searched for a needle in a haystack, he wondered. And if so, what a grand feeling it must have been to have found that one needle buried amongst mounds of straw. Such a triumph. Exactly how he'd feel when he found Kaylee.

"Come on, squirt, rise and shine." He jiggled Molly's shoulder early the next morning.

She rolled over and mumbled something unintelligible before clearly stating, "I don't want to go to school."

"Good. You're not going to school today."

Molly turned back, opened her eyes and stared at him. "Why not?"

"Because you and I are going to Miami." He opened her closet and pulled clothes off hangers.

"To see Kaylee?"

He glanced at her. The look of hope in her eyes was almost as hard to take as her tears that first night. Ever since then she'd taken to heaving huge sighs and showed little interest in her usual activities. Every night she ended her prayers with the same fervent request. "And God, please make Kaylee come back."

"That's right. We're going to go find her. And I'm going to ask her if she'll come back here to live with us."

"And be my mommy?"

"Your mommy. My wife. Now scoot."

Molly needed no further prompting. She dressed in record time, agreed to munch a granola bar and sip from a juice box on the road in lieu of a real breakfast. Rick stopped at the station and left a note on the door. *Out of town emergency. Back soon.*

He had nowhere to leave Brutus on such short notice, so the dog was along for the ride.

In the motel room in Miami he thumbed through the yellow pages. The sheer numbers of hair salons was daunting. How would he ever find Kaylee? He'd quizzed Molly incessantly, but she had no memory of Kaylee mentioning the name of Tillie's salon.

He lay awake that night long after Molly had fallen asleep and Brutus snored soundly nearby and considered how to make the search easier. By morning he had a plan.

He started with the chambers of commerce, and when that yielded no results he searched the city and county records of business licenses, searching for a beauty salon owned by anyone named Tillie or Matilda. He couldn't imagine what else Tillie would be a nickname for.

Sitting next to him, Molly patiently dialed phone numbers of hair salons on his cell phone, asking, "Is Tillie there, please?

Then is Matilda there, please? Is Kaylee there, please?" and sighing each time. With one of the fat pencils from her school bag she crossed each salon off with a black mark as she went.

"Daddy, this isn't working. We don't even know where she is." Molly's lower lip jutted out.

"Time for a break, huh, squirt? How about ice cream? Any kind you want."

Molly heaved one of her huge sighs. "Okay."

While they waited in line, Rick had a thought so obvious he almost kicked himself. He still had Max Ferguson's cell phone number programmed into his phone. He'd used the phone's auto dial to reach Max the day Dwayne Holcumb had come to town. Max was involved with Tillie. Max would certainly know how to reach her. He had no time to contemplate why he hadn't thought of this before.

He punched in the auto dial and listened to a recorded message informing him that the party he was attempting to reach was not currently available. He could either leave a message or dial another number in case of an emergency. Reluctantly, Rick left a message, the memory of Max telling him what a putz he was still quite vivid. Max would rub his nose in the mistakes he'd made with Kaylee, but if it allowed him to find Tillie, which in turn led to finding Kaylee, it would be a small price to pay.

He bought Molly ice cream and they went back to the motel room. The Disney Channel was airing *101 Dalmations*. While Molly watched it with the volume turned to low, Rick picked up where she had left off calling salons.

After an hour and a half he had a hit when he asked for Tillie. He tried to play it cool, but inside he felt exultant. He'd found her. He'd found Kaylee. Finally.

"Tillie Gruden." Her voice was crisp and professional with just a touch of an accent similar to Kaylee's.

"Is this the Tillie who has a cousin named Kay Lee Walsh?" Next to him, Molly sat up. She turned the TV off and watched him with anxious eyes.

"Who is this?"

"This is Rick Braddock. I live in Perrish, Florida. Kay Lee was staying with me last month while her car was being repaired."

"Oh, Rick! Yes. Kay Lee told me how kind you were to her."

"Is Kaylee there? Could I speak to her?" He nodded at Molly who drew closer.

"She's not here, Rick. She decided not to stay in Miami after all."

"What?" Rick exploded. "Then where is she?" Had she gone back to Tennessee instead?

"All I can tell you is she left yesterday. She decided to pursue another opportunity. She was still working out the details and didn't want to jinx it, but she did promise to call in a few days. Shall I ask her to call you?"

Disappointment seeped into every pore of Rick's body. He sagged as if someone had let all the stuffing out of him. "Yes, I'd appreciate that. Thank you, Tillie. And oh, if you don't mind me asking, Tillie's not your first name, is it?"

She chuckled. "No, it's not. It's not even my middle name."

"Then how... Sorry, it's none of my business. It's just that I had a hard time tracking you down. All I had to go on was the name Tillie and that you owned a hair salon in Miami."

"South Beach, to be exact. But it's no secret. My middle name's Matilda, which believe it or not, I consider an improvement on my first name."

Rick couldn't help but smile. Kaylee's cousin had the same kind of appealing openness as Kaylee. He had to ask. "Which is?"

"Myrtle," she groaned. "Myrtle Matilda Gruden. After my mother's two favorite aunts."

"Mystery solved. Thanks, Myrtle."

"Good-bye, Rick. And if you catch up with that girl before I do, you tell her to call me, you hear?"

"Will do. Bye, Tillie."

He hung up to find Molly's gaze zeroed in on him. "Is Kaylee lost, Daddy?"

He shook his head and opened his arms. She crawled into them and laid her head on his chest. "I'm sure Kaylee knows exactly where she is. All we have to do is find her."

Chapter Thirty-Seven

Kaylee was so excited she could hardly stand it. She imagined the looks of surprise on Rick's and Molly's faces when she told them she'd decided to stay in Perrish. Except what if Rick's surprise turned into something else? He'd practically shoved her onto the road to Miami. Maybe he wouldn't be pleased at all that she'd decided to return so soon.

Better to find that out sooner than later, Kaylee decided. But when she stopped by the gas station the morning after her arrival, Rick wasn't there. She read the note on the door and hoped whatever the emergency was, it wasn't too serious.

By the next day, thanks to the flyers she'd spread all over town, word was out the salon was back in business. She had a few walk-ins and the phone rang with inquiries.

Kaylee knew she'd made the right decision.

Still she fretted over Rick and Molly's absence. Rick's parents lived in Arizona. Perhaps one of them had fallen ill. According to the locals, as she discovered later that day, it was distinctly out of character for Rick to disappear without a moment's notice to anyone.

Kaylee drove by his house twice. What had happened? Where were they?

Friday morning she cruised past the garage on her way to the salon and her heart nearly stopped. The lights were on. The garage bay doors were open. Rick was back.

She circled the block. Butterflies kicked up in her stomach. It seemed like forever since she'd seen him. But it had only been a few weeks. What would she say? She'd have to tell him the truth. She didn't think she could live without him. She didn't want Miami. She didn't want glamour and sophistication and sunsets on the beach. She wanted him. And Molly. And a good life in a small town.

She wouldn't pressure him for a commitment. She'd agree to take it slow. If only he'd give them a chance.

She got out of her car and started toward the garage. Rascal Flats crooned from the radio. Rick was at the counter at the back, absorbed in whatever it was he was doing.

Perfect, Kaylee thought. She could sneak up on him. She slid her arms around him from behind and stood on tiptoe to peek over his shoulder. She felt his reaction race along her body. She blew a grape-flavored bubble, popped it in his ear and grinned, yanking the wad of gum back into her mouth.

"Hey there, stranger. Long time no see. Where ya been?"

He turned around and she'd never seen that look in his eyes. He wasn't amused. He looked haunted and...desperate. "Geez, Kaylee." He picked her up and hugged her to him so tightly she couldn't breathe. "Where have *I* been? I've been looking for you."

"You—you have?" She wasn't exactly sure what reaction she'd expected from him, but it hadn't been this. He was so *serious*. So *emotional*.

"Where did you go? I went crazy looking for you." Her feet touched the floor again, but he was still holding on to her like he'd never let go.

"I went to Miami, but now I'm back here. In Perrish. Rick, what's wrong?" She stroked the back of his head. He was starting to scare her. Had something happened? Something bad? Had something happened to Molly?

She forced his head up and looked into his eyes. "Rick, what is it? Is it Molly? Is she okay?"

He shook his head. "Molly's fine. Nothing's wrong. Except—except, I thought I'd lost you."

Kaylee smiled, trying to lighten the mood. "You didn't think you could get rid of me that easily, did you?"

He clutched her back to him and buried his face in her hair. "We looked everywhere. Drove to Miami, called damn near every salon in Dade County looking for you."

Kaylee bit her lip. "Oh, Rick, you didn't."

He eased back a little and looked at her. "Damn right I did. Me and Molly and Brutus looking for a needle in a haystack."

"But you found me," she pointed out.

He cupped her head in his hands. "Actually, you found me," he corrected. He kissed her lips. "Funny thing was, I didn't even know I was lost until you came along."

"Rick, stop it. You're scaring me."

"Am I? Why?"

Kaylee squirmed under his intent regard. "I don't know. Because you're being sentimental, and silly and—and—"

"Honest," he finished for her. "Which I've avoided doing for a long time. I never wanted you to go to Miami. I wanted you to stay, but I was afraid to ask."

"Afraid I'd say no?"

He nodded and glanced away for a moment, looking over her shoulder.

"Are you still afraid?" she asked gently. He looked back at her. "Terrified," he whispered.

And then he did something she'd never in a million years expect macho Rick Braddock to do. Holding her hands in his, he got down on one knee and looked up at her. "Kaylee, will you marry me?"

Kaylee swallowed her gum along with the lump of emotion clogging her throat. "I thought you'd never ask."

Dear Readers,

Samhain Publishing first published *A Month From Miami* as an ebook in 2008 and in print in 2009. Samhain closed its doors in February 2017 and returned publishing rights to its authors. I had such a love of this story, I decided to update the cover and do some minor editing and re-release it. If you have enjoyed *A Month From Miami*, perhaps you will also enjoy the story of Rick's twin brother Ray in *A Forever Kind of Guy*. See the excerpt below.

You didn't know Rick had a twin brother, did you? Neither did I until after *A Month From Miami* had already been published.

You can find *A Forever Kind of Guy* here: **http://books2read.com/author/barbarameyers/subscribe/1/33163/**

Thanks for your support, and as always, if you enjoy my books, please take a moment to post a review on the site where you purchased it and/or on Goodreads.com. Reviews are *always* appreciated. I love hearing from readers, too. Contact me through my web site, barbarameyers.com.

All the best,

Barbara Meyers

ABOUT THE AUTHOR

When not writing fiction, Dr. Seuss-like poetry or song lyrics, I work part-time for a worldwide coffee company. This is where I disguise myself behind a green apron and trade lattes for story ideas.

I am still married to my first husband and have two fantastic children. I'm originally from Southwest Missouri and now reside in Central Florida.

To learn more about Barbara Meyers, please visit www.barbarameyers.com

Other Books by Barbara Meyers

A Forever Kind of Guy
What A Rich Woman Wants
Training Tommy
Misconceive
Not Quite Heaven
Scattered Moments
Cleo's Web
White Roses in Winter
Phantom (Manuscripts Under the Bed)
If You Knew (Red Bud, Iowa, Book One)
If You Dare (Red Bud, Iowa, Book Two)
A Family for St. Nick (Christmas Novella)

Barbara Meyers writing as AJ Tillock

The Grinding Reality Series
The Forbidden Bean (Book One)
Cool Beans (Book Two)

Please enjoy this excerpt from
A FOREVER KIND OF GUY

Hayley Christopher swiped gloss across her lips and stared at herself in the bathroom mirror.

Why do I bother? she silently asked her reflection.

Her plan for the future dangled just out of reach like a rabbit in front of a greyhound. She wanted to race forward, shake the Florida sand off her feet and arrive in Los Angeles ready to start her life over, but something always held her back. Ten years ago it had been a man. Though she'd vowed never to sacrifice her dreams for a man again, she hadn't counted on a little boy getting in the way of her second chance.

Just a few short months ago she'd been ready to escape Jacksonville and the life she'd once had with Trey. Her bags were packed. An airline ticket awaited her. She'd planned to step off the plane in L.A. and never look back.

Marriage to Trey derailed her plans the first time. Now she'd allowed her semi-orphaned, step-nephew Fletcher to block her path. But she hadn't had a choice, had she? With his mother OD'ing on heroin, dying in her arms, begging her to take care of him, to protect him from his violent father, what was she supposed to say? "No, Steffie, sorry, I've got a new life in L.A. waiting for me"? Everyone else had turned their backs on Stef and for good reason. Hayley couldn't. She'd made a promise to watch over Fletcher without realizing what it would mean.

The other options were to leave Fletcher with strangers, or worse, at the mercy of his father Carlos, should he ever get out of jail. She shuddered at the thought that Carlos might make good on his threats against her. That he'd hurt his own son in the process. The poor kid had been traumatized enough in his young life. While she knew she wasn't the ideal candidate to take custody, at least Fletcher knew who she was, though they'd hardly bonded in the few months she'd had him. They probably never would.

As long as he was with her, Hayley knew Fletcher wouldn't be mistreated and he'd be kept away from his father. With any luck at all, he'd be adopted by the kind of family Hayley herself had always dreamed of. A mother and father. Siblings. There'd be a big backyard with a swing set. Dinner on the table at six every night. Maybe even a dog.

Sure it was a dream. It hadn't come true for her, but maybe she could make it come true for her stepsister's son. If Carlos ever came looking for Fletcher, he'd be long gone, absorbed into the system with a new name, a new family and tightly sealed records. Somehow she'd make that happen. And afterward she'd move forward with her own plans. She and Fletcher would both be free of their pasts.

She stowed the lip gloss and mascara in her makeup case and stared at her reflection once more. What was the point in wearing makeup or making an attempt with her hair? Why did she bother putting cute workout clothes on?

"L.A. Someday. Soon," she promised herself as she did every morning.

She sat down on the closed toilet lid to wrap the Ace bandage around her swollen ankle. Giving in to a burst of exuberance after teaching one of her aerobics classes yesterday had been a mistake. Her professional cheerleading days were several years behind her, and she was getting too old to do back flips. She should have known better.

Life as she'd known it was over, she reminded herself. Some days there seemed no point to anything.

The doorbell rang. She heard Fletcher move away from where she'd left him on the sofa watching cartoons.

"Don't open the door, Fletch," she called. "I'll be right there."

Quickly she finished wrapping her ankle, making sure the self-securing bandage would stay in place. Who could be ringing her doorbell? She knew virtually no one in tiny Perrish, Florida. Oh God, she hoped it wasn't more bad news. Bad news had been following her for too long, showing up when she least expected it. Maybe the ringing of the doorbell heralded a change in that pattern.

She grabbed the despised crutches and maneuvered her way out of the bathroom, wincing when she bumped her injured ankle with the tip of the crutch. She'd needed the crutches for less than a day but it was long enough to know she hated them.

Four-year-old Fletcher stood to the left of the front door, his attention focused on whatever was on the other side of the slender pane of sidelight glass. Hayley moved closer to see a man hunkered on the other side making funny faces at Fletcher. She glanced down to see Fletcher's reaction. His expression was the one he usually wore of serious concentration, but a ghost of a smile played around his lips. At least Hayley wanted to think he might be close to a smile. It'd been a long time since he had.

There was no chain on the door, so Hayley debated for a moment about whether to open the door to a strange man. It was broad daylight and he looked harmless enough. He straightened when he heard the deadbolt slide back.

They stared at each other for what was probably a split second but felt like a lifetime. Hayley felt the ripple run through her. She'd experienced *the ripple effect* twice in her life. Once with her ex-husband and the first time with— "Hi, I'm Ray Braddock," he began.

—Ray Braddock when she was fourteen. She'd been a brand new student, a freshman at Jannings High School. He and his twin brother Rick had been the hottest boys in the junior class. She'd worshiped Ray from afar, though she'd never actually met him. But every time she saw him, the ripple effect slammed her full force.

Okay, she told herself. *You can do this. You are not attracted to him. The last thing you need is a man in your life. Men are bad news. Men cause pain. Men mess up your plans. The ripple effect means nothing.*

The ripple effect is evil.

"Hayley Christopher." Good. That's good. She remembered her manners. She remembered her name. Now if that excitement fluttering in the pit of her stomach would cease and desist, she'd be fine.

"I know."

Her radar shot out a warning. "You know? What do you mean, you know? How would you know my name?"

"From the property management company. I—"

"Oh? I can't believe they gave out my name. They have no right. Who I am and where I live is my business and no one else's. There must be some kind of law—"

"Whoa. Slow down there. I hired the property manager. I'm the owner of the property. I live in the other unit." He nodded toward the other half of the duplex.

"You—own—wait a minute. What?" The other half of the duplex had been vacant during the short time she'd lived there. Or so she thought.

As if sensing her distress, Fletcher moved closer to her, wedging himself between her leg and her crutch and clutching her thigh. He sent out one of his trademark, almost inaudible whimpers of inquiry. Awkwardly, she patted his shoulder. "It's okay, sweetie."

Ray rescued her from her confusion. "I was out of town for a while. So I hired the property manager. But I'm back. Starting next month, you can pay your rent directly to me."

"Oh. Okay."

"What happened to you? Do you need to sit down?" Ray gestured at the crutches and Fletcher hanging onto her. "Want me to come in for a minute?"

Hayley couldn't take her gaze off her landlord. He'd been good looking as a teenager and he still was. But his handsome face had more character now. Tiny lines radiated from the corners of his eyes. As she recalled, he'd been leaner than his brother, and that hadn't changed. He looked tanned and strong and capable.

But he also looked sad. And a bit lost.

Maybe that's what I look like too. It was certainly how she felt most days. Giving herself a mental shake, she tried to regroup and say something reasonably intelligent.

Inviting him into her personal space was out of the question. "No. That's okay. I'll make the rent checks to you from now on. Was there anything else?"

"Is everything all right with the place? Appliances? Plumbing? Air conditioning?"

"Everything works. I'm not crazy about some of the decorating choices, but it's nothing critical." *Except the bathroom wallpaper,* she added silently. *It's hideous.* She'd seriously considered doing the next tenant a favor by ripping down the wallpaper in the bathroom. Bare drywall would be an improvement over the garish flowered foil.

"All right, then. Here's my phone number." He handed her a plain white business card on which he'd written his name and the number. "Let me know if you have any problems."

She took the card. Her fingertips touched his. She ignored her reaction.

Not.

"It's only you and your son, here, right? Fletcher? Is that his name?"

She glanced down at Fletcher, who was staring up at Ray. "Yes. Uh, well, sort of."

Ray's brow furrowed, but she didn't feel required to explain her relationship with Fletcher to him. "How do you know his name?"

"The property manager."

"Oh, right. Okay."

Ray stood there a moment longer. Hayley wondered what else she should say. She couldn't think of anything. Her mouth went dry. Her brain became addled. Every nerve ending she possessed went on high alert and sent mixed signals, scrambling her thought process.

Invite him in.

Make him go away.

He's hot.
You'll get burned.
Step closer.
Stay away from him.
"Do I know you?" he asked.

Hayley stared at him.

He studied her intently. "You look kind of familiar. Like maybe we've met before."

Great, she thought. Even relocating this far from Jacksonville, she couldn't get away from the negative publicity.

"Do you follow sports?"

"Well, yeah—"

"The Jacksonville Jacks?"

"Not so much lately—"

"Then you probably know that according to every reporter in the greater Jacksonville area, I'm the ex-pro cheerleader, gold-digging, cheating hussy their beloved quarterback Trey Christopher divorced. You probably recognize me from some unflattering photos that ran in all those rags the past couple of years."

Ray's gaze remain fixed on her as if he hadn't been listening. "No, it's not that." He cocked his head a bit and narrowed his gaze.

"What do you mean 'it's not that'? What else could it be?"

"I haven't read a Jacksonville newspaper in about two years. Are you sure we've never met? Maybe when we were younger?"

He couldn't possibly remember her, Hayley thought. *Why not?* Her subconscious asked. *You remember him.*

"You mean like in high school?"

"I think I'd remember you if you went to Jannings Point."

Hayley's ankle began to throb, warning her she'd been in an upright position for too long. Plus she needed to leave for work shortly. "I did, but I was a couple of years behind you. I don't think we ever met."

"Maybe not. But I still feel like I know you. Anyway, I'll see you around, I guess." Ray turned and exited the small screened porch and headed back to his side of the duplex. He stopped halfway and turned back to her. "Let me know if you need help with anything."

I most certainly will not. She knew from her experience with Trey exactly what happened when she relied on a man. Even if she wasn't too good at it yet, she relied only on herself now, and her plans called for her to keep it that way.

Of course it would have to be raining, Hayley thought with a sigh as she parked in front of the duplex that evening. She had a trunk full of groceries, a throbbing ankle, Fletcher in the back seat and her beloved crutches to contend with. The rain was the icing on an absolutely splendid day. She turned off the wipers, yanked the key from the ignition and stared at the water droplets beading against the windshield.

First Ray Braddock had shown up at her door this morning, which had caused her to think about him off and on all day.

Since she couldn't teach exercise classes with a sprained ankle, the director of the Y had relegated her to front desk duty, which she hated because it meant she was stuck there checking ID's, handing out towels and answering the phone. After lunch he'd sent her to help out in the child care center, giving her a chance to see how Fletcher was doing.

Fletcher had simply clammed up after her stepsister's death a few months ago. Hayley couldn't imagine what Steffie's son had been exposed to in his young life that would cause him to refuse to speak. There didn't seem to be anything physically wrong with him. Hayley had done what she could for Fletcher, rescuing him from the hovel of an apartment where Steffie had been living with Fletcher's no-good father, who was now in jail. For the time being, she could watch over Fletcher until other arrangements could be made. It was the only thing she could do for poor Steffie.

But nothing Hayley did brought Fletcher out of his self-imposed shell. She marveled at the strength of will he possessed to keep himself from speaking. He didn't interact much with other kids even in the daycare setting. Mostly he played alone with building blocks or trucks or puzzles. Outside, he went his own way on the playground, observing everything, showing enthusiasm for nothing.

Sometimes she felt the same way. As if she had an invisible bubble around herself. She could see out, observe other people interacting normally, developing relationships, falling in love, believing in the same romantic fantasy she'd once believed in. But she had no enthusiasm for, or personal interest in, any of it. Not anymore.

Refusing to brood any longer, she got out of the car, retrieved her crutches and released Fletcher from his car seat. Too bad the imaginary bubble wasn't waterproof. She popped the trunk and handed two of the lightest bags to Fletcher.

"Take these to the porch, honey. I'll be right there."

Resting her crutches against the bumper, she stood on one foot to rearrange the other bags in the trunk so she'd be able to pick them up and balance fairly equal weight on either side, and manage the crutches at the same time.

"Need some help?"

Hayley jumped back at the unexpected male voice and figure that appeared next to her. She made a too-late grab for the crutches, wobbled awkwardly on one foot and fell backward, landing on her butt in patchy, wet gravel.

"Ouch!"

A pair of male feet in beat-up flip-flops stepped directly into her line of vision, and her eyes traveled up a set of muscular legs. Baggy khaki shorts and a wrinkled black tee shirt did nothing to disguise his tall, athletic build.

"Sorry, I didn't mean to startle you."

He bent down to help her up and her gaze flew to his face, his dark eyes, the straight, almost-black hair that fell across his forehead. This morning she'd noticed he was overdue for a shave, either by laziness or design, and that fact was even more pronounced now. Not to mention damn sexy.

He touched her and she froze.

That all-too-familiar tingling started, while butterflies began flapping their wings in her stomach.

Stop it! Stop it! *Stop it,* she warned herself. She'd been burned by those same feelings once already. It wasn't going to happen again.

With hardly any help from her, Ray got her on her feet and slid her crutches under her arms. "I'll get these," he informed her, as he gathered up her damp grocery bags. "You go on ahead."

What a lovely sight she must make. Her butt was sopping wet and probably muddy. The rest of her was merely rain damaged.

She got the door unlocked and let Fletcher go in ahead of her. She was only too aware of Ray behind her, heat radiating off him through his damp clothes.

"You can leave everything on the counter," she told him, indicating the kitchen. The living area of the duplex was a large open space with the kitchen tucked in one corner, featuring a counter that overlooked the seating area and dining table. There was a laundry room on one side of the space and a short hallway on the other that led to a bedroom at either end and a bathroom in the middle. "There are clean towels in the laundry room if you want one. I'm going to go change." She held out her hand to Fletcher. "Come here, Fletch. Let me dry you off."

In the bathroom, she sat on the closed lid of the toilet again and propped her crutches against the wall. Fletcher was damp from the rain but not soaked. She wrapped a towel around him anyway, drying his hair, face and arms. She held the edges of the towel around his head for a second before parting them.

"Peek-a-boo."

Fletcher stared at her.

She tried again, closing the towel and quickly opening it. "Peek-a-boo." His brow knit in puzzlement. Hadn't Steffie ever played games with him, had fun with him? Had he ever laughed, or had he simply forgotten how?

"It's okay, Fletch." One of these days he'd smile. She'd make sure of it. She patted his damp shirt. "You want to put on a different shirt?" He shook his head. She knew the green tee-shirt he wore with a picture of a frog on it was his favorite. She gave him a quick hug. "You can go play. I'll be out in a minute."

In her bedroom, she berated herself for getting flustered before. She yanked a pair of jeans and a denim shirt out of her closet and scolded herself as she stripped off her wet shorts and tee-shirt. "Since you aren't trying to impress Ray Braddock, what do you care how you look?" She stared at her reflection in the mirror as she buttoned the shirt. Damn, she looked good. The rain made her complexion even more dewy and healthy-looking. She scrunched her damp hair and clipped it up off her neck. Stubborn tendrils drifted out of the clip to hug her neck and temples.

Some days she cursed her reflection, and some days she thanked God for it.

"I don't care how hot he is, you are to stay away from him." She shook her finger at her image in the mirror. "Don't encourage him. Don't flirt with him. Don't get involved with him." She yanked the jeans over her hips and zipped them. "He's your landlord and your next-door neighbor. Behave yourself."

Satisfied she'd effectively covered herself from head to toe in denim and armed herself against any masculine charm that might present itself, she joined Fletcher and Ray in the kitchen.

Hayley saw that Ray had unpacked her groceries and put the refrigerated and freezer items away. Everything else he'd left on the counter. The plastic grocery bags were bunched together in a little ball. He'd put himself on Fletcher's level once again, and the boy nodded at something Ray had asked about the toy truck he had in his hand.

Ray glanced her way and she wondered if her imagination was playing tricks on her, or did his gaze eat her up as she approached?

Warning bells went off in her head when Ray straightened and his stomach growled long and loud.

Irritated with her reaction to him, she crossed to turn on the oven. "Helping me with my groceries wasn't a ploy to invite yourself to dinner, was it?" she asked over her shoulder.

Ray's stomach gurgled again and she turned around. He looked a tad bit guilty. "Not entirely, but I'm open to an invitation. What are you having?"

Hayley extracted two pizzas from the freezer, much too aware of her culinary deficiencies. "I'm sure you'll get a much better meal at your place."

Behind her, she heard Ray sigh. "I've been out of town for a while, and my cupboard is bare. But that's not a very good excuse for barging into your dinner plans, is it? I'll catch you later, okay?"

He started for the door with Fletcher trailing after him. He ruffled

Fletcher's hair. "Bye, buddy. I'll see you later."

"I didn't say you had to leave," Hayley called out. Too late. The door closed behind him. "Dammit!"

She grabbed her crutches and hop-skipped to the porch. Ray had already crossed to his porch and had opened his door. "Hey." He stopped and turned toward her. "I never said I wouldn't feed you dinner." Since he'd helped her bring in her groceries in the rain, she owed him even though the last thing she wanted to be was indebted to him. He stayed where he was. "Don't make me come over there," she threatened, only half joking.

The rain had let up to a light sprinkle, but the overcast sky added an extra shade of gray to the evening light. They stared at each other. *He's not going to make me beg him to come back is he?* Hayley wondered. The nerve. Why, when everything she'd learned in the past year had taught her to avoid men like Ray Braddock, did she sense herself giving in, making the next move, which technically should have been his?

"I'm making frozen pizza. And I usually manage to burn it. Still interested?"

"Burnt frozen pizza? That's my favorite."

But still he stayed on his porch, his door half open. Hayley groaned. Why didn't she let him go, back to his bare cupboards and growling stomach?

Why? Why? Why?

Why was he hanging back if he was supposedly starving? She'd come to the door, essentially told him he was welcome to eat with her and Fletcher. What else did he expect from her?

This was as much effort as she was willing to make, and she was already mad at herself for it.

Could he possibly be as skittish as she was? Maybe he was warning himself to stay away from her. Perhaps he, too, had a healthy fear of history repeating itself.

Fletcher edged up next to her, poking his head out so he could see Ray.

As if Fletcher's appearance helped him decide, Ray closed the door and came back to her side of the duplex. "I guess, since you asked so nicely, I'd love to stay for dinner."

Biting her lip, refusing to smile, she muttered "Idiot" under her breath as he followed her and Fletcher inside. The thing was, she didn't know who she was referring to when she said it.

CPSIA information can be obtained
at www.ICGtesting.com
Printed in the USA
BVHW071017180321
602885BV00005B/540